# After Eli

*Books by Terry Kay*

The Year the Lights Came On
After Eli

TERRY KAY

# After Eli

*Boston*

HOUGHTON MIFFLIN COMPANY

1981

*Library of Congress Cataloging*
*in Publication Data*
Kay, Terry.
After Eli.      I. Title.
PS3561.A885A68      813'.54      80-27577
ISBN 0-395-30854-2

Printed in the United States of America

S 10 9 8 7 6 5 4 3 2 1

*For Tommie, who has endured
and loved and believed*

Everything that deceives may be said to enchant.

PLATO

# Acknowledgments

No one writes a book alone. People give to the effort, and in their giving a writer discovers patience and discipline and, ultimately, hope. There have been many who have given unselfishly to this work and I am grateful to each. Three people most especially have been important: Jonathan Galassi, whose editing greatly improved feeble passages and who helped me find a deeper love for writing; Irene Tumulty, officially an agent, but more privately a friend who said, "You can, you can, you can . . ."; and Sheri Gunter, who listened day by day, sentence by sentence, and who gave me energy because she cared.

# After Eli

# 1

FOR TWO DAYS the Irishman had watched the house and waited.

The house was below him, on a flat shelf of land that spilled off the mountain like the after-matter of an ancient volcano. A stream, as slender and wild as a break of lightning, curled from the mountain around the house, turning sharply below the shelf. In the sun — when the sun was high — the stream glittered like a silver necklace dangling from a throat of trees. He knew the water would be cold and sweet and clean.

The house was old. Its unpainted lap-plant siding had darkened into weathered ribs and the roof was covered with rusting sheet tin. The spine of the roof sagged in the center. The front of the house had a porch, full-length, covering the front door and windows like a lip. The two side windows were small and high in the walls; windows made for seeing out, not in. There were two chimneys, holding the house between them like bookends. He had seen smoke from only one of the chimneys; it would be from the kitchen.

There were three other buildings: a barn, a corncrib, and an outhouse. And a well, sheltered by a roof of wood shingles. A barbed-wire fence looped in a circle from the back of the barn, crossed the stream, and disappeared into a windbreak of pines. He had seen a cow and a calf and two mules in the pasture, and pigs in a slab fence outside the wire fence. There were chickens, also, but no dog. It was strange there was no dog.

In the two days he had watched the house from the mountain, the Irishman had noticed only one man and a woman there. He knew they were young — not long married, he believed. In the mornings, the man walked to the side of the road at the foot of his house, where the shelf fell into a strip of level valley, and waited for a truck. The truck was filled with other men who seemed tired and methodical. In the late afternoon, before sundown, the truck returned, slowing but not quite stopping, and the man slipped from its tailgate and walked to the house without looking back. Sawmill hands, the Irishman decided. In the day, from where he camped on the mountain, he had heard the dull, ringing cry of saw blades from far away.

The woman was not often outside. On the first day the Irishman had seen her at the well, dressed only in her slip. She seemed thin. Her elbows were drawn into her sides, and her shoulders were stooped. The silk shine of her slip flashed like frost in the sunlight and the Irishman remembered a woman in another place, whose body had signaled to him its unending secrets. She, too, had been thin.

\* \* \*

He did not know why the house had stopped and held him for two days. He was tired, he knew that. And the rest had refreshed him. But it was more than being tired. It was the house itself. The house intrigued him. It yearned to speak, and he could not leave until it did. A soft and distant music played in the Irishman when he watched the house. It had the sound of a single lute, with high, splitting notes breaking into soprano voices and the soprano voices were whispering secrets to him. There was something about the house. Yes. And the voices would tell him. He knew the voices would tell him if he did not hurry them. The voices had always told him, and he trusted them. The Irishman knew patience. Patience was his artistry and his genius.

He sat on the ledge of the mountain, protected from the March wind by a granite cave, and waited for the house to trust him with its secrets. He did not know where he was in the great Appalachian range. North Carolina, he thought. Perhaps Georgia. The mountains were brown and borderless and he had traveled for weeks through small villages huddled to themselves like vagrants needing companionship. He himself was a vagrant, skilled only in his patience and in his gift for belonging to the moment and place of his wandering. It was his nourishment and his way of survival in the lean years of the late thirties, and the Gypsy urge that led him from village to village became a life that was both poetic and cruel. He lived as animals live, with intense calculation and with an unerring sense of the indefinable world scurrying about him like so many bugs.

Then, late in the afternoon of the second day, the Irishman knew he had waited long enough.

\*　　\*　　\*

He stood on the road before the house at the last finger of sunlight, when the mountains were caught in the cupped dome of gray coolness. He wore his knapsack loosely over his left shoulder and carried in his right hand a walking stick with an intricate carving of a gargoyle on the knob. He waited until the man had closed the barn door and was walking back to his house with the pail of milk.

"Ho, there, friend," the Irishman called cheerfully.

The man whirled quickly toward the voice. The milkpail shook in his hand. He stared at the stranger on the road, but did not speak.

"Ah, I've put the fright in you, I have," the Irishman said. "I'll be askin' your forgiveness."

"No need," the man replied weakly. "Wadn't expectin' nobody out here."

The Irishman dropped his knapsack from his shoulder and pushed his left hand into the small of his back.

"Fact of the matter, you're a bit better off than I am," he said.

"Leastways, you're knowin' where 'here' is, and I could be standin' at the pearly gates with a hand-printed invitation and still be turned about."

"Where you headed?" The question was timidly asked.

"By and by, I'm hopin' it's to Atlanta and then on to sunny Florida," the Irishman answered. He laughed and added, "That is, if I'm even in the right part of the blessed globe."

The man stared at him. The fear in his eyes faded. He said, "You goin' to Atlanta from here, you better grow you some wings. Take you a couple of days on foot just to get in the right direction."

The Irishman sensed the relaxation. He could see a smile playing across the man's face. The man was younger than he had thought, perhaps twenty.

"No doubtin' it," the Irishman cried comically. "It's the luck I'm havin', and you'd think an Irishman would be a bit more blessed than that, now wouldn't you?"

The man grinned broadly. He looked quickly toward his house, then back to the Irishman.

"That's what you are, ain't it?" he said. "Knowed it was somethin' other'n what's around here. You Irish from over in Ireland?"

The Irishman extended his arms above his head and lifted one leg in the air.

"Just the same as you, my friend. Same as the Good Father made Adam himself. Arms, legs. Two apiece."

The man looked again toward his house and the Irishman followed his eyes. He could see the woman standing in the shadows of the screen door like an abstract painting.

"Well, friend, good to speak to you," the Irishman said. "If you'd be kind enough to point the way, I'll be off, thinkin' about pickin' up some wings along the way."

The man hesitated. He switched the milkpail into his other hand.

"Late to be travelin'," he said. "You want, you can put up

here in the barn tonight and share some supper with the wife and me."

The Irishman reached for his knapsack. He counted the pause between the invitation and his movements. It was an old cadence with him, like a rhythmic dance. Then he shook his head easily and lifted the knapsack to his shoulder.

"Good of you to offer, friend, but it'd be burdensome, it would, what with the times bein' bad, and that's somethin' Michael O'Rear won't see happenin'."

The man did not answer immediately. He looked again toward his house, toward his wife.

"Ain't no trouble," he replied suddenly. "Not if you don't mind some spare eatin'. Ain't much. The wife's been a little sick and I ain't pushed her to put much on the table."

The Irishman smiled. He kicked playfully at a rock in the road. He looked away into the darkening mountains, as though contemplating the offer, then turned back to the man.

"Well, you're a sight kinder than I'm thinkin' I'd be under the circumstances," he admitted. "But I'd be lyin' if I didn't say it sounded good, me bein' weary and longin' for human company to share some words with."

A boy's satisfaction fluttered across the man's face. He said, "Caufield's the name. Lester Caufield."

"And me you call Michael," the Irishman replied.

\*     \*     \*

To Lester Caufield, who was easily impressed, Michael O'Rear was impressive.

Michael laughed and told tales that could have been read from books of stories. He had a voice that was thunder from a cave and whisper from the wind, and his words sounded like a poem read by an actor, or a preacher's prayer skimming about in space in search of God. And words. Irish words. Like music.

And there was another thing about Michael O'Rear: You believed him. It was more than what he said, it was the way he looked into you when he said it. Lester had never seen such eyes. They changed with his voice, like seasons, and Lester knew they were eyes that had seen farther across sadness and joy than any other man had ever seen. Michael's eyes danced, then softened. And they looked into you. *Into* you.

Lester Caufield found in Michael an immediate friend, and felt wholly comfortable with him. Michael had been a merry guest at supper. He had praised the meager meal with soft blessings of wonder and gratitude. He had spoken of faraway places, of homes and suppers in other mountains, and of how it was possible to sit at another man's table and feel the pulse of his life. And he was gentle. Lester liked the gentleness, and he had seen the same wonder in his wife's silent, watching face. Michael had spoken her name — Mary — with a broken syllable that rolled musically from his mouth. *"May-rie,"* he had said. *"May-rie."*

After the supper Lester had taken a jar of whiskey from a pie safe and motioned for Michael to follow him to the front porch. Lester sat in a straight-back chair and Michael slipped to the porch floor, leaning against the doorjamb with his shoulder, his legs stretched and crossed comfortably at the ankles. Lester read Michael's face as he stared into the pit of the wooded night. There was melancholy in Michael's eyes; he seemed to be seeing into another mountain in another place.

"You come along at a good time," Lester said, offering the jar of whiskey.

"And it's luck, I'm thinkin'," replied Michael. "I've been long enough on the road, wanderin', with no one to talk to but my own good self and the creatures." He swallowed from the jar. The homemade whiskey was sharp and strong. He laughed and his body shook. He added, "Trouble is, the creatures come to makin' more sense of it all than I did."

Lester nodded. "Creatures ain't bothered by things," he said philosophically. "May be why they make sense."

"True enough," agreed Michael. "I've thought the same myself, many's the time." He pointed with his hand toward the woods. "See that squirrel nest in that oak? About halfway up."

"Yeah. They all over the place," Lester answered.

"I've been lookin' at them for the last few days," Michael confessed. "Think about squirrels. They build and stay put. Most of the men I've known, they wander all over." He looked at the whiskey jar in his hand and swallowed again. "You're a good man, Lester Caufield," he whispered. "A good man. You and your Mary. Takin' in a stranger to feed and bed in hard times. Not many you'll find in the mountains who'd do such. I know. I'm a travelin' man who's been on the ups and downs. You're good people, you are."

"My daddy always told me don't never open the door to somebody you don't know," Lester admitted, "but it seems right to me to be neighborly."

"No, I'll be havin' none of that," argued Michael. "It's more'n bein' neighborly. You're out of the ordinary. You're what the Irish would call righteous."

Lester laughed.

"Somebody ought to tell the preacher that," he replied lightly. "Don't reckon the preacher thinks so. Especially about me. The wife, she's a churchgoer." He leaned his chair close to Michael and whispered, "Reason she ain't out here. She don't take to drinkin'. Says it's first-rate sin. But this jar was give to me by my cousin as a weddin' present and I couldn't just drain it out. Reckon I knew somebody'd come along to help with it." He leaned back and looked up into the night. "Well, hell, she ain't no more'n a girl yet," he mused. "Me and her been wed a month now, I reckon. She ain't used to takin' me, if you know what I mean, especially when I have me a drink or two. She's scared to death I'm gonna get up for a hunk and split her wide open."

Michael did not answer. He lit a short-stemmed pipe and smiled and nodded and continued to stare into the darkness. He could hear Mary in the kitchen. He thought of Lester pushing himself into her and his body tensed. He remembered watching her from the mountain and the frost color of her slip.

"Matter of fact, you pass along that jar and I'll take me a sip right now," Lester again whispered. "Don't make a damn to me what she says. I'm feelin' good for the first time in days, and tomorrow's Saturday and I ain't goin' to work. I don't take a drink while you around, ain't no way I'll get to. She's started throwing a fit if I do it by myself."

Michael handed him the jar and Lester wiped his sleeve across the mouth and turned it up to his lips. He swallowed twice.

"Good, ain't it?" Lester said proudly.

"True enough, it is."

Michael could feel the music flowing inside him and the soprano voices ringing in his head. And then the night rushed through him like a ghost and he could sense the singing of small night animals and the cooling, green perfume of grasses and trees breaking through the membrane of early spring. He breathed deeply, suddenly, filling his lungs. The house seemed to rise and yawn and enfold him. The voices were becoming a scream.

"Know what I been sittin' here thinkin' about?" Lester asked easily. "Come to me at supper, out of the blue. I been thinkin' how you seem like a fellow who used to live around here."

The screaming in Michael stopped abruptly.

"Another Irishman in these parts?" he asked lightly.

"Wadn't no Irishman, far as I know, though I reckon there's the blood around," answered Lester. "He was reared around here. I recall him from when I was a boy, and I heard tell a lot about him since. He used to be somethin'. Told some good tales. I reckon he left for good seven, eight years ago. Some say he's dead. Some say he ain't."

"A wanderin' man, he was?"

Lester nodded and swallowed again from the whiskey.

"I reckon he was more'n that, you get right down to it," he

replied. "From what I hear tell, ol' Eli was about anythin' you could think of. He was a charmer, all right, but meaner'n the Devil hisself, if he had to be."

"Fact is, I've been called the same," Michael said brightly.

"Well, I be damn," exclaimed Lester. "Sounds like I'm callin' you names, don't it? Don't mean it that way. I mean Eli was a talker, made people feel right. That's what I mean. Same way you do. And he was always smilin', same as you. You ask anybody around here, they'll tell you. Way I remember him, he even had the same kind of easy look you got." He laughed. "Hell, down in Yale they'd probably throw you in jail for bein' like Eli."

"Then I'll stay out of Yale, wherever it is," Michael replied.

Lester giggled. He toyed with the jar of whiskey.

"Just goin' on with you," he said. "Don't make no difference what Eli done, he was a man to listen to." He paused. "Ain't thought about him in years," he added.

"Well, no offense taken, friend," Michael said. "It's true enough, I'm a talker. Proud of it, if you twist the fact out of me. It's the way I've made my way, everythin' from readin' Milton to little ladies on the tent Chautauqua to — "

"What's that?" Lester asked innocently.

"The tent Chautauqua. It was like a travelin' show. Music and actors doin' plays and readin's. Died out about ten years ago, I'd say, what with radio and the Depression. But it was somethin' to see, Lester Caufield. Somethin', all right. Me, I'd be readin' from some good Irish poet, or actin' in a play, and the ladies would be swoonin' and the nights were lovely, they were. Not been the same since. Little left that I can find but some carnival barkin' at the circus."

"Never run across it," Lester confessed. "Only thing around here's some revivals, and when that ain't on, some drinkin' done down at Pullen's, down in town."

"Times change," Michael said simply. "Maybe your friend took off on some tent circuit of his own likin'."

"Eli? Don't nobody know, I reckon. He wadn't Irish, I reckon, but he had him a streak. Tale around the hills is he come back home last time with a whole suitcase of money he stole somewheres. Hid it on that farm of his — down the road five or six miles — and then he lit out again. But that was some time ago, like I said. He ain't come back since."

Michael shifted his weight, leaning forward from the doorjamb. He folded his arms around his knees and locked his right hand over his left wrist. His eyes sparkled quickly and played across Lester's face.

"Ah, a buried treasure, it is?" he said. His voice had the exuberance of a child's question.

Lester nodded and returned a child's smile. He glanced over Michael's shoulder through the screen door, then motioned Michael closer with his head and whispered, "Them Pettit women say it ain't so, but ain't nobody believes 'em. They's been some snoopin' around, times bein' what they are, but ain't nobody found nothin'. Harley Nixon tells around how he got shot at one night, thinkin' they was gone, but them women don't leave the place all at one time, not even goin' to church."

Michael returned the whisper: "Is it a goodly sum?" he asked.

"What they say. Ten thousand dollars, some say. Five thousand, according to others. Word is Eli took it from a bank up in Kentucky, but don't nobody know for certain. Way he talked, he could've been lyin' just for the hell of it. Eli loved to do his talkin' and word is he told around that it was hid in his luck place. But that was the way Eli was."

Michael could sense a drama moving in his mind. Flashes of a house he had never seen, of faces, of secret, hidden places. His heart pumped hard against the muscles of his throat and he could feel the palms of his hands warming.

"And the women?" asked Michael, forcing his voice low.

"Couldn't call 'em all women, I reckon," replied Lester. "I ain't seen 'em in a while, but there's Eli's wife — Rachel, she's named. And there's Sarah, the daughter. I expect she's sixteen or seventeen now, a couple of years younger'n my Mary. Always been a little weak, like Mary."

"Just the two of them?"

Lester shook his head and laughed sharply. He sipped from the whiskey, smacking and sighing as he swallowed.

"One more," he said. "Dora. She's the sister to Rachel. Old maid. Tale is, she's the one you got to watch out for. Keeps a shotgun handy and damn well knows how to use it. Besides, she's quaint, I hear tell."

"Quaint?"

Lester shrugged his shoulders. He rolled the whiskey jar in his hands and thought about his answer.

"Well, maybe that ain't the way to say it," he replied. "She's always starin'. Got a mean eye. Meaner'n Hell." He laughed. "Reckon that's the reason she never got no man. That'd be more'n a man could stomach, wakin' up every mornin' to some woman starin' a hole through him." He laughed again.

A chill ran through Michael. He could feel the glare of a woman's face.

"But, hell, it wouldn't be that I'd be scared of," Lester added. "It'd be that damned ol' shotgun. I'd be careful, I was you. You got to go by when you light out in the mornin', if you goin' on down to Hiawassee." He snickered gleefully. "Don't you go strayin' none when you pass that house off the road, say five or six miles on down. You'll see it. Sets up on a little hill in a bunch of oaks. First farm down the road is Floyd Crider's; next one is the Pettits'. Ol' Floyd ain't gonna do nothin' more'n wave his hand. I ain't givin' you no promise on them women." He snickered again.

Michael's inner eye framed the image of three women, and his mind repeated their names — Rachel, Sarah, Dora. He said, "It's a good thing there's some fear in them, I'm thinkin'. Women livin' alone could be in the Devil's danger if they're not careful what's about them."

"And them women could be what the Devil's danger is," Lester replied, snorting into the mouth of the jar. He shook his head lazily and stretched his shoulders against the hard brace of the chair. The whiskey had entered his mind and muscles and the night was becoming heavy. He rubbed his hands over his eyes and yawned. "Anyhow," he added, "it's somethin' how much you put me in mind of Eli, what I recall of him."

"Well, I take that as a compliment, all but the part about him bein' a rogue, that is," Michael replied. "That part I'll leave to the next traveler down the road."

Lester laughed suddenly. He hiccupped and his eyes floated sleepily to Michael.

"Yes?" Michael said.

"I was just thinkin' how you was lucky to come walkin' up here instead of up to the Pettits' place," Lester mumbled. "Dora might've blowed you to kingdom come before you got the chance to say hello."

Michael pulled himself from the floor of the porch, smiling at the thought.

"Now that's the truth," he agreed. "That's the truth. Maybe my luck's changin', and it's luck I've been livin' by all these long years, Lester Caufield. Pure luck."

\*    \*    \*

He did not have a watch, but Michael knew by the ticking of his patience that it was after midnight. He had planned carefully. It was time.

He rolled quietly from the cushion of straw and folded his bedding neatly and tied it beneath the top flap of his knapsack. He then pushed the straw back into the stack — a habit of erasing where he had been.

He stepped silently across the barn and slipped out of the door into the barnyard. There was only a rim of a moon, like a silver scratch. It was cold and dark, the kind of darkness he needed.

Luck, he thought. Yes, blessed luck, as he had said to Lester. There was no dog to worry about. Nothing for warning. That was first. And it was Friday. Being Friday would give him time. The rest would be simple. He had studied the door carefully; it would be no trouble. And there would be time to follow the stream and lose himself in the mountains before Monday morning and the truck of men.

He placed his knapsack and walking stick at the foot of the steps leading to the porch. He took the steps slowly, pushing his weight on the supports. Then he was across the porch and at the door. He reached for the knife scabbarded to his belt. He slipped the blade between the doorjamb and lock and pried gently. The door broke open without a sound.

He was inside, moving in a crouch, skimming the room with his fingers. The bedroom was before him, its door open. He could hear the heavy breathing of whiskey sleep rising from Lester. He wondered if Lester had taken his wife.

Michael smiled. A pleasing Irish melody rose in the back of his throat and the words flowed into his seeing like sheet music — *"I have loved you with poems . . . I have loved you with daisies . . . I have loved you with everything but love . . ."* The music was a serenade of joyful sadness and it filled Michael with memories. His skin tingled with a rush of excitement. He stood at the bedroom door and stepped lightly to the foot of the bed. Lester was asleep on his left side, his right arm tucked against his chest. Mary lay beside. She was awake. She stared at Michael in horror, unable to move or to make a sound. Michael winked and warned her with a low, hissing "Shhhhh." He bent to Lester, catching him on the shoulder with his left hand, rolling him quickly, the knife in his right hand flashing in one clean stroke through Lester's throat. Lester's body quivered. The blood gurgled and spewed as Michael rolled him onto the floor. He turned to Mary, whose open mouth was frozen in a mute scream, and the Irish melody in his own throat escaped in a hum.

"Well, now, you're a lovely sight, close up, you are," Michael said softly, easing onto the bed with his knees. "Young as the mornin', you are. Just the thing a man would be needin' before he's up and off."

He moved effortlessly across the bed, singing quietly to himself as he worked, casually pulling away the bedcovers with his left hand, playing with her flannel nightgown with the tip of the knife blade. He was unhurried, almost gentle, as he slipped the blade into the gown and slit it open.

The smile in his face faded as he looked at Mary's body. "You're a sickly one," he said bluntly. "Not tit enough to feed a sparrow." He smiled again as his left hand swept lightly over her breasts, tipping the tiny pink nipples. "But it's not tit I'm in favor of," he added. "Not when there's more for the havin'." His hand dropped to Mary's underpants and he tore at them roughly, lifting her from the bed. The knife whipped quickly, slashing at the garment, and then his hand was on the soft feather hair and his fingers were gouging at the tight opening.

Mary cried at last.

# 2

THE BOY WAS SITTING on the back of the moving wagon, slumped forward at the shoulders as an old man would sit. His elbows pushed into his thighs and his fingers laced his hands together like bootstrings. His legs dangled from the bed of the wagon and he wagged them unconsciously in small air steps as he stared between his knees at the grass bridge in the center of the hard dirt road, unrolling in a pale green ribbon beneath the spoked wheels of the wagon. There was no expression on his face.

The boy's father sat up front on a plank seat hooked to the side gates of the wagon. He had a thin back and he, too, was slumped forward, exactly like the boy, but his feet were propped on the front gate of the body and he held the rope reins of the two mules loosely in his hands. The wagon between the boy and his father, sitting with their backs to one another, was empty except for two axes and a large fertilizer sack filled with sweet potatoes.

*   *   *

Rachel Pettit stood at the front window of her house and watched the wagon moving slowly along the road. She knew it was Wednesday. Floyd Crider was a calendar. If it did not rain, he arrived always on Wednesday, always in the same hour, always at the same languid pace, always in the same hesitant mood. Floyd intrigued her. She was grateful for his attention and his concern, yet he intrigued her because, of all the men she knew, he was the most guarded and private. He was a male Crider and that was the way of the male Criders, as though it had been bred into them; it was a substance in their blood, passed down from generations in the darkness of mating. If you were a male Crider, you were born to silence and to a hollow, distant face with eyes covered by a dull film of surrender. And if you were a male Crider, you did not change. You lived and died in a monotone that was as empty as a sigh.

But Floyd had been a caring neighbor. Since Eli had disappeared, Rachel had learned to depend on Floyd for the safe man-presence he offered, as well as for the occasional man's work demanded by the farm. His sense of obligation, sealed by the common borders of their land, was as absolute as an Old Testament law: It was the work of good deeds to watch and to help. And slowly, Rachel had learned Floyd well. She did not impose; she waited. She would not speak until Floyd spoke. She would not ask his advice about the farm until Floyd insisted that he be allowed to help. And she never spoke of Eli. To speak of Eli would have been to whimper and she could not whimper before Floyd.

Each Wednesday, when it did not rain, Floyd escaped the unending oppression of his failing land and made a visit to the town of Yale, and it was his habit to stop at the home of Rachel Pettit. Each Wednesday Rachel would hear the wagon, and she would stand behind the curtain of the window in the front room and watch as Floyd stopped his wagon fifty yards away at the mouth of the road turning into her house. He would sit and observe the house, expecting Rachel, or Dora, or Sarah, to greet him. He would sit and become uncomfortable and remove his hat and fan the air into his face. But he never looked at the boy, though the boy was always with him, always sitting in the back of the wagon, looking down.

And then Floyd would cup his hands to his mouth and call out: "Ho, anybody home?"

Rachel would not answer him at first call. Never at first call. "Yo-hoo. Anybody home? Rachel? You there?"

In all the years, Rachel had always been there.

* * *

"Yo-hoo. Anybody home? Rachel? You there?"

Rachel stepped to the screen door. She knew Floyd could not see her from the road. She called, "That you, Floyd?"

"Yes'm. It's Wednesday."

Rachel pushed open the door and stood beneath the frame of the doorway.

"Mornin', Floyd. Jack. Come on up. We're all here," she replied.

Floyd clucked to the mules and pulled them into the narrow road leading to the house. He stopped the mules at the edge of the yard and tied the rope reins to the hand brake. He then climbed slowly off the wagon, using the front wheel for steps.

"Thought somethin' might've been wrong when you didn't answer right off," Floyd drawled, looking beyond Rachel. It was one thing Rachel had long known; Floyd could not look into her eyes when he spoke.

"Nothin's wrong, Floyd," replied Rachel. "I was in the back of the house. Didn't realize it was Wednesday again. Week's gone fast."

"Time gets by and you don't know it, I reckon," Floyd said. "It sure does. More I live, the faster it goes. A man don't know how little time he's got unless he's got a little age on him." He nodded authoritatively and mumbled, "Uh-huh, uh-huh."

Rachel moved to the corner of the porch, above the steps. She leaned against a support post.

"Y'all all right?" she asked. "Mama Ada feelin' better?"

"Doin' good. Doin' good. Have to help Mama around a little bit, but she's feelin' good. Sure is. Y'all all right?"

"Fine, Floyd. Fine. Sarah and Dora's out back, workin' out there in the garden."

"Keeps me worried, y'all bein' up here all alone," Floyd said.

"Nobody's bothered us, Floyd."

"Can't tell, though. Sure can't. Times bein' hard."

Rachel knew what he wanted to say but could not.

"It's been two months since the Caufields was found," she replied patiently. "Whoever done that must've passed on through."

"Could be."

"Well, we're fine, Floyd."

"Uh-huh."

Floyd stood nervously beside his wagon. His fingers moved absently to the blouse of his overalls and he withdrew a tobacco sack. He began to build a cigarette with the precision of an artist, his long, hard fingers moving gently over the thin paper, cupping it, tapping it full with shredded tobacco leaf, folding it in a single twist. Rachel watched him, fascinated by his skill.

"Me'n the boy's goin' to town," Floyd said as he lit the cigarette. "I heard tell there was a man wanted some oak shingles cut. Thought y'all might be needin' somethin'. Maybe you got some quilts you want carried to the store."

Rachel looked at Jack Crider sitting on the back of the wagon. He had not lifted his head. He seemed preoccupied.

"No," she answered. "Nothin' today, Floyd. I'm grateful, just the same."

"Sure wish Dora wadn't so dead set against lettin' me and the boy cut up some wood for y'all," Floyd said slowly. "Wouldn't take us but a little while."

Rachel smiled. She said, "Don't suppose it's hurtin' us, Floyd."

Floyd sucked smoke from his cigarette. He looked around the yard, his eyes carefully examining the buildings. He pinched the cigarette from his lips and dropped it and ground it into the dirt with his shoe heel.

"Almost forgot," he said quickly. "Got a sack of sweet potatoes in the wagon. Me'n the boy finished cleanin' out the hill a couple of days ago. Got more'n we can use." He turned to the wagon before Rachel could reply and effortlessly lifted the heavy sack and shouldered it. Floyd was small and thin, but strong.

"You didn't have to do that, Floyd," Rachel protested.

"Wadn't no need in lettin' 'em go to waste."

"I know they're good. Sarah loves sweet potatoes."

"We had us a heavy crop last year. Made up the biggest hill we ever had," Floyd said. "Where you want me to put 'em?"

"You don't mind, in the storeroom."

Rachel watched Floyd nod and drop his eyes from her face. She knew him; yes, she knew him well. Part of his caring was overplanting his garden, though his sharing of goods was always spaced and calculated, presented with timid excuses of having more than needed for his own family. It had become a familiar ritual between them: the gift hurriedly offered like an embarrassment, countered by protest, then excuse, then acceptance. The two could have been players in a motion picture, repeating a memorized script. There was never any improvisation or invention; it was always the same.

Floyd followed Rachel to the screen door, waited for her to open it, then entered the house.

The house was wood-warm. Its walls and floors and ceilings had cured into the soft tan of time and use. The smell of wood smoke and cooked foods and cleaning soaps coated the house and expired from the walls like a living thing, a breath. But there was no odor of a man, nothing of the musk of the field laborer, or of the sweat brine of the sawmill hand. The breath of the house was sweeter, more delicate, like evenings of early spring flowers or the perfume of lilac water on hands. It was a house that belonged to three women and contained only their presence.

There were five main rooms to the house — the living room,

the kitchen, and three bedrooms, one for each of the women. A narrow corridor led from the kitchen along the back of the house to the small sideroom used for storing canned goods and food supplies, and to Dora and Sarah's bedrooms. The largest of the rooms, belonging to Rachel, was at the front of the house beside the living room. Rachel's room was both bedroom and workroom. Two heavy quilt curtains had been tacked to the ceiling, almost precisely dividing the room. One side was for sleeping, the other for sewing and quilting. Most of the hours of Rachel's life were spent in the divided halves of the room. Once there had been a door leading from her room onto the porch, but Floyd had boarded it, with Rachel's permission. "Makes me feel some better," Floyd had said flatly.

*   *   *

"House looks good," Floyd said routinely as he walked through the living room into the kitchen and to the sideroom. It was more than a compliment; it was a litany spoken by a man who had helped build the house, had repaired it, tended it with a craftsman's pride. It was something Floyd always said.

"Dora scrubbed the walls this week," Rachel replied.

"She's a worker," acknowledged Floyd, placing the potatoes against the wall in the sideroom. He added, "Woman like Dora, she'll scrub the wood off." He blushed at his weak humor.

"She likes to keep busy," Rachel said. "She and Sarah's been out in the garden all mornin'."

Floyd looked instinctively through the window of the kitchen. He saw Dora and Sarah working in a small, flat field beside the barn.

"Been a lot easier if she'd of let the boy come over and run the middlebuster," he said. "Would'n've took but a couple of hours. Make a better garden, bein' plowed deep."

"Dora's got her ways," Rachel replied simply.

"Yes'm."

"I appreciate the potatoes, Floyd. I'll cook some tonight."

Floyd shifted nervously on his feet. He said, "Long as I'm

here, I might as well take a look at that well pulley. Make sure the boy done it right." He looked at Rachel and then quickly away. "If it ain't no trouble," he added.

"No trouble at all," Rachel answered. She had forgotten about Jack repairing the well pulley. It had been a month and Floyd had not mentioned it before. "But it's fine," she said. "Jack's handy when it comes to fixin' things."

"He's all right, I reckon."

"You want to look it over, you can."

Rachel opened the kitchen door and stepped into the back-yard. Floyd followed. She crossed the yard to the well. Dora and Sarah stopped their work in the field and stared. Floyd lifted his hand, a pointed finger, in greeting. Sarah returned the wave timidly; Dora turned to her work with the heavy steel hoe.

"Sarah's growin' up," Floyd said.

"She is," agreed Rachel. "She's a woman now. I wadn't much older when I got married."

Floyd nodded. He turned to the well and began examining it. He did not know why, but he had always thought of the well as Eli's single triumph on his farm. Eli had battled for it, cutting through granite and clay, going deeper for water than anyone in the valley. He had used dynamite and a shovel and scoop bucket and had worked tirelessly. He would not listen to advice to move the well, not even a few feet. "This is where Rachel wants it," he had declared, "and, by God, this is where it'll be put, if I have to bore a hole to China." He had persisted and one day his shovel had caved into an underground river as cold as winter. The next day Eli had called in every neighbor within five miles to sample his water.

Floyd had helped Eli cover the mouth of the well with a box of fieldstone, planked across the top by oak shelving. And then the windlass of chestnut, with the winch driven through the tight center eye of the wood's age circles. The winch had a cog wheel with a drop wedge for locking the windlass and holding the bucket. It was the first windlass lock anyone in the valley had ever seen.

Floyd ran his hand over the lock and the windlass. The chestnut had been burned smooth by the rope. He dropped the bolt and locked the windlass and pulled with his weight against the rope, looped over the repaired pulley. The pulley was attached to a crossbar that Eli had cut from a blackgum and had nailed solidly beneath the roof of the shelter.

"Looks good," Floyd judged. "I was rememberin' when Eli dug out this well. Cut through some hard rock, but he done it. Got him the sweetest water in the mountains, to boot. Always like stoppin' by for a drink."

Rachel's face opened quickly, like a blink, then closed. She was surprised. Floyd had not mentioned Eli by name in years, and she had always understood his silence; it was a matter of respect, of avoiding the absence in her life. At least she had always believed that. It could have been that Eli was an absence in Floyd's life. He had been Floyd's friend. It did not matter that Eli told other people fantasies to please them, he had always been truthful with Floyd.

"You helped Eli dig it," she said, deliberately repeating her husband's name.

Floyd dropped his head. He mumbled, "I was around. Hauled off the dirt over yonder where that fig bush is."

Rachel stared at the bush. It was in full leaf. She remembered when Eli had planted it and had laughed that it was a stick and would never grow. But he would please her. If it was figs she wanted, it was figs she would have. The bush had survived and had grown an umbrella of limbs and leaves, and each year it pushed figs out of its covering like sweet bronze candy.

"That's been a few years," Floyd said, shaking his head philosophically.

"Yes," whispered Rachel. Then: "Floyd, you worry too much about us."

Floyd did not answer. He toyed with the bucket on the plank covering of the wellbox.

"Don't think I'm not grateful, but we can take care," Rachel added. "We have for a long time."

Floyd nodded and looked across the yard to Dora and Sarah.

"Be good if y'all had a dog of some kind," he said seriously. "Them Caufields didn't have one. It got killed a couple of days earlier, I hear tell. Kicked by the mule."

"Maybe," answered Rachel. "But I don't know what good it'd do. If Sarah didn't spoil it lazy, Dora'd probably run it off."

There was a pause, a taut silence stretching between them.

"I remember Eli likin' dogs," Floyd said softly.

Rachel was again surprised. Floyd had again spoken of Eli by name.

"You ever want one, let me know," he added. "We got too many to keep fed, anyhow."

"I will."

Floyd wiped the sleeve of his forearm across his face. It was a nervous habit Rachel had recognized for years. It meant Floyd was ready to leave.

"Gettin' on in the day," he said. "Me'n the boy got to go on, I reckon. Maybe find that fellow wantin' some shingles. I got some white oak cured out and a little bit of hickory."

"I'm glad you stopped by, Floyd. I appreciate it," Rachel told him.

She walked with him to the wagon. The boy was sitting exactly as he had been. Rachel spoke to him: "Tell your mama I said hello, Jack." Jack nodded.

"You need anythin', you send Sarah over," Floyd said, untying the rope reins from the brake. It was another of their memorized lines.

"I will," Rachel promised.

*   *   *

Rachel watched, arms folded, hugging her breasts, until the wagon rolled into the main road and disappeared around the knoll that had once been planted in corn. The sun was on her.

She lifted her face and closed her eyes and stood unmoving in
the warmth. Her breasts felt full against her arms and she
shuddered at a remembered touch that flashed through her
body like a chill. She could see Eli in the translucent screen of
her closed eyes, his face burning with laughter, the roar of his
voice thundering inside her mind. His fingers were touching her
lips, her face, her arms, her back. His mouth pulled from the
brown vessels of her nipples and his hair was warm under her
chin. Then his face fluttered and was gone and she could sense
only the fevered heat of early summer. There were earth sounds
around her, swirling in the undetectable rush of time, and she
could feel something shrill piercing her, filling her.

\* \* \*

Floyd did not see the man standing inside the gray-green of the
wood's shadows. Floyd's eyes were fixed ahead, at the tip of the
wagon tongue balanced between the two mules. He was thinking of Rachel Pettit. He had said too much to her, had been too
insistent. He had spoken of Eli, which was not his right. His
duty was as neighbor, but not to give advice. He crouched
forward on the wagon seat, feeling the shame that he feared
more than any other emotion. It was not right to pry, he told
himself bitterly. It was never good to speak more than necessary. And he had. He did not know if he should return to the
Pettit house. Or if he could.

\* \* \*

The man stepped into the edge of the road after the wagon had
passed, then quickly back into the undergrowth. He was not
certain: Perhaps the boy sitting in the back of the wagon had
seen him. The boy had looked up, then down again, but if he
saw him, he did not react. Even if the boy had seen him, it could
not have been clearly, not enough to recognize him again. For
days, he had been careful not to be seen. It would be foolish to
blunder after being so careful.

"Ah," he said aloud, "don't go rushin' things, Michael O'Rear. You've work to do."

He shrugged the sudden tightness from his shoulders and pulled at the bill of the cap on his head. Then he turned in the woods and started his slow climb back up the mountain. He began whistling. Softly. Gaily.

# 3

MICHAEL STOOD without moving and watched the rattlesnake.
He knew the snake could kill him; still, there was something
majestic about it. It was coiled into a rope of thick muscle that
quivered like a blood pulse and its tail hissed a sickening warning. The whirring of the rattles mesmerized Michael. It was as
though the tail performed rites of a ceremony as ancient and
dark as time. Circe's magic, thought Michael. Sweet as death,
the rattler's song. The snake's head danced against its swollen,
dark body. Its mouth opened and closed in a white smile and
its teeth glistened. Its red-string tongue slithered like a whip.

Michael was not afraid of the snake. It was an even match.
The snake had quickness and its vial of poison and its Devil's
noise; he had size and strength and a pinning stick. The stick
was long — six feet, at least — and Michael had trimmed one
end into a fork, where two limbs had branched away.

He gouged gently at the snake's head and whispered teasingly
as he turned the stick in his hands: "Shhhhh. Be quiet, my little
one. You'll get your bite soon enough. Soon enough."

The snake's body tightened into a hard knot. Its head sank
backward like a raised fist. Michael knew the snake would
strike soon. He tapped above the snake's head, then flipped the
stick quickly and pushed hard, catching the snake behind the
hard bone of its jaws. The snake's body writhed, turned upside
down, uncoiled, convulsed, fought hard to pull its trapped head
free, and if not free, then off. The instinct for suicide in trapped

animals was great and Michael knew it. He pushed steadily as he eased down the length of the stick to the snake.

"Easy up, now," he said to the snake. "No need of fightin' it. Not now. Not now. You lost it. Fair and square."

The snake's body lashed at the pinning stick, wrapping it in a death choke. Michael reached across the stick and caught the snake behind its flat jaws with his right hand. He squeezed hard with his fingers and the snake's mouth gaped open and he could feel the long ribbon muscles contracting as the snake swallowed involuntarily. He stood, lifting the snake still coiled to the pinning stick.

"Ah, you're a beauty," Michael said proudly. "A four-footer, I'd wager, and you've killed your share, you have, of rats and lizards. Swallowed 'em up whole. And I've got another swallow for you."

He chewed into the wad of tobacco leaf in his mouth, squashing it flat. He could feel the burn of the leaf against his tongue, and his mouth filled with saliva. Then he turned the snake's head to him. He pinched the snake's mouth open against the stick and spit the brown juice of tobacco deep into the snake's throat. The snake's head twisted angrily and its venom dripped from the tips of its teeth as the juice slipped into its body.

"That's enough," Michael said gently. "Just enough to calm you down. That's all." He waited patiently until the snake's body began to relax and loosen on the pinning stick. "Don't go dyin' on me, now," Michael coaxed. "You're not to go dyin'. Not yet."

He uncoiled the numbed snake from the stick and dropped it carefully into a thick cloth sack. He tied the top of the sack with a leather strip and looped it around the gargoyle head of his walking stick. Then he shouldered the stick and began walking happily through the woods.

*     *     *

It had been seven days since Michael had begun his surveillance
of the house of the three women. The house was an unplanned
fortress, standing on the tip of a plateau that rose like a wave
against the mountains behind it. It was surrounded by oak and
chestnut trees, with a hairline of pines running from the mountain down into the belly of the valley. The trees around the
house clustered like sentries, their highest limbs interlocking in
fingers of leaves, and the house, as well as its inhabitants, was
protected by an isolation that seemed almost mystic. Michael
knew of isolation. He understood it. Isolation enforced order
and habit, a rhythm of days that rolled into other days until it
created a monastic sense of timelessness. And so it was with the
house of the three women. Their waking and sleeping ticked
slowly on an internal clock of repetition.

The only intrusion had been the wagon with the man and the
boy. Neighbors — the Crider man Lester Caufield had described — Michael judged. He had watched from the woods
below the road as the man disappeared into the house with his
bundle of goods, reappeared at the well, and then left. And then
he had taken the risk of stepping into the road above the creek
and having the boy see him. But that had been a small risk.
Only, he was intrigued that the boy had not moved from the
wagon and that Dora and Sarah — he had easily identified the
women on his first day of watching them — had not left their
work in the garden to speak to the man with Rachel. There was
something to be learned from their behavior. Michael replayed
the actions again and again in his mind; intuitively, he knew it
was a pinspot of weakness and it would serve him well.

Each day he had watched and waited and lived comfortably
in the lush growth of the mountain. He was not unsure, as he
had been when he had camped above Lester Caufield's house.
Lester had told him what he needed to know. Lester had told
him of Eli — how he was like Eli — and of the three women,
and he had known immediately. He could be patient. He had
waited two months since the Caufields. He had traveled up to

Knoxville and worked in a tannery before returning to the mountains, and had plotted his drama with exacting detail. For two months he had repeated the names of the women. He had drawn the features of their blank faces in his mind and had heard their voices and cast them in their roles. And now he was ready.

The mountains had been cold and harsh before, in March; now they were warm by day and cool by night and the air was as sharp and clean as ice. Michael did not mind the waiting. He had learned of the ecstasy of being alone. Each day he worked with his knife, carving a figure from a heart of cedar that he had found in the woods. The carving relaxed him, narrowed his vision to exacting detail. And it satisfied an artistry that often confused him because it seemed to belong to another person. But it was patient work and patience was necessary. Rest. Think. Listen. There could be no blundering. It would be fool's work to blunder. Fool's work, and Michael O'Rear was not a fool. When the curtain parted, he would be prepared. He would not be a stammering fool. Rest. Think. Listen.

\*　　\*　　\*

On the eighth day, in early morning, Michael covered his campsite and packed his knapsack. The snake was in the sack, which was hanging from a limb. He slipped his walking stick through the loop of the leather strip, tied it securely, lifted the sack from the limb, and placed it on the ground. The snake squirmed and rolled weakly. "Soon, my beauty," Michael whispered. "Soon."

At midmorning he began the long, circling trip around the farm, and at noon stood above the house. Soon Sarah would emerge from the house and drive the cows from the barnyard to graze in the open field below the woods. She would sit in the shade of a great cedar tree and watch over the cows until Dora called her from the house, almost precisely two hours later. It had been the same every day Michael had watched the house. It was the routine he needed, the way of introduction that would take him among the women. He sat in the shadows and waited and ate part of a trout cooked the night before and stared intently at the house below him, trying to imagine the rooms and the furnishings in them.

He did not move until he saw Sarah leave the house and cross to the barnyard. Then he untied the sack and eased the snake onto the ground, catching it carefully behind the jaws in the narrow of its throat. He slipped his knife from its sheath with his left hand and forced the blade into the snake's opened mouth, behind his needle teeth. He began massaging the snake's head with his right index finger and the milky venom oozed from the snake's teeth, across the knife blade. "Get it out," he whispered. "Don't be leavin' more'n a drop or two. You wouldn't want to kill Michael O'Rear, now would you?"

He looked toward the house and saw the cows plodding up the hill, followed by Sarah. He eased the knife from the snake's mouth and wiped the blade across the fur back of a moss stand. Then he turned the snake's head toward him and winked. "Now's your vengeance, little friend," he said in a low voice. "Do it well." He turned the snake's head quickly and thrust its mouth on his left arm, above the wrist. He could feel the snake vibrate with a sudden life as its teeth sank deep into the muscle of the arm. A hard pain exploded in his body and he yanked viciously at the snake, ripping it away from his arm. The snake hissed and he snapped its head against the ground and then crushed its skull with the heel of his knife. The snake's dying body rolled in a wrapping motion, like a screw, thrashing in the pine needles. Breathing heavily, Michael caught his arm above the wound and watched the snake die.

He could hear the cows nearing him. He moved quickly, gathering the snake and rolling it in a loose coil ten feet behind the spot where Sarah always rested. He positioned the snake's head over a rock and covered the rock with leaves. It would work, he thought. He could slip his hand beneath the crushed head and flip it high, and the snake would appear to be alive. That would be enough. The rest would be convincing. He stepped back and judged his work. He was pleased. He felt the ache grow in his arm and he realized the weak poison was seeping throughout his body.

\*     \*     \*

Sarah was happy to be outside. She had worked that morning in the house, across from her mother at the quilting frame. The work was slow and monotonous and her mother had retreated into the silence that often fell over her like a shadow. Once, when she was younger, Sarah had asked her mother about the mood and Rachel had replied, "You'll learn it soon enough." Sarah had known this was not an answer, but a warning of something that would sour with the passing of time. It was a fear to be endured, like the stories she had been told by Dora about monthly bleedings when her time for the cycle had begun. Sarah had not questioned her mother again about the aloneness she pulled around her like a garment; afterward — instinctively, in perfect imitation — she, too, had begun to slip into her mother's silences.

She walked past the grazing cows to a soft sandbar she had heaped into a cushion beneath the cedar that stood alone in the line of pines lacing the edge of the woods. She sat lazily, her knees up, stretching her body forward to feel the pleasing strain of muscles pulling in her shoulders and back. A very small breeze washed across the side of her face, like a breath. She crossed her arms over her knees and leaned her head against her elbows and listened to the easy beat of her heart echoing in her temples.

When she heard the man's voice, her body started violently. She rolled forward, to her left, turned on her hands and knees and looked up. He stood not fifteen feet away. His right hand was raised, palm up, toward her. He pointed to the ground with his left hand.

"Shhhhh," Michael whispered. "It's a rattler, long as my leg."

A scream exploded from Sarah's throat. She scrambled awkwardly backward, crawling on her hands and knees.

Suddenly, the man before her dove to his left, his arms locked in front of him like a shield. She saw his knees hit the ground and his hands fight something before him. She heard him cry, saw his shoulders recoil, then fall forward again. She saw the snake spin through the air and fall heavily, and then the man was over it, swinging a rock. The rock fell again and again against the ground. Sarah could hear the pounding and feel it thundering through her hands.

Then he slumped back into sitting. He was breathing harshly through his mouth, his head nodding as he inhaled and exhaled. His face was flushed and perspiration dripped from his forehead. He held his left arm stretched out before him.

It had happened so quickly, in splinters of seconds, faster than Sarah could comprehend. She stood cautiously, staring at the man. Then she turned and began running down the hill.

Michael smiled as he watched her run. He closed his eyes and replayed the assassination of the snake, and as he did, he could hear a ripple of applause building into a chorus.

\*   \*   \*

Michael was leaning against his knapsack when Sarah arrived with Rachel and Dora. He had tied a handkerchief above the elbow of his left arm and twisted it tight against the artery. The vessels of his forearm bulged in blue cords under his skin and the puncture wounds of the snakebite had blistered into purple dots.

He raised his face to the women and a feeble smile played across his mouth.

"You hurt bad?" Rachel asked tentatively, stepping near him.

"Not hurt, but bit sure enough," answered Michael.

Rachel's eyes flicked to his face, to his voice, to the song of his accent.

"Let me take a look," she said. She knelt beside him and took his arm. She touched the outer circle of the festering wound, pressing it gently.

"We got to cut it," she told him. "Bleed the poison out."

Michael nodded. He rested his head against his knapsack and closed his eyes. His mouth was dry and his face burned with the heat of the mild poison spreading through his body. He had not believed it would affect him, but it did not matter. Perhaps it was better that it had.

"Won't take but a minute, but it's got to be done," Rachel added.

He nodded again. He could hear movement about him, could feel other hands on his arm pulling away the handkerchief above his elbow. A stinging rush of blood spread into his forearm. Another woman — Dora — spoke. Her voice was stern and heavy.

"I'll do the cuttin'," she said. "I got the knife."

He felt his arm being lifted and balanced across a lap. Then he felt the quick draw of the blade on his skin, over the bite. His body trembled and his fist closed tight. Blood began to seep from the cut, dripping down his arm like a thick paint.

"We'll let it bleed a spell and then get you down to the house," Rachel said bluntly. "You could go into a fever."

"Rachel."

It was Dora's voice and it was a warning.

There was a pause, a silent struggle between the two women that Michael could feel. He opened his eyes and looked at Dora. Her narrow face was cold with contempt.

"You needn't go to worryin'," he whispered. "I'm grateful to you and on the word of them that's holy, you got no danger to be facin'. I couldn't do fight with the weakest of God's creatures right now."

"Nobody's worried," Rachel assured him calmly. "Not

many people come through here we don't know, that's all."

Michael smiled his understanding. He closed his eyes again and flexed his fist to force the blood out. He could hear footsteps in the leaves around him.

"Mama, here's the snake," Sarah said. "He — he killed it."

"It's big," replied Rachel. "Must've had plenty of poison."

"Don't go touchin' it," warned Dora. "Snakes look like they're dead sometimes when they ain't."

Michael moved against his knapsack. He forced a smile.

"Sure enough," he agreed. "That's the truth of it. Snakes, you can't tell about. That's somethin' I've learned travelin' about, and it's a strange lesson for an Irishman. There's not a single snake in Ireland. Not one."

"Don't talk," Rachel said. "Don't move around. It'll just spread the poison that much quicker."

"I'm at your mercy and grateful for it," replied Michael quietly. "Whatever it is you want, I'll be mindin', but I don't like bein' thought of as a stranger. My name's Michael. Michael O'Rear."

Rachel opened his handkerchief and refolded it into a bandage. She wiped away a string of blood that had matted in the hair of his arm.

"My name's Rachel," she said reluctantly. "Rachel Pettit. The girl, she's my daughter, Sarah. Dora's my sister. Dora Rice."

"You're kindly people," insisted Michael. "It's providence that puts you here, it is."

Rachel did not reply. She pressed the handkerchief over the cut and held it.

*   *   *

It was late afternoon before the women moved Michael from the woods to the house, using a mule and a hauling sled with steel runners. Sarah had returned to the house for water and bandages and a salve to apply to the cut, and Rachel had cleaned and dressed the wound. But the women had said nothing. They had sat away from him in silence, and as he rested, Michael had tried to close the distance of their presence by the telepathy of his imagination, to force the ghost of his inner eye to narrow on their faces, to enter their bodies through their breathing. But he could not. He had thought of them for two months, but still they were far away, removed by a mystique that covered them like a transparent lacquer. He did not know what it was, but he knew the drama was forming and he knew his role.

*   *   *

He was guided by Rachel into her room, through the quilt curtains, and to her bed.

"Take off your shoes and lay down across the top quilt, Mr. O'Rear," she told him. "We'll get you some food and I'll change the bandage."

"It's Michael, please, and don't be troublin' yourself."

She looked at him evenly.

"You got bit helpin' Sarah," she said. "We owe watchin' after you." She turned and left the room.

Michael removed his shoes and stretched across the bed. The bed was soft and cool and had the clean smell of fresh cloth. He smiled easily and cupped his hands behind his head, pushing against the pillow. It was beginning. His own private Chautauqua. He had made his entrance and met his audience. And he had done it with a prop too daring to disbelieve.

He wondered if the women had taken the snake's rattles as a prize.

# 4

RACHEL WALKED OUTSIDE, alone. It was dark, in the early smoke of night, and a chill had fallen over the mountains like a cloud. She thought of the man in her bed. It was not an illusion, not a trick of her mind. It was not restlessness. The man in her bed was very like Eli.

It was in his manner, in the toss of his head as he talked, in the music of his voice. It was in the bold sculpture of his smile and in the energy that expired from him like heat.

Eli, she thought. She inhaled deeply and the perfume of the night made her shudder. Eli's presence had been intoxicating to Rachel, suffocating her with its sweet scent of promise, opening her body as if it were ripe fruit splitting at his touch. He had done so much wrong, had lied so often, had taken from others with such ease and without regret, yet she had not been able to resist his presence and she had forgiven him willingly, eagerly.

The man in her bed was very like Eli.

Dora had recognized it also.

Dora had said, "Send him away. It'll come to no good."

"We can't," she had answered her sister. "What he done was for Sarah. We owe him."

"Mark me," Dora had warned. "Mark what I'm tellin' you. It'll come to no good."

Her caution had frightened Rachel. Dora was older only by

six years, yet somehow she seemed eternal, without youth. She
had always been sullen and suspicious, as though possessed by
a psychic power from some lightless world spinning in her
mind. She had come to live with Rachel and Sarah five years
earlier and had brought with her an atmosphere of fear and
bitterness as deadly as acid.

Rachel walked slowly in the white sand of the yard. She
heard again her sister's words: "Mark me. It'll come to no
good." Dora had never trusted Eli. To Dora, Eli had been evil,
and now there was another man, very like Eli, and she could
sense in him a terrible danger.

Rachel had said nothing to Dora of the dark message. She
knew speaking of it would only free the phantoms in Dora's
mind, and her visions would become more fearful.

Perhaps Dora was right. It was an odd coincidence. She had
been thinking of Eli. Floyd had mentioned his name and she
had been thinking of him, and the memories were intimate and
hurtful, and she wondered why she could not control his force.
Perhaps Dora was right. Perhaps it would come to no good,
having someone so like Eli to care for. But if there was a danger,
it was a danger to her alone, the danger of memory aroused.
The man in her bed would soon recover and be gone and that
would be the end of it.

She stood beside the fig bush and looked up along the horizon
of mountains that were ink-blue against the gray sheet of night.
Her eyes moved carefully over the mountains and her memory
separated profiles of bodies and faces hidden in the sagging rim
line. Eli had found the profiles for her. He had drawn them with
his finger, forcing her eyes to follow as he traced them across
the velvet of darkness. "There's another," he had said proudly.
"You see it? There. Plain as it can be, just like the Indian said."
It was the same as seeing pictures in the stars, he had told her,
only better. "Look hard. There's his face. See it? And there's
his chest. And his legs and feet, toes pointed straight up. Plain

as can be. You see it?" Yes. Yes. She had seen the profiles and, yes, it was better than watching stars. Stars were dots that had to be connected with imaginary lines; the profiles of the mountains were full and endless. No one else knew about them, Eli had whispered. No one. It was a lost story told by the old Indian, and it would die in the secrecy that he shared with her. She knew of the old Indian. He had died many years before. He had been gentle but demented, and things that could not be explained were always believed to be the work of the old Indian, because the old Indian could see into time. No one else knew, Eli had said, but the old Indian had told him the faces and bodies of the mountain rim had once belonged to a race of clay giants who ruled the earth, until they began boasting that their monarchy included the heavens also. Then they were made to lie down and stare forever upward into the awful eye of God, and they had become grotesquely disfigured and covered with the feathered hair of trees. That was how the Great Smokies came to be, molded from the bodies of clay giants. And they had names: Hail, Thunder, Rain, Fire. Yes, Eli had said seriously as he laughed, that was why there were such words, because there had been such giants.

Rachel turned from the fig bush and walked to the well and pulled the heavy wood covering from over the opening of the wellbox. She looked into the black tunnel that Eli had dug into the ground — stubbornly, proudly dug, until he reached a vein of the sweetest water in the valley. She wondered if the man in her bed was as stubborn and proud. She wondered if he could see faces in mountains.

\*　　\*　　\*

In the night Michael removed the bandages from his arm and peeled open the cut with his fingers. He rubbed the palm of his hand over the lips of the wound, smearing the seeping blood across the razor line of the slit. His arm throbbed from torn tissue and he lay back against the pillow and breathed slowly to quell the nausea. Then he rebandaged his arm and slept.

By morning the cut was puffy and infected. There was no fever, not to the touch, but Michael lay still in bed, his eyes floating beyond the faces of Rachel and Dora, as though wandering in a semiconscious dream. His breath was shallow, through his mouth. He did not answer Rachel's questions as she cleaned and wrapped his arm.

"The fever's in him," Dora said, pressing with her hands against his throat. "Could be he's got a weak heart."

"Maybe it's the snake poison," replied Rachel.

Dora did not answer. She stared into the cloud of Michael's eyes, searching for something she could not see.

"We better get him covered up. Bring the heat back out," Rachel added. "Maybe get a spoon of whiskey in him."

"Maybe that's what he wants," Dora replied cynically.

They covered him with two quilts and fed him three table-spoons of clear whiskey, and then they left the room.

He could hear their voices through the walls. The voices were muted, wordless, but he could tell they were arguing. He blinked his eyes rapidly to moisten them, then he adjusted his head against the pillow and a smile danced across his face.

\* \* \*

For two days the wound split and bled and the signs of fever rose and fell in him at will and he was careful to maintain the appearance of a coma in the presence of the women. It was a risky performance, yet there was a joy in playing it — the skilled actor against his audience, flashing nuances like card tricks, balancing pauses against the rhythms he could feel pulsating throughout the house. Michael did not know why, but he knew there was someone else about to enter the scene.

That person was Mama Ada Crider.

She was a very old woman. Very withered. Very small. Her chest was concave and her back bowed in a cat's stretch. Her face was emaciated and white as bone, her lips cracked and dry, her eyes deep and dull and covered with cataracts that looked like drops of silver.

Mama Ada had the power of healing. She could stop bleeding and draw fire and blow away thrash. And she could do something no other person in the mountains was able to do: She could drive poison from people or animals. She used an Old Testament scripture that had been taught in secret by her mother, taught with an exactness that was the perfect print of her mother's voice in word and intonation. And Mama Ada had never taught the secret to anyone. Her children had been sons, not daughters, and the dominion over poison was a gift of mother to daughter. The scripture and its precise saying was locked in her mind like a God-whisper and its cosmic power would be sealed with her death.

To the people of the Naheela Valley, it was not a witch's power, not a thing of satanic worship that Mama Ada possessed. It was a command that had been poured over her at birth like an anointment. And it was mighty. There were stories about her. She could order snakes to stretch out like sticks and they obeyed. She had blown fire from people whose skin had bubbled in whelps as black as ash, and the burn had dusted away in fine powder. She had cured the thrash in babies too sick to open their eyes, whose parents had given them up for dead.

Rachel knew of the stories, had been told them as myths, but she knew them to be true. She had seen the power. It had happened when Sarah was a baby. Sarah had fallen and struck her face against a table, and her nose had begun to bleed profusely and would not stop. Eli had wrapped Sarah in a sheet and put her in the wagon and driven to Mama Ada. The sheet was soaked red and Sarah's body had become limp, but the blood would not stop. It flowed in spurts, gushing with each heartstroke, and Mama Ada had sat calmly in a chair on the front porch of her home and held Sarah across her lap. She had bent forward over the baby's face, her eyes closed, and she had whispered something no one heard. Before she opened her eyes again, the bleeding in Sarah had stopped. The only thing Mama

Ada had said was, "Wadn't no need to bring the child out. You could of just told me and it'd been the same."

*   *   *

And now Mama Ada was in the room with Michael, seated beside the bed in a chair taken from the kitchen. Michael watched the scene from behind the false veil of his unfocused vision. He could smell the musk of death on Mama Ada like a dampness. Rachel and Dora lifted his arm and removed the bandages and placed it on a pillow at the edge of the bed. Then Mama Ada reached for the arm and ran her fingers over the cut. Her fingers were brittle and as cold as the skin of a reptile.

"Leave me t'be," she said in a weak, ruptured voice.

And Rachel and Dora stepped away to the foot of the bed, against the quilt wall, and watched as Mama Ada pulled her face to Michael's arm.

Michael could sense her lips moving close to him. He could feel her cool breath against his arm. He wondered with amusement how he should react to the old woman and her hocus-pocus of deceptive divinity. Her fingers fanned over the wound in a spider's touch, meticulously, like a reader of braille. Then her fingers stopped and she cupped the palm of her hand over the cut and blew on his arm, circling her own hand. It had the feel of a cool, gentle wind. Michael's body quivered in surprise. A lightness entered his arm and swam up his shoulder, across his back, and along the corridor of his spine. His left hand snapped open by a command he could not control and his fingers spread wide, straining the muscles. He could feel an electric shock numbing his fingertips. His mind whirled dizzily and his head rolled against the pillow. A word he did not know filled his mouth and broke through his lips in a guttural cry.

Suddenly Mama Ada dropped his arm. Her hands snapped open, palms down, and her thin fingers began to tremble. Her eyes widened and her tiny, dry mouth cracked open in a tight circle. Her hands turned up and she began to push weakly against an invisible force above Michael's body. Her head twisted left, to her shoulder, and a feeble cry — a whine — rose from her mouth.

"Mama Ada?" whispered Rachel.

"Watch her," Dora warned.

Mama Ada sank back against the chair and her head bobbed in a rubbery seizure. Her hands fell to her sides and she closed her eyes tightly.

"Be gone, be gone," she cried. Her eyes flew open and she stared into Michael's face. Her arms and hands rose again and she waved them in a swimming motion, stroking the air, pushing it aside. "Be gone," she repeated, whispering.

"Mama Ada? What is it?" Rachel asked, stepping toward her.

"Somethin's there," Dora said quietly. "She feels it."

"Mama Ada?"

"I told you," snapped Dora. "There's somethin' about him."

The swimming motion of her arms slowed and stopped and Mama Ada stared fearfully into the space beyond Michael. Her arms closed in front of her, under her chin, as though pinned to her body. She began to bend forward at the waist, falling.

"Get her," called Dora, moving quickly.

Dora and Rachel reached Mama Ada before she toppled from the chair. They held her and let her head rest against her own shoulder. Her eyes were widened in terror and her breathing was deep and erratic.

"Go get Floyd," Rachel said to Dora. "She looks bad."

\*   \*   \*

It was morning, in the prelight of day. Michael leaned forward, his elbows on the oilcloth of the table. He held a cup to his mouth, breathing in the rich vapor of coffee.

"Ah," he said peacefully. "It's the fullest I've been since I took a mind to splurge my last few dollars at a restaurant in Memphis. It was a feast like this, all right. Little restaurant with tablecloths made out of two colors of pink. And the waitress wore a starchy little white uniform with pink lace. Even on her cap, it was. She was turned up and snooty at my bein' so scruffy-lookin', but when I ordered the evenin's best, plus a half-bottle of imported pink champagne to match the pink tablecloth, why, she changed her mind. Couldn't have had better service if I'd been the blessed Pope, mind you."

"It's good to see you eatin'," Rachel said. "After not takin' a bite the last couple of days."

Michael replaced the cup in its saucer and nodded.

"But it's not to be taken as a slight," he replied. "I don't have much recall of the past few days, to be truthful. Just some flashes of light, like the heavens openin' up, all bright and shiny after a rain. I guess it was the poison that that blessed lady drove out. It's a miracle, I'd say. In Ireland, she could be sainted for such a gift."

"Mama Ada's helped out lots of folks," Rachel said. "It's her way."

"Well, she's got me beholden to her. There's no other way of puttin' it," vowed Michael.

"You feelin' better this mornin', Mr. O'Rear?" asked Sarah.

"Fit as a fiddle," Michael answered merrily. "Fit enough to dance the day down and still have some left for night. It's one thing I do, Miss Sarah, I bounce back. Why, I knew a fellow once — a Britisher, he was — who caught the malaria soldierin' down in India, and he'd get those chills so bad, you'd have to strap him down to keep him from vibratin' away. Then he'd get the heat and they'd have to wrap him in wet sheets. But, quick as that, he'd be up and about. Sassy as the soldier he was. And I'm the same."

Sarah laughed quickly. Her eyes flashed.

"You'll be goin' on, then?" Dora asked bluntly.

Michael let the weight of the question crush the room. Then

he smiled easily and replied, "Yes, Miss Dora. I'll be goin' on, soon as the sun peeks up."

"Not today," corrected Rachel. "Not till you get some strength back."

Michael shifted in his chair. He rubbed the snakebite wound with his right hand.

"Miss Dora's right," he protested. "I've got to be movin' on. Likely I've missed out with the circus job in Florida, but there may be a ragtag carnival along the way."

"The circus?" Rachel said.

"The circus, indeed. Wouldn't you know? I'm a barker."

He stood up with a grand sweep of his arms and struck a comical pose.

"Ladies and gentlemen, right this way," he sang. "See the famous women of the mysterious East. Dancin'. Wigglin'. Tellin' strange stories with the wavin' of their arms. Right this way. Careful there, fellow, you're lookin' faint-hearted, you are. Maybe it's the merry-go-round for you."

Michael finished his chatter with a bow and a flourish and sat down heavily in his chair. Sarah laughed gleefully, covering her mouth with her hands. Rachel and Dora stared at him in surprise.

"I hope you'll be forgivin' me," Michael said. "Bein' off-color like that in front of ladies. It's circus talk and it fits me the way a church hymn fits a good preacher. Just part of bein' what I am, it is."

"It's — it's no harm," Rachel stammered.

"I'm takin' advantage of your good carin', carryin' on so, but the spirit's flown up in me like a sparrow, and bein' Irish to boot, well, it's just hard to keep down."

"Nothin' wrong with feelin' some of life," Rachel said hesitantly.

The mood changed in Michael like color. His smile fell. His voice softened.

"But I'm bein' less than a gentleman," he apologized. "I've

raved about things to feed my own selfish feelin' and I've not asked about the three of you."

"Nothin' to say," Dora remarked.

"There's always somethin' to say to others, Miss Dora," corrected Michael. "Always. For one, I've been wonderin', since I've got some senses back, about your menfolk. There's been none around that I've seen. Could it be they're off workin'?"

The room froze. Sarah's stare locked on Michael. Dora turned away. Rachel stood at the table and began stacking the breakfast dishes.

"I'm askin' your forgiveness if — " Michael began.

"No," interrupted Rachel. "It's — it's a fair question." She placed the dishes before her on the table and faced Michael. "Fact is," she said, "my husband — Sarah's father — has been gone a few years now. Off somewhere. He was always that kind of man. The wanderin' was in him."

Michael stood slowly. He turned away from the table and walked to the kitchen window. Outside, the mountains were washed pale with morning.

"If I could've guessed, I wouldn't've asked," he said slowly. "It's not of my matter, and I've clouded this good house with hurt by bringin' it up. I'm shamed by it."

"No reason," Rachel replied. "Wadn't no way for you to know."

Michael shook his head.

"But I am shamed. Ought to be," he mumbled. "Here you've taken in a stranger, and a man at that, and that stranger's been more fool than grateful. And there's the neighbors — that fine old lady and her family. They must be thinkin' the worse, and I'm shamed by it."

Dora's voice cut the stillness like a whip.

"That's took care of," she said. "Rachel seen to that."

Michael turned back to the women.

"How?" he asked.

Again the room froze. The question lingered. Rachel stared hard at her sister.

"How?" repeated Michael. He heard the urgency of his own voice and tried to control it.

"I told them you was Eli's cousin," Rachel confessed. "He — Eli — is my husband."

"O Holy Father," Michael whispered desperately. "I've caused you to be bearin' false words before your neighbors." He dropped his head. A shimmer of delight arose in him.

"It's been done," Dora said flatly. "None of us'll say different."

"What you done was for one of us," argued Rachel. "You talk about bein' beholden to Mama Ada; we're beholden to you. It's all we can do. You'll not leave until your strength's back."

Michael paced the small room. He ran his fingers through his hair. A small clucking sound, a protest, rattled in his throat.

"It's not right, it's not," he said. "Bein' alone in the house with the three of you. Not the least." He stopped his pacing abruptly. "Miss Sarah, if you'll be bringin' me my knapsack and goods, I'll feel better bein' outside, in the barn."

"There's no need — " Rachel began.

Michael's raised hand stopped her.

"Exceptin' how I feel about it," he corrected. "There's some decency left, I'd hope. The barn's fine. The barn's better'n any night I've seen in weeks, save the softness of your own bed."

Sarah moved in her chair. She started to rise, then sat back. Her eyes darted from Dora to Rachel.

"Mama?" she said.

"Do what he wants," ordered Dora. "A man's got a right to his pride."

Rachel nodded once and Sarah rose and left the kitchen.

"There's a room out in the barn," Rachel explained methodically. "We used to have a worker when Eli was home, a man he bailed out of jail one time. They put up a little room in one corner, out of the way, with a stove and a rope bed. We keep the place picked up and the mattress aired. Out of habit, I guess."

Michael heard the monotone of her voice, the note of resignation, of invisible surrender, to her sister. He saw the curl of a smile in Dora, though the muscles of her face did not move.

"You're an understandin' woman, Rachel," he said gently. "I'd feel better about it, and it'd do me good, bein' outside. Maybe there's some light work around I can do to help out today. Nothin' heavy, mind you. Just somethin' to get the blood flowin' again. I know the needs of my own body; work's good for it."

Rachel carried the dishes to the work counter. She would not look at him, or Dora.

"We'll see," she said. "Dora knows about the outside work. I do the quiltin'."

"We'll be hoein' in the garden," Dora replied. "You can help out some if you feel up to it."

"I do," Michael said. Then to Rachel, in a whisper: "I'm sorry about your husband, your Eli. Him bein' a wanderer. I've some of the same blood in me, I'm sorry to say, travelin' the world over like I've done. It's a bad sickness, it is. Worse than any fever. Could be you told the truth in part; could be me and your Eli are cousins of a kind."

The words drove into Rachel. It was like a voice in the back of her mind. He was very like Eli.

Sarah reappeared in the kitchen, struggling with the knapsack. Michael took it from her, lifting it lightly with one hand.

"Now, what's the matter with me?" he said gently. "Askin' a lady to carry the burden of a junk collector. I'd do better burnin' it in the trash than carryin' it around like it's a king's prize. Shows what a man thinks of himself, pickin' up bits and pieces along the way just to prove he's been there. Truth is, not a thing in it's worth the price of a smile. Exceptin' my greenery for Saint Paddy's celebration."

"What's Saint Paddy?" asked Sarah.

"Saint Paddy? Ah, child, it's the soul of the Irish, it is. Saint Patrick was the patron saint of Ireland. Grand as the sight of the Almighty himself."

Michael turned the knapsack in his hand like a toy. He dropped it into a chair and unlaced the top.

"But there's somethin' else in here," he said secretively. "Somethin' I'd be grateful if you ladies would let me share with you. Made by my own hands, they are, and it'd be my honor to make a gift of them."

He pulled back the cover of the knapsack and reached deep into it and withdrew a small box tied with a string. He held the box up in front of him and smiled proudly.

"It's little enough," he announced, "but next to my greenery for Saint Paddy's Day and the carvin' on my walkin' stick, it's the best I've got."

He untied the box and removed the top.

"Close your eyes, Sarah," said Michael.

Sarah obeyed, like a child.

"Give me your hand," he said.

Sarah cupped her hands before her.

He reached into the box and picked out a green paper flower and placed it in her hands.

"It's a shamrock," he told her. "The flower of the Irish. And I made it with my own two hands, to sell on the streets of New York City."

"It's — it's pretty," Sarah said softly, turning the paper flower in her hands. "I never seen one."

"It'll bring you luck — but only paper luck, I'm afraid," Michael replied happily. "The real thing, now that's another story. That'd be a blessin'. Here, ladies, there's one for each of you. Woman I worked for in New York City said I should've been an artist. Said I was the best at makin' paper flowers she'd ever seen. We sold 'em by the baskets, I'll tell you."

Rachel and Dora accepted the flowers silently.

"It'd make me feel good inside to know you'd be rememberin' Michael O'Rear whenever you look on these in days to come," he said gently. "The people I'm fond of, I leave a shamrock, like it was a fancy callin' card. Like Johnny Appleseed markin' out his travels with apple seeds."

"They're pretty, like Sarah said," remarked Rachel. "We thank you for them, Mr. O'Rear."

Michael smiled broadly. He retied the box and pushed it back into the knapsack.

"Miss Dora," he said, "let's have at that garden before the sun gets up and makes a puddle of us all. Get it done while the dew's up and then I'll be for findin' a fishin' pole and bringin' in a string of fish for supper."

Dora dropped the shamrock she held onto the table and stared coldly at Michael.

"Whenever you're ready," she said.

\*   \*   \*

Michael's presence filled the day, with the playfulness of his stories, the booming of his song, the drum of his laughter. And Sarah circled him like a butterfly, awed by the exaggerations of his endless adventures. She was girlish and giddy and her small voice, flooding with questions, was as free as a bird sitting on the shoulder of a limb, singing into the ear of a tree.

Rachel worked inside at the quilting frame and listened. She could feel the power of exuberance building like a parade, with brass and cymbals, march-time and costumes of shimmering colors. The parade was a man very like Eli, whose step had the heavy sound of an announcement and whose shoulders seemed to crowd even the out-of-doors. It was good, she thought. It was very good. She wondered only if Sarah would become intoxicated by the man, as she herself had become intoxicated by Eli. No, she decided. No, he was far too old. Sarah would see him only as someone who was fascinating. And that, too, was good. Dora's warning did not matter.

At night, Rachel and Sarah sat on the front porch and listened as Michael recited Irish poetry and told them of his years on the tent Chautauqua. His voice was that of a man who had been often alone and was unashamed to speak aloud for the joy of his own sound. It was a time that passed quickly, too quickly, before Michael went to the barn to sleep.

*　　*　　*

Rachel woke before morning to the sound of a lusty Irish tune whistled in the field below her bedroom window. She wrapped her cotton robe around her and peered through the window. Michael was in the field with a shovel, marking the ground with shallow holes.

"You're up early, Mr. O'Rear," she called through the screen.

Michael whirled on his heel and faced the window. He could not see Rachel through the screen.

"True," he replied. "I've rested my fill, I suppose. Couldn't stay asleep another minute, not with all that's waitin' to be done, and with the day screamin' to be lived."

"You feelin' better?" she asked.

"Better, Rachel. Better. A fellow once told me that a man what lived in the mountains would be a bit of a loon to want to be anywhere else, and I'm believin' I know what he meant. It's a lovely time of the day, it is. Like lookin' into the face of the Almighty. Take a breath, Rachel. You can feel it."

Rachel breathed deeply, obediently. The air was sweet.

"What're you doin'?" she asked.

Michael raised his shovel like a flag and pointed along a line from the road across the field.

"Well, I'm doin' somethin' that should've been done a long time ago, Rachel," he answered. "I'm markin' out for a fence. Put in a fence and there'd be grass aplenty for grazin', and it'd be a help to the land. It struck me last night, when I found the rolls of barbed wire in the barn, just sittin' there. It's the least I can do before movin' on."

"That's doin' too much, Mr. O'Rear," Rachel protested. "You don't owe us — "

"Only my life," he interrupted. "Only my life. And it's Michael. Save the 'mister' for the preacher."

\* \* \*

Dora moved noiselessly into Sarah's bedroom to stare out the side window of the house. Sarah sat on the edge of her bed, listening to the conversation between Michael and her mother.

"What's goin' on?" Sarah asked Dora.

"Nothin'," Dora answered.

"Why's he up so early?"

"He had somethin' to say."

"What?" Sarah was confused and sleepy.

"He's tellin' the world that he's here and that he's to stay around awhile," Dora replied bitterly. "As long as he wants. That's what he's sayin'."

# 5

MICHAEL'S FENCE was not an ordinary fence.

He did not build it as other men would have. Other men would have cut and set the posts and then stretched the wire, and the fence would have been completed. Michael built his fence in parts, in spans, posts and wire together. He wrestled it from the ground slowly and deliberately, urging it into shape with a performance that made it seem gravely important. Each post, each stretching of wire, declared the need for the fence and each act of its building was accomplished in festive excitement, like the discovery of an obscure but rare truth.

In the retiring peace of late afternoons, Michael coaxed Rachel and Sarah to walk the fence line with him as he surveyed his progress with an artist's anxiety for perfection.

"That'll be redone," he would thunder. "And that. Fool that I am for doin' such sorry work."

The fence would be solid, he vowed to Rachel. It would last longer than any of them.

It would be what a fence should be: for keeping out as well as keeping in.

"There's a tune to it," he said proudly, plucking at the taut wire. "Listen, Sarah. Listen. You could sing to it, you could. Wait till the wind comes up. It'll be like a Gypsy band playin' violins. Wind music like you've never heard. You'll be sleepin' to it at night. You'll see."

\* \* \*

The fence seemed to possess him. He poured his energy into it madly. He behaved as though time did not exist, and if he recognized the awkwardness his presence had created, he ignored it. It was the fence that mattered. The fence. It had become a kind of private staking line, like the boundaries of an animal's roaming. The fence had his scent, his signature, his coded warnings against invasion. The fence was his. And the three women watched him from a distance, each with her own questions. There was a man among them. Nothing was the same. The air sizzled and popped with an electric charge that flowed from him like a storm, and his voice began to hypnotize the space about him with the driving cadence of a march song.

And the space about him, and the three women who lived in that space, began to accept him.

*     *     *

"Funny how that fence is in me," Michael confessed one night. "Like it's me I'm plantin' down instead of posts. Like the tighter the wire pulls, the more it holds me in. Here I am, hangin' around like a stray cat, puzzled at not up and leavin' like I've done lifelong. But it's a job that's got a hold on me, ladies. It has at that. And I'm hopin' my stayin' to do it hasn't put a strain on you."

"No," Rachel answered hesitantly. "No. We got our work to do. Nothin's changed."

But there had been changes. Imperceptible changes of mood and habit. Michael filled the eye of their subconscious seeing like an inescapable force. He was in their thinking and in their tensions and there was no way to exorcise him. They could only watch. And wait. There was an unknown and it was gathering beyond them.

The unknown arrived with Floyd Crider.

*     *     *

On the first Wednesday of his work with the fence, Michael recognized Floyd's wagon on the road that led into Yale and hurried from the field to meet Floyd at the turnoff leading to the house. Rachel watched from the window as Michael and Floyd talked. She knew Floyd was uncomfortable by the way he sat forward on the wagon, rolling the rope reins in his hands. He would have to be, she thought. Though she had told the two men of one another, Michael was a stranger and Floyd was awkward around strangers. Michael's voice was strong and his accent confusing and when he spoke he animated his words with bold gestures. Floyd would not know what to say. He would be embarrassed. She watched as Michael pointed to the fence he was building and waved his hand along an imaginary line that circled above the house and skirted the edge of the woods. Then Michael stood quietly beside the wheel of the wagon and listened to something Floyd was saying. After a few minutes, Floyd left and Michael returned to his work. Rachel stood at the window watching him. There was something unusual about Floyd's visit, she thought. He had talked with Michael more freely than she had believed he would. Maybe Floyd was more comfortable around men, even men like Michael. But that would be expected. Still, there was something missing in the routine of Floyd's visit. Jack, she thought. Jack was missing. Jack was not with his father. She could not remember when Jack had not been with Floyd. She walked to the kitchen and poured water into a glass fruit jar and carried it across the field to Michael.

"I saw you talkin' to Floyd," she said as he drank from the jar.

"Ah, he's a fine man, he is," Michael acknowledged. "Askin' if we had any needs, sayin' he was pleased to see the fence goin' up. Said he remembered when Eli bought the wire and they'd talked about it, just the place I'm puttin' it. Even volunteered to bring his boy over and help out, but I told him it was a vow I'd made to do it myself."

"He's been a good neighbor," replied Rachel.

Michael nodded.

"A better man you couldn't find, I'd wager," he said. "I asked about his dear mother. Said she wasn't up to her health and he'd be lookin' for the doctor to come out and see her."

"Mama Ada?" Rachel asked with surprise. "Floyd's always sent us word when Mama Ada gets sick. We take turns stayin' with her. Dora even gathers up some herbs she likes takin'."

Michael's face furrowed in worry.

"Could be askin' in the doctor's just a precaution," he said. "He didn't seem overdistressed, the way he told it. Said she hadn't said much since that day she took the poison out of my arm. But he's a quiet man and I was ravin' on about the fence. Could be I didn't hear the fear in him."

Rachel looked toward the sun. It was late morning, in the same hour that Floyd always arrived at her home on Wednesdays. It was hot and clear above her, but in the west a line of thunderheads rolled like tall, white bubbles floating on a dark underskin. There would be rain before the day ended.

"Floyd don't bring in the doctor unless he's worried," Rachel said. She turned to Michael. She saw the flash in his eyes, like a change of light. "We'll go over," she added. "Me and Dora and Sarah."

"I'd like to be goin' with you," he replied.

"No," she said sharply. Her voice betrayed her. "It'd — it'd be better if it's just us this time," she stammered.

He said: "That's a point. Me bein' a stranger. It could make things ill at ease. Is it a far walk?"

"A few miles," Rachel told him. "When Floyd gets back from town, Jack can drive us home in the wagon."

"You need two mules, you do," Michael said. "Just the one for plowin's not enough. You need to be able to get about, even if it's just a short way to town or to Floyd's."

"Floyd does for us when it's needed," she replied quickly. "Takin' the quilts in to sell, pickin' up what we need. Helpin' out when Mama Ada's sick is little in return."

Michael's voice was very soft: "Rachel, I understand it.

That's how I been feelin' about the three of you. What I'm doin's little enough."

She was caught in the force of his gaze and could feel him entering her like a ghost. She stepped back without realizing it and her arms crossed over her breasts in an unfamiliar reflex.

"I expect we'll be back later in the day," she said weakly. "It'll depend on how she is."

"Stay what's needed. I'll be fine."

She hurried away. A half-hour later Michael saw the three women leaving the house and walking along the road. He was hidden in the apron of the woods, where he had stacked the young blackgums cut for his fence posts. He leaned against an oak tree and watched them disappear around the bow of the road. A cool, constant breeze flew in from the west, pulling the thunderheads. He felt a calm settle over him, a relief from the fury of his false obsession with the fence. He had calculated well, but there was the price of his energy and it had tired him. Now, at last, he was alone on the farm. He lifted his face to the breeze and began to sing softly to himself as he walked toward the house:

*"I have loved you with poems . . . I have loved you with daisies . . . I have loved you with everything but love . . ."*

\* \* \*

The house was locked against him. He paced the length of the porch and fought the rage that exploded like pain in his head. This was Dora's work. Staring, suspicious Dora. Bitch Dora. But it did not matter; it would be simple to pry the lock. It was his anger that bothered him. It would not be good to uncage the anger. He had worked too hard.

He slipped the lock and searched the house quickly but found no sign of Eli's treasure. Outside, it was beginning to rain and he left the house and went into the barn. He made a small fire in the iron stove and placed a pan of water on top to boil. He needed to relax, to think. He sat in a chair beside the stove and lit his pipe and watched the film of steam build over the water. He told himself he had not expected to find Eli's money so easily, that only a fool would hide a great sum in a likely place. And Eli could not have been a fool. Lester Caufield had said as much and he knew it from the behavior of Rachel and Sarah and Dora. Eli would have been shrewd; hiding the money would have been a game with him and it would be found only when the riddle of his plotting was solved. Game against game, thought Michael. Game against game. And Eli was a worthy foe.

He made a strong tea of sassafras root and stirred in a spoon of honey. The tea was rich and sweet. He lay across his bed and listened as the rain pelted the oak-shingled roof above him. The inside of the barn was dark in the storm and though the room built for Eli's worker had been partitioned and the iron stove installed and a window cut in the side of the barn, a remote chill still swirled in the corners and over the rough wall planking. Michael placed the cup on the floor beside him and pulled a blanket over his legs. He closed his eyes and listened and his thoughts began to swim with the sounds of the storm. He saw Mama Ada, felt her fingers on his arm and smelled the damp warning of death. Sarah's laughter. Dora watching him — knowing. Yes, he thought with amusement, Dora knows. Or thinks she knows. Far away, thunder rumbled like a growl and Rachel's face rose in Michael's mind, smiled at him, then faded. The fence sang a falsetto whine in the wind. The well bucket blew over and clattered against the rock siding of the wellbox. He was above the house of Lester and Mary Caufield and the stream glittered like a sunflash. The rain fell hard, beating dully against the wood frame of the barn. Mary was under him, screaming. Sick, frightened Mary. So tight she bled and he had bruised himself in the shoving. A brilliant blink of lightning snapped its whiplash in the field below the house and Michael sat up abruptly in bed. He could feel himself growing full against his trousers and the cramped binding made him ache.

He twisted on the bed and unbuttoned his trousers and freed himself. He lay back, touching himself lightly, and began a slow milking of the flared head. A pleasant, floating sensation grew in his chest. Suddenly, his body froze. A sound that was not a sound, but a prelude, whistled through the room. He buttoned his pants and rolled from the bed and caught the handle of his knife. He could hear the faint straining of chains and the scraping of wagon wheels. He slipped the knife back into its sheath and moved quietly across his room, into the barn and to the barn door.

The wagon was driven by Floyd Crider. Rachel was with him, huddled under the makeshift tent of a heavy tarpaulin. The rain lashed at them in sheets and Floyd wrestled to control the frightened mules. He pulled the wagon close to the steps of the front porch and Rachel shook free of the tarpaulin and ran into the house. Floyd tapped the reins over the mules and the wagon bolted forward, in a circle, then back to the road.

From a splintered opening in the barn door Michael could see Rachel through the side window of the house. She closed the front door and stood looking out the window at the barn. Then she pulled something over her head and opened the door and ran into the rain toward the barn.

Michael stepped away from the door, into the shadows of an empty feed stall. He could hear Rachel's running steps splattering in the water. The door opened quickly, then closed against the wind. She stepped cautiously toward the room and stopped.

"Michael?" she called.

He waited for the echo of his name to die. Then he said, "I'm here."

The sound of his voice — not from his room, but from the shadows — startled her. She whirled and cried out and stumbled backward.

Michael jumped from the stall, catching her. He held her close, gently.

"Hush, hush," he whispered. "I've put the fright in you,

bein' hid away like that. It's only me. That's all. Nothin' more."

Her body shuddered like deep sobbing and then it relaxed.

"That's better," he said quietly. "Fact is, you scared me almost as much, not expectin' you back in such a storm. That's why I was hid out in the stall, to see who it might be. Then when I knew it was you and you called out my name, I was in a quandary about lettin' you know where I was without puttin' the fear in you."

He laughed easily and rubbed her back with his hand.

"It can't be done, you know," he added. "I've had many ghosts tell me that. There's times when you'd be believin' the very angel of Hell has you in his sight and it could be nothin' more than a bug lookin' you over."

She pulled away from him.

"I know," she said. "I didn't mean to scream. I'm sorry."

"Sorry? For what? Well that you did. But you look more like you've been drowned. Come along now. I've some strong tea and honey and a fire in the stove. You need to warm yourself, unless I'm wrong."

She hesitated and looked at the barn door, then back to Michael.

"Yes," she replied. "I do. The rain's cold for summer."

He turned and led her into his room.

"Sit by the stove," he said. "I'll put more wood in and get you some tea and you'll be feelin' dry inside out in a few minutes."

She dropped the shawl from her shoulders and sat close to the stove and watched as he pushed two pieces of wood into the hot coals.

"Mama Ada's near to death," she said at last. "Floyd's gone back to town to see if the doctor's come back. He was out this mornin'."

Michael shook his head sadly as he poured the tea into a cup.

"It's a pity," he said. "Grand old lady such as she is. Helpin' out the world and then not havin' the same kind of help when she most needs it."

"Floyd brought me by to find some of Dora's herbs that Mama Ada's been askin' for. He said he'd have the doctor stop by in his car and pick me up."

"Bad as it's stormed, I'd be doubtin' if a car'd make it over the roads," replied Michael. He stirred the honey in the tea and handed it to Rachel.

"Floyd said he'd come back if the doctor couldn't be found," she explained. She held the cup in her hands and stared thoughtfully at the deep amber liquid. The rain echoed in the room like a hum.

Michael could feel the awkwardness of her silence. He knelt before her and gently pushed the cup to her lips. She swallowed without looking at him.

"What you're sayin' is that it won't matter," he whispered. "Is that it?"

She nodded.

"I thought as much," he said. "The time is on her. I knew it was near when she drove the poison from me. Somehow in that strange other world of bein' half-alive, I knew it."

She began to cry, though without sound or expression.

"It's the way of things," Michael said softly. "She's lived long and good. Let her go with those memories cheerin' you."

Her hands began to tremble and he took the cup and placed it on the floor. He touched her face and her hair.

"Did you know?" he whispered. "Your hair's shinin' with rain. Clear as a mirror, it is. You can see yourself in hair that's shinin' with rain. It's true. You look hard enough and you can see yourself."

She shook her head against his hand.

"Please," she mumbled. "Don't — "

"Hush, now," he replied gently. "Cry it out. That's what you've been needin', Rachel. You've been needin' it for too many years. It's all dammed up inside, like some terrible river."

"No — no, I can't."

"Can't what? Can't feel? Is that what you've managed to teach yourself, Rachel? Not to feel?" He caught her face and forced it to him. "No matter what you say, I won't be believin' that," he said. "You tell me that and it's like damnin' yourself, it is. You ask all the questions you want, make up all the reasons in the world, and you won't be findin' anything to hide behind that's big enough or wide enough to deny feelin'. Ah, Rachel, Rachel, I know. I've spent too much of a worthless life learnin' it the hard way. Maybe that's why bein' here, on this place, means so much to me. Knowin' the feelin' that's in you, beggin' to come out."

Rachel dropped her eyes from him and rolled her face in his hand and began to weep openly. He pulled her to him from the chair and held her and took the surrender of her crying until it became an even breathing.

"It's a blessin', it is," he murmured. "It's like drinkin' you in, havin' you let out the hurt like that. Do you understand, Rachel?"

She nodded against his chest and the yes shot through his body like a shout. He could feel the hammering of his heart quicken in his upper chest and the sudden blood-rush filling his loins. He turned on the floor to touch his body lightly against her.

"I know how you're feelin'," he said. "All the don'ts and all the wrongs and all the sins you're tellin' yourself. Especially now. Now, with that grand old lady dyin' — maybe dead this very second — and here you are miles away, bein' held by a man who's a stranger, and you given to another who's been away all these long years. So many doors closin' you in, lockin' you up."

Her body stiffened. She lifted her head from his chest and pushed with her hands against his arms.

"I — I've got to go in the house," she said weakly.

"No." His voice was a command, and Rachel's head recoiled as though slapped. She raised her elbows before her in the tight space separating them and began to pull away.

"No," Michael said again. He caught her arms and pinned them to her sides and forced her to face him. "Not now. Not this close to bein' free." His eyes flashed. A blue light danced across their pupils and his mouth closed forcibly over hers. She tried to turn her head but could not. And then he released her.

He sat back on the floor and looked at her. His eyes softened and a mask of weariness fell over his face.

"I'm sorry," he whispered. "I've not the right, forcin' you like that. It's me who's the weak one. Givin' in to such needs." He looked around the room and listened as the rain beat against the barn.

"We all got needs," she said quietly. "We all do."

"Some means more than others," he replied. "Times like this — rainin' times like this — my need is to be held." He smiled faintly. "It's a baby's needs, I suppose, exceptin' I'm no longer a baby and a man's needs are not so easy to put to rest."

She reached for him and touched his face with her fingers.

"I remember," she said simply. "Eli — " She paused, expecting to regret having said his name, but there was no regret. "Eli always said it was a man's way of goin' back to the womb. I liked that."

Michael did not answer. An old fear pumped in his chest like a murmur. His breathing deepened and a cold crown of perspiration seeped from his hairline. He could feel her fingers on his face, purring with the softness of an even, searching stroke. There was another woman who had touched him, a bitch woman. A porcelain whore woman who had lived in a circle of mind-mirrors. Haughtily arrogant. Gifted with ready answers. Always right. Always. Lying with her ready answers, cooing "maybes" from the serene shadows of her righteousness, but flint-hard. A temper as brutal and unfeeling as an assassin's. She had been a predator pecking at his flesh with her talk of giving. A killer. A goddam killer. Holding her promises to his head like a cocked pistol, laughing secretly as he groveled and drooled and worshipped at her feet. But she had made a mistake. She had taken another man to a place that had been theirs and he had watched them fuse in love. And he had left them buried in the sand of an ocean.

"Michael?"

Her voice pulled him again to the room in the barn. He reached for her touching hand and turned it to his mouth and kissed her palm.

"Michael."

*       *       *

Afterward she lay beside him on the narrow bed. Her nipples, which had opened to him like the tips of a brown bloom, ached pleasantly from the drawing of his mouth and she could feel his quick spill drying on her skin. Her face was buried in the pillow of his chest and she waited for remorse to fall over her like a judgment. But there was no remorse. There was only the rain and the remote chill of the barn and the remembered tenderness of the man beside her.

# 6

GARNETT CANNON drove his car slowly, in low gear. It had stopped raining, but the soft dirt of the road had become a thick slush puddling in the narrow ruts of wagon wheels, and the Ford slithered dangerously between the deep gullies. Garnett cursed angrily and held tight with both hands to the top of the steering wheel.

He cursed the weather. He cursed being a doctor. He cursed two days and two nights of no sleep. He cursed his hands and his mind that had not been able to save the leg of a farmer in Young Harris. Damned pitiful fool. Doctoring himself until gangrene ate into him like rot. Goddamned idiot. Gagging on the stench of his dead leg when five dollars could have saved it. Two dollars. But there were too many remedies free for the taking and the man's family had scoured the woods for yellow-root and ginseng and red oak and pokeberry and God knows what else. Garnett twisted his shoulders to drive away his fatigue and anger. It was all a goddam waste, he thought. Damned mountain voodoo. And if it didn't work, they all happily died, blessed by the sure knowledge that it was the Time. God a-calling. Like a yodel across the valley. Come on, good son, sweet daughter. Says here in the Ledger it's the Time. "Damn it all to hell," Garnett muttered as the car slipped sideways and then righted itself. God had to love them. Nothing could kill them. Nothing. It had to be God's doing, keeping them tucked away like moles, letting them grub for life day after day, like the Jews in Egypt making straw and mud bricks. But the Jews had Moses, for God's sake, even if he was tongue-tied. God got the Jews out, didn't he? Hell, Moses would get kicked out if he came into these hills. Nothing would make them leave. And God was keeping him there, a last-minute attendant with his pills and powders and sharp steel blades. He wondered why he stayed, why God would not crook his great finger and beckon him to some fine place where he would be embraced as an arbiter of life rather than a consultant to death.

He looked out his car window at the wet green hills, waving in the storm's after-wind. The great trees were shimmering with a waxed brilliance and the late afternoon sun shattered across the sea of leaves like a crystal dance. A deer ran free along a ridge above the ruins of a logging field.

"Dammit," he muttered.

He had been asleep when Floyd had knocked timidly at his door. Quaking Floyd Crider, standing inside himself, begging in a voice so quiet and afraid it was almost unintelligible. Like some grunting deaf-mute. Except the deaf-mute would smile and flash his fingers. But Floyd did not have to say anything. He could have pointed with his big toe and Garnett would have understood about Mama Ada.

Garnett both feared and respected Mama Ada Crider. She was not like the other mountain healers. Whatever Mama Ada did contained mysteries greater than science and witchery. He had reluctantly, and secretly, sought her help to cure thrash in babies, and the mouth boils had disappeared without the single application of any of his grand medicines. He had examined her work in dozens of patients who seemed incurable, or who thought they were incurable. He had heard them tell of a sensation that rushed through them like a water that was not water. Yet it was not emotion or high-crying agonies syncopating with the cosmic winds of the universe. Mama Ada's healing was done as calmly and as simply as removing a splinter from a hand, without any pledges to obey the rules and regulations of a prescribed hereafter. The patient walked away. That was all. There was no celebration, no preening, no worship.

But Garnett knew he did not understand these people. He was not born among them. He had not inherited the right to belong.

He eased the car into the narrow mouth of the road leading to Rachel Pettit's home and an odd energy — a curiosity — awoke in him. He had known Rachel for years. Rachel and Dora had been the only children of Harley Rice, the first patient he had treated after opening his office in Yale. Rachel was a girl then, just before her marriage to Eli. She had been beautifully tan, with rich chocolate eyes, and he had teased her about being Portuguese. She had laughed merrily at the strange word and made him repeat it in syllables. She would tell Eli, she had promised; it was a word Eli would like. Later, when Eli began to disappear and tales of his exploits filled Pullen's Café with their folk-hero embellishments, Garnett saw less and less of Rachel. He knew she sold quilts and worked miracles with a sewing machine, but her dark beauty had softened and the easy laughter had left her. She had waited many years for Eli to reappear like a valiant from war and that retreat had left her isolated and silent. She lived with Sarah and Dora and the legend of a buried treasure, and it was well known that the only person Rachel communicated with was Floyd. Until now, Garnett thought. In Yale, the people spoke of a man who was Eli's cousin. An Irishman. He had been bitten by a rattlesnake and Mama Ada had saved his life and he had stayed to work at building a fence on the farm. To the doctor, the report was humorous. He knew the Pettit family. If the Irish strain was in their bloodline, it was older than the invasion of the Angles and Jutes and Saxons. But no matter. A man would be good for Rachel. It was a damned shame to have a full woman withering like a prune over some insane act of loyalty. Maybe she's rolling in the grass with him five times a day, Garnett thought. If so, the Irishman was a lucky bastard.

Garnett laughed sharply. His fatigue was leaving him.

*   *   *

Rachel sat with Michael on the front porch of her home and watched the Ford crawl up the mud road like a black turtle. She was tense. She wondered if her face or her voice would betray her and if the doctor would know without asking that she had made love to the man sitting beside her. The doctor was a wise man. Her hands tightened on the small cloth sack of herbs that she held in her lap.

"You're not to be worryin'," Michael said quietly. "There's no wrong in givin'. Remember that, Rachel."

She did not look at him.

"Will you remember that, Rachel?" he asked.

"Yes," she answered shyly.

"Then be for smilin' for the good doctor," he replied cheerfully.

"I — I can't," she said. "I'm thinkin' about Mama Ada."

"I know," agreed Michael. "And I'm bein' selfish." He stood at the edge of the porch, above her, and waited as the car slipped into the yard.

Garnett switched off the car's motor and shoved the door open with his shoulder. He walked carefully across the yard, keeping his eyes on the ground.

"What you're seeing is one of God's miracles, Rachel," he said, stepping across a puddle of water. "A damn fool doctor and a broken-down Ford out in weather that would've grounded Noah." He looked up. "How are you?" he asked sincerely.

Rachel stood, holding the sack of herbs against her.

"Fine," she answered softly. Then she said, "This is Michael

O'Rear." She paused. "He's Eli's cousin, from over in Ireland," she added.

Garnett studied Michael's face like a painting. He gave Michael an old, practiced nod, a doctor's habit.

"Irish?" he said. "I almost married an Irish girl once. She was a nurse. Prettiest thing I ever put eyes on. Tied up a bandage like a Christmas package. She loved ballet and made me take her every time one would be around, up in Boston. Then one day I got a letter from her, telling me to go jump in Swan Lake. I heard later she up and married a lawyer and had twenty or thirty children, and gave that poor fool fits."

Michael smiled broadly. He extended his hand to the doctor.

"Likely he'll be deservin' a peaceful place in Heaven, if she's the same as some of the scrappy ones I've known along the way," he replied. "It's a pleasure to meet you, Doctor."

"Same," Garnett said. "It's good to hear the accent again. You a drinking man, Mr. O'Rear?"

The surprise of the question rose in Michael's face. He looked quickly to Rachel.

"Don't pay the question any dues, Mr. O'Rear," Garnett continued. "It's the way I am, and the reason I ask is because me and some of the gentlemen of this community get together occasionally at Pullen's Café after the dinner crowd leaves. It's a disgrace of a place at mealtimes, but at night it's the best in the way of a tavern you'll find anywhere around. In fact, it's the only one. Thought maybe you'd come in and join us one night. Help me convince these damn stone-age minds around here that it's nineteen thirty-nine and Hitler's about to pull us all into a war."

"That's kind of you," replied Michael. "I'll be doin' that. One night soon, I'll make my way in."

The doctor nodded. He said, "Good." Then, "Come along, Rachel. Bring that sack of ground-up roots and stewed leaves and eel skins or whatever it is this time, and let's get going. Believe it or not, I love that old woman. If there's anything that real medicine can do, I'd like to say I did it."

Rachel followed Garnett. She did not speak to Michael.

"I'll be waitin' to hear," Michael said as Garnett opened the door to the Ford.

"I'll bring them back when I leave," Garnett told him. "By the way," he added, "the fence looks fine."

"It goes slow, but it goes," replied Michael. "You're a good man, Doctor. For doin' all this, I mean."

Garnett looked across the yard to the barn. He saw the thin swirl of smoke coming from the stovepipe cut into the side of the barn room. He laughed easily.

"It's not being good, Mr. O'Rear," he said. "It's the nobility of the calling." He slipped into the car and closed the door and drove away.

\*　　\*　　\*

They did not return until the following morning. Michael watched from the field as the Ford circled the yard, stopped, then drove away. He waved at the car from his distance but did not know if the doctor saw him. Then he jabbed the posthole digger into the soft ground, still wet from the storm, and walked briskly toward the house.

Dora was at the well, pouring water into an enamel bucket. She looked old and tired and Michael knew she had not slept. He wondered if she had questioned Rachel about their time alone together. No, he decided. No, she would not have. Not at the home of Floyd Crider. Not with the old woman dying.

"Good mornin', Miss Dora," Michael said brightly. "It's good to see you back. How's Mama Ada?"

Dora stared at him coldly. "No better," she answered.

"Ah, and it's a pity, it is. And the doctor? What does he think?"

"He never said. Went back to town for some more medicine."

"He's a good man," Michael remarked. "It's easy to tell. He'll do what he can."

Dora lifted the bucket from the wellbox.

"I'll carry that, Miss Dora," offered Michael.

"I can do it," Dora answered evenly.

Michael stepped away. Their eyes met and she saw the rage flutter in him, then quiet. He smiled gently.

"I know the three of you must be tired to your very souls," he said. "I'll be workin' in the field. The diggin's easy after the rain. Tell Rachel and Sarah I'll see them in the afternoon."

"The fence," Dora said suddenly. "When's that fence goin' to be built?"

The expression did not change in Michael's face.

"Soon, Miss Dora," he answered softly. "Soon."

He watched as Dora crossed the yard and entered the house. He could see the vague outline of Rachel standing close to the screen of the window, staring out at him.

*　　*　　*

It was late in the day when Sarah found him resting in the woods beside his stack of blackgum posts. He was stretched across a soft bed of pine needles that he had raked together with his fingers, watching a bluejay darting through the limbs of a hickory. It fought for balance on a twig, flapped noisily, screamed, then dove away from the tree.

"Mr. O'Rear?" Sarah said quietly.

Michael rolled to his right and in one move was on his feet, leaning forward in a coil. He recognized Sarah and stood upright, laughing.

"You 'most had a corpse on your hands, Sarah, girl," he said. "Comin' up on me, not makin' a sound like that."

"I'm sorry," she said.

"Them's words I don't like hearin'. Never be sorry, Sarah."

"But it scared you."

"And well it should have, me daydreamin' like I was when I should have been workin'. It's water you've got, is it? And that was what I was thinkin' about. Whether to go to the house or to the creek, and, lo, here it is."

Sarah handed him the jar of water and stood away from him as he drank.

"It's good," he said. "Nothin' better, and I've had my share of ale, bein' around the circus. But nothin's as good as good water."

"Mama said you'd be thirsty," Sarah mumbled. "She started to bring it up, but she told me to."

Michael smiled. He knew what he could expect from Rachel — reserve, caution, withdrawal. She had violated her loyalty to Eli and it would need time to heal.

"Your mother's a carin' person," he said. The smile widened on his face. "And a givin' one," he added lightly. "Don't know that I've ever met a better lady, in every way."

"Mama made Dora go to bed," Sarah told him.

Michael placed the jar on the ground and sat beside it, curling his feet beneath his legs.

"It's good she did," he replied. "Miss Dora looked weary enough. She must've not slept."

"She tried doctorin' Mama Ada with some herbs, but they didn't work."

"Your Aunt Dora knows a lot about herbs, does she?"

"Some. She makes me take some. Used to, when I was little."

"Well, you're a woman now. Pretty as a flower."

Sarah smiled. She shook her head and turned to look across the field below the woods.

"What's that?" bellowed Michael. "You denyin' you're pretty as a flower?" He laughed easily. "Just goes to show you're not lookin' at yourself in the right mirror."

"A mirror's a mirror," she answered. "They all the same."

"And that's where you're wrong, Sarah. There's all kinds of mirrors. Why, in the circus there's a house of mirrors that can make you look fat or skinny, or wide or tall, or like you've got two heads instead of one. There's all kinds of mirrors, but there's only one that's worth seein', Sarah."

She stared at him suspiciously.

"What's that?" she asked.

He stood and stepped to her and took her face in the palms of his hands and lifted her eyes to him.

"It's the mirror in the eyes of the man who cares for you, Sarah," he replied. "You'll see it someday. Someday, you'll be lookin' into some lucky man's eyes and you'll see yourself dressed in a robe and a crown and you'll know you're a true princess, you will."

His eyes pulled her into him and she stood without moving against his palms.

"Do you believe me, Sarah?" he asked gently. "How do you think a butterfly comes from a worm? By believin' it's got beauty inside it that no one else can ever see. And that's the way it'll be with you, Sarah." He leaned forward and kissed her tenderly on the forehead and then released her. "Now that's a private kiss, Sarah. Just between you and me. Just to tell you there's one man who already thinks you're a butterfly. Will you keep it that way? Between us? Not tell your mother or Miss Dora, because they'd not understand. Just between us? Will you?"

She nodded.

"I — I've got to get on back," she said hesitantly. "Mama wants me to watch for the doctor's car. When it comes back up the road."

"I'm thankful for the water, Sarah. I'm glad it was you that brought it up."

"Mama — Mama said we'd better not miss the car goin' back. She — she's worried about Mama Ada."

"I'll help out later," he said.

Sarah looked at him, then turned and ran from the woods.

"You're a butterfly, all right," Michael said to himself. He smiled. "Ready for spreadin'." He began to whistle.

*     *     *

The doctor's car passed by the house in early evening, speeding recklessly over the rough dirt road, and Michael sat until late night with the three women on the front porch of the house and watched for the car's return, but it did not appear.

The following morning, as he left the barn for breakfast in

the fading darkness, Michael saw the weak yellow beams of headlights drifting slowly in his direction, as though searching the ground in resignation. He knew intuitively that Garnett Cannon's funereal pace was his own private processional. He decided he would not speak of seeing the car; the news would come soon enough.

\*   \*   \*

The first bell struck as they were completing breakfast.

It was a very faint chime, a dull, metal ringing that floated into the kitchen and then died away.

Dora spread her hands over the table, palms down, in a hushing gesture, and lifted her face to the ceiling. No one moved.

Then a second bell. And a third.

Rachel pushed quickly away from the table and slipped through the kitchen door into the backyard. Sarah and Dora followed. They stood together outside, facing the sound, facing Yale.

A fourth bell. And a fifth. The three women pulled closer.

Michael watched them through the window and listened attentively. He did not understand what was happening, but he knew there was a private message in the ringing, that each striking of the bell spoke to them in a dreaded voice.

Again and again the bell struck. Minute after minute, like a drugged ticking riding up the funnel of the mountain valley, echoing faintly. And then it stopped.

Dora turned away and walked back into the house. She paused at the door and looked at Michael, then passed him and went into her room. Sarah stood beside her mother and began to cry. Rachel held her and said nothing.

"Is there somethin' I could do?" Michael asked gently from the kitchen door.

"No," answered Rachel. Then she added, "Mama Ada's dead."

"That was the ringin'?"

Rachel nodded yes. She embraced Sarah, taking the girl's face to the cradle of her throat.

"Are you for certain?" Michael asked.

"There were eighty-five rings. That's how old Mama Ada was," Rachel told him. "When somebody dies, they ring the bell in years, so people'll know."

Michael walked to Sarah's back and put his hands on her hair and stroked it.

"It's a sad day," he whispered. "But the best thing to do for sadness is to let go of it, Sarah, and not be ashamed of it passin' through you. Stay close to your mother. She'll be needin' you as much as you'll be needin' her."

Rachel looked into his face, then dropped her eyes and pulled Sarah closer.

"I'll be workin' in the woods, if you'll be needin' me," Michael said. "You've things to do. The wake and the funeral, and it's best for me to keep from troublin' you, bein' I'm not family or friend of the sweet lady."

He left them standing in the yard. He crossed the field and walked in the hem of the woods until he was above the house, at the place where Sarah had guarded the grazing cows. He sat with his back against the giant cedar and surveyed the valley. A haze covered the land in its thin fog-skin and the sun broke over the mountains like an unfolding Chinese fan.

"Ah," he said to himself in a relaxing sigh, "it's a lovely day, it is. A lovely day."

*　　*　　*

The minister sat behind the pulpit in a tall chair with the wingspread of ornate angels carved in the thick oak tips above his shoulders. He stared transfixed at the opened coffin before the altar. His legs were crossed at the knees and his hands rested, left over right, on the kneecap. His hands were large and the knuckles were disfigured with knots of arthritis. His skin looked bleached against his black suit and the dark mahogany of the chair. He was white-haired and old and the flesh under his small eyes sagged from too much crying for Jehovah to forgive his sinful people.

He watched numbly as the fuzzy figures of mourners moved slowly before the coffin, peering into the shallow wooden pit for a quick eye-stop of memory. They looked and shook their heads and forced their faces to turn their bodies away and returned to the church pews in a dragging walk of holding back the terrible final moment — not realizing the terrible final moment was over. He watched as they marched before him, swaying, one by one, old and young, in the custom of a last praising. They came in a prescribed order — first friends, then neighbors, then relatives, until only the family remained. And then Floyd and his wife and children, the last of the processional, gathered in a tight bow at the coffin's edge and drank with their eyes from the still, small figure that lay like a flower on a white pillow. Floyd reached timidly across the space of his life and his mother's death and touched her face lightly, almost involuntarily. A film of tears filled his hollow eyes and someone tugged at his arm and led him away to the front pew.

A baby whimpered and was stifled against a mother's shoulder. An old man coughed. A woman cried in a soft monotone, like a brook. The minister nodded once and the pianist began to play a subdued lead, and three people, a man and two women, stood together beside the piano, facing Floyd, and began to sing "What a Friend We Have in Jesus." Their voices were high and harsh.

The old minister closed his eyes and leaned his head against the flying angels of the tall mahogany chair. The words and music and the voices of the song were like an extension of him. He had heard it hundreds of times at hundreds of funerals. His mind repeated the words with the voices and his right index finger tapped the rhythm against his kneecap.

Then the song was over and he opened his eyes and stood slowly and walked to the pulpit. The Bible was open before him but he did not look at it. He lifted his face to the exact center of the ceiling and his lips parted and his throat quivered with the beginning of a word.

"The Lord is my shepherd; I shall not want — " he recited in a voice that rose in a roar from his chest.

"Yea, though I walk through the valley of the shadow of death, I will fear no evil — "

His voice rumbled in a song cadence and the words were flung far across the small church, driving the sword of David into the breast of every listener.

He ended the psalm with a breathless "Amen" and stood trembling, washed in the rush of the echo: ". . . dwell in the house of the Lord forever." He stepped from the pulpit and walked unsteadily to the front of the coffin. He looked once into the frozen face of Mama Ada and gently whispered, "Ada."

He watched her for a long moment, as though expecting a reply, and then he turned to the congregation.

"Ada," he said again. "Ada liked singin'. Told me once to bury her with singin', with a sermon about singin'. Said to make it soft and sweet, like precious Jesus. Said to make it loud and strong, like God laughin'. Said to tell people to go to her grave-side with singin' on their lips and in their souls."

He raised his deformed hands before him and locked them at the wrists. He stared at a pinspot of the ceiling, the space-map linking him to God, and his mouth opened and his voice flew from his throat like a wind.

"Sing your songs, O people," he said happily. "Sing of light, not darkness. Sing of joy, not sorrow. Sing in celebration, not in lamentation. Sing with spirits soarin', not laggin'."

A voice from the congregation muttered, *"Amen,"* and the minister bowed his head and pulled his hands to his chest and smiled triumphantly.

"Death's not a draggin'-down angel to them that's fearin' God," he began again, quietly, patiently. "Death's not mean-faced to the lover of Jesus' name."

*"Amen. In Jesus' name."*

"Death's a turnin' loose of everythin' that's knotted up and tiresome. Death's a heart filled with laughin' to them that's been hurt with burdens. Death's a roomful of happy faces to them that's been alone. Death's a whirlwind trip over the whole universe to them that's never traveled anywhere except in dreamin'."

*"Praise God."*

"Death's a clean mountain mornin' to God's child. It's the first snow of first winter. It's spring's bloom. It's summer's goodness. It's autumn's harvest."

*"Glory be to God."*

The old minister paused and his head lifted and his smile broadened and his arms spread in an embrace of the room. His voice became a whisper.

"Death's just God's way of showin' His believers what it's like to be forever achin' with happiness. O my people, happiness. Happiness in bein' free of all this old world's pain. Bein' free of anger. Bein' free of fear. Bein' free of always wantin' more."

*"Free, dear Jesus, free."*

"Death. Death. Old, old Death. Where is he, anyhow? Where's his hidin' place? Up in the mountain? Somewhere in town? Down by the river? Where's his hidin' place? What is old Death, anyhow?

"Death's not some ghost, sneakin' in when it's pitch-black night.

"O my people, that's not what old Death is.

"Death's God's mercy comin' on the quiet, swift wings of sweet, sweet angels. O yes, my people. That's what Death is."

*"Sweet Jesus."*

The old minister stepped forward in the aisle. His eyes swept the congregation and he nodded happily. He turned to Floyd.

"Sweet, sweet angels, brother Floyd. Picked by the Almighty God Jehovah, Himself. Gentle angels who hear God's message and do God's will with gladness. Gladness because they know, brother Floyd. O my people, they know.

"They know what's ahead for the good. The good like Sister Ada. They've been on the bosom of God, restin' their weary heads against His great, wide shoulder, and they've felt His blessedness. And they've heard the songs God sings like a baby's lullaby when the fightin's over and the day's done.

"O yes, my people. Sister Ada liked singin'. So sing up for her. Not for mournin', but for praisin'. Sing her to rest. Sing her loose from this place. Sing her on her angel's trip through the valley of the shadow of Death, up through the Naheela Valley, up over the mountains. Sing her on up until she dwells in the house of the Lord forever and leans her weary face on the great, wide shoulders of the Almighty."

He was suddenly spent and his voice broke and he struggled for breath. He stepped back and leaned one hand on the coffin and fought the light dots of pain in his brain. Then he looked into the coffin and smiled and whispered, "Ada."

# 7

GARNETT CANNON stood aside from the choir of mourners in the June heat — in the cemetery of names he had once touched and squeezed and probed — and he felt a loneliness he had never known. He watched the gravesiders moving among themselves in a daze, tightening the close circle around the deep rectangular hole. It was a tableau of an eternal rite and Garnett knew their most private feelings: Who would be next? He saw their eyes darting about them, searching for the premonition that floated in the air like a specter. There was an eerie sense of expectation, as though a burial bouquet of dark flowers would be flung above their heads and fall into the hands of one of them.

They stood in generations. The toothless old, bent at the neck, frail as twigs. The tiring. The strong, with chesty bodies and burned work faces. The very young, afraid of the singing at the graveside. They were the whole of humanity, thought Garnett. From God's beginning myth to the last child spewed down the liquid tunnel of its membrane shell, breaking loose from its hot cavity. They were all of all people. They were the royalty and the remnants of a noble mutation caused by accident or God. Garnett was not certain which. God, he supposed. He did not know if he believed in God, but he did believe in the frustration that made his guts, if not his voice, cry out.

He stepped back to the shade of an elm and slipped the knot

of his tie. Perhaps God was just a word, he thought. Perhaps the whole gold-leafed, red-lettered tale was a primeval illusion and Mama Ada would rot like a diseased potato and nothing about her would move a single inch from the oak box with its brass handles and hinges.

He fanned his face with his hat. The crowd was singing "Stand by Me." He knew he would go early that night to Pullen's Café and drink long and bully the crowd with his view of the world beyond the valley. The men would listen respectfully until he accused Roosevelt of being a Hyde Park demigod, and then they would shake their heads in their disapproving manner and mutter, "Now, wait a minute, Doc. Ain't no need to go that far."

But Garnett loved the men of Pullen's Café. He loved their tolerance and their stubbornness. He loved the literature of their stories. He loved the peace they seemed to bring with them like a silent companion. It was a mystery why they enjoyed peace in Pullen's. Perhaps it was a fraternal thing, but without the Greek or the initiation. Mountain quid pro quo: Something for something, but there was no one who cared to measure or test the something, and that, in its own way, was peace.

The singing stopped and there was scripture and a prayer and the coffin of Ada Crider was lowered into the grave and the crowd began to walk away.

Garnett saw Rachel standing alone, waiting for Dora and Sarah to join her. He thought of the Irishman. He pulled his hat on his head and walked to her.

"Rachel," he said in greeting.

"Doctor," she replied solemnly.

"It hurts to lose her," he confessed. "Maybe more than anybody since I've been here. I loved that old woman."

"Yes. Me, too."

"Are you all right?" he asked. He did not care if the question sounded personal. Being personal was his business.

She nodded.

"Just wanted to know," he replied. "Been a long time since you've been in to see me. Not since Sarah was born, I guess."

"I've been well," Rachel said. "So's Sarah."

Garnett looked across the cemetery to where Sarah stood obediently beside Dora and a group of older women.

"She's grown almost," he remarked. "A woman now. And pretty. Got Eli's fairness, but she looks like you just the same." He removed his handkerchief from his pocket and wiped the perspiration from his eyes. "By the way," he added, "I was glad to meet that O'Rear fellow. You tell him I meant it about coming down to Pullen's. If he's Irish — and he is — he'll like it."

Rachel looked at him suspiciously, but his eyes were scanning the leaving crowd.

"I'll tell him," she said.

"Good."

Garnett began to walk away. Then he stopped and said, "If you need me, Rachel, let me know." He turned and left without waiting for a reply.

*     *     *

The fence stretched like a backward question mark across the field and in a widening semicircle above the house. Michael worked steadily in the heavy, thick heat, but he had changed. He no longer walked the fence line at night with Rachel and Sarah and no longer boasted of his workmanship. His voice had lost its merriment and he often sat for long periods without speaking, absently carving on a block of wood. He seemed distant and solemn and restless, and his silence was as commanding as his bluster had been.

He was a wind that had calmed and his moods affected each of the three women differently.

To Rachel, it was a prelude to his leaving, the last calling of the wanderer's instinct. It had been so with Eli and Eli had left many times. She had been controlled around Michael in the days following Mama Ada's death — never touching, never asking, never signaling. She had lain awake at night and felt the imprint of his body and thought of the short, dark distance between them and she had plotted going to him. But she could not. She could not risk discovery, nor could she risk absolute surrender to him; surrender would have meant the confession that Eli was only part of her, not all. She loved Eli, she repeated to herself again and again, but here was this other man; here was Michael. And she fought his presence with a practiced coolness. She could not go to him and she knew he could not come to her; he was the kind of man who waited, who tortured women with his patience. Still, she yearned to hold his face and bring it to her breasts and feel him thrusting deep within her. She wondered if he thought of leaving because she would not go to him at night.

To Dora, there was warning in Michael's behavior. He was planning to stay. After the fence, there would be no reason to remain, but Michael would not leave and Dora knew it. He needed to invent an excuse and he would find one. Dora watched him closely. She knew that he would not simply pass among them as a casual visitor would; when he left them, there would be scars.

Sarah was not suspicious. She was in awe of Michael. To her, there was nothing mysterious about his silence. He had grown accustomed to them and to his surroundings and had settled comfortably into an involuntary rhythm, like breathing. Michael belonged. He belonged there, among them. And he was not always quiet. Not with her. He was different when she brought him water in the glass jar and they sat together in the canopy of trees. Then he was relaxed and joyful. He laughed with her and told her colorful stories of his travels and he always kissed her on her forehead and pledged her to secrecy. Michael treated her like a woman, looked at her as a woman, spoke to her as a woman. It was man to woman, not man to girl. Even in his gentle teasing, his eyes were telling her of urges that swam between them like dreams. And Sarah began to feel their privacy growing inside her, like an internal fitting of a joyful expectation. To Sarah, Michael belonged and he belonged especially to her. It made her angry when she heard her mother or Dora speak of the change that had infected Michael like a disease. She said nothing, but she began to grow apart from her mother and aunt, and at night she sat in her bed and thought of being alone with Michael in another place.

*　　*　　*

And then Michael's somberness vanished as suddenly as it had fallen on him.

"I've been long enough in a fit of sorrow," he announced one morning. "That good lady's dyin' — Mama Ada — was a hurtin' thing. Kept takin' me back to my own mother's death, back across to Ireland. Was why I couldn't go to the wake or the funeral. There's them that can take dyin' and understand it and there's them that draw up like a sleep, but they don't sleep. I'm that kind. But it's been long enough. I'm back to thinkin' about the livin', not dyin', and tonight I'll be takin' the good doctor up on his invitation for the café."

His burst of exuberance startled Rachel. She looked automatically to Dora, as though seeking approval of the man sitting across from her.

"Gettin' away from the work'll do you good," she said. "You've put in a lot of days."

"I have, Rachel," he replied. "But it's been good for me. Good for my thinkin'. A man needs to leave somethin' to be proud of and that fence is mine." He laughed easily and drew butter across a biscuit with his knife. "Not much for a man to brag about leavin', a fence, but it's more'n most men I've known around the circus. Only thing they leave is sawdust and some broken-hearted ladies wonderin' whatever happened to all the promises they've been told."

"When's the cows goin' in?" Dora asked curtly.

Michael bit from the biscuit and chewed slowly. His eyes danced over Dora with amusement.

"Why, Miss Dora," he said, teasing. "Sometimes a tiny little bird voice tells me you've got your doubts about the finishin' of that fence."

She dropped her eyes.

"Ah, now, Miss Dora. Am I right? Could that be a bit of the truth? Why, I don't blame you. Not in the least. Here's this braggart of a fellow, always boastin' about somethin' or the other, tellin' stories that'd shame the lies of a sailor, and he's fussin' around with a barbed-wire fence that another man could've put up in a week. Huh, Miss Dora? Am I right?"

Dora's lips twitched. Her face reddened in anger.

"Why sure and it's the truth," Michael continued lightly. "I've done it bit by bit, turtle-slow, so's I could sit at this fine table and in the company of three handsome ladies, and not have to be roamin' about the world, steppin' over elephant droppin's in some canvas tent."

Dora's eyes snapped up.

"Don't nobody know the truth better'n them that says it," she said hatefully. "It's not my house and not my business."

Michael leaned forward, toward her. The smile was still on his face.

"Miss Dora," he said softly, "I told you not long ago, it'd be soon. And it will be and then I'll be off, but when I go I'll be leavin' somethin' that'll make me remember havin' been here. That's the whole of it."

An awkwardness crowded the room and the table. Sarah slumped in her chair and her eyes darted from Dora to Michael. She saw the intense war between them and for the first time she disliked her aunt.

"Dora don't mean nothin'," Rachel said quietly. "Havin' you around's been good for us. And it's not just the fence. It's all the other things you've done to help out. I guess we needed it more'n we think."

Michael looked at her, into her, and she was with him again in the barn, with the storm driving them into a fusion of touches.

"It's a fine thing you've said, Rachel," he replied. "A fine thing. And it does away with whatever gloom I've been in." He turned to Dora. "Miss Dora," he said, his voice soft and low, "could we be friends? Just for the short time left on the fence? Could we do that?"

Dora had not felt his voice before; she did now. It spread through her and over her. She could sense it rising in her throat and covering her face. There was no portent of danger in him, no reason for suspicion.

"I didn't mean nothin'," she whispered.

"I know it, Miss Dora," he said. "I know it."

There was a pause. Rachel interrupted it. She said, "That's better. Much better. And it'll be good for you to go to town tonight. We all feel that way. Don't we, Sarah?"

Sarah pushed away from the table and stood. She dropped her face to the dishes before her.

"I guess," she mumbled. Then she added, "I don't know about them things." She turned away from the table.

*     *     *

He walked in a strong, even stride along the road leading into Yale. It was good to be away from the farm. He had too long played his drama, with its laborsome, foreboding nuances of mood — which he wore like drab costumes — and the role had tired him. He needed another setting, another audience. He needed the company of men and the relief of their loosened imaginations. The doctor had said that Pullen's was a café by day and a tavern by night, and a tavern was not only a place to drink, but a place to become known, a place where recognition floated around the room, as nondiscriminating as a whore selling attention. It was a place where men could be proud of being men and where there were none of the encumbrances of etiquette, with its feather touch and hammer heaviness. Michael was at home in taverns, even taverns such as Pullen's. He was a master of taverns.

It was a gray-light hour, in the first damp scent of night when the sounds and colors of day segued quietly into evening. The hour was clean and Michael was clean. He wore a shirt that had belonged to Eli. It had been washed and starched and pressed neatly by Rachel. Or Dora. He did not know which. It could have been Dora. He had broken her like an animal and he had been amused by her daylong, clumsy attempts to apologize for her suspicions. Dora would no longer trouble him, he thought confidently. Dora could become an ally, if he wished, if he used her properly. He worried only about Sarah. Sarah had been sullen all day, as though betrayed. He would have to be careful with Sarah.

He thought of the shirt he wore and of Lester Caufield's drunken remark about being arrested in Yale for being like Eli. He wondered what Eli had been like — outside the legend. Were they alike? Or had people forgotten Eli and remembered only the stories about him?

Michael was certain of one thing: Lester Caufield's easy gossip about Eli Pettit's hidden treasure was true. It had to be. Rachel had very privately given him two wrinkled one-dollar bills before he left for Yale. For his evening, she had said. Because he deserved it. He knew Rachel did not have money for such gifts; it had to come from Eli's cache.

It was a gray-light hour and Michael stood at the outskirts of Yale and felt intensely alive.

The township of Yale had been built on a crown of black land that rose like a ripple across the Naheela Valley. It was a small town with exactly one dozen buildings fitting into two even lines — six and six — on opposite sides of the road. The

Naheela River ran narrow and deep at the back of one line of buildings and Yale Mountain rose like a billowed shirt behind the others across the street. The street through the middle of town had been paved less than a year and it gave the town a look of importance.

Michael had no trouble finding Pullen's Café. He saw Garnett Cannon's Ford parked out front, beside a truck with dented fenders. He walked past the truck and looked at it curiously. He had seen it before, but where?

Then he remembered: It was the same truck that had taken Lester Caufield into the mountains each morning and returned him home each evening.

The café was crowded when Michael entered. He stood in the doorway, hands on hips, smiling broadly, and surveyed the room. Two uncovered electric light bulbs hung from cords in the center of the room, casting severe streaks of light and shadow across the men hunched over their beer or whiskey. The sound of the room was the bass of many voices, and Michael felt immediately at home.

"Irishman!" The voice came from across the room. It was Garnett Cannon.

"Doctor," Michael answered cheerfully, waving a hand. "Let me get my eyes about me and I'll find you, wherever you're hidin'."

The room fell silent. None of the men had met Michael O'Rear, but he was not a stranger to them. They knew of him, knew of the fence and the snakebite and Mama Ada's healing and his kinship to Eli Pettit. What they did not know — could not know — was that they had been waiting for him.

The doctor's voice boomed from his corner table.

"Well, by God," he said. "Let a man with some refinement in his voice come in and say a word or two and it strikes the whole place dumb as a stroke." He shoved his way among the tables and walked to Michael.

"Good to finally make it in, Doctor," Michael told him. "I

think I've been needin' it." He accepted Garnett's extendeu hand.

The doctor pulled Michael beside him and turned him to the staring faces.

"Gentlemen — and I use the term in jest — this fine fellow from the Shamrock Isle is Michael O'Rear," he announced. "You've heard of him, no doubt, the way you gossip like women. He's a cousin to Eli Pettit, a former citizen of our fair community and the only person I know of who could drink for a week and never pick up a tab."

A murmur of laughter rolled across the room. Michael knew the men were accustomed to Garnett Cannon's condescending manner. He knew also the men enjoyed it.

"Mr. O'Rear here is the mystery behind that fence going up around Eli's field," Garnett continued loudly. "Which means something will, at last, happen to that patch of land. If I remember correctly, Eli planted exactly one corn crop there and as Job Franklin would say, he didn't make enough crop to wipe his ass on the cobs."

More laughter. Freer and fuller.

The doctor caught Michael by his left biceps and squeezed hard with his fingers, feeling for the pulse of the artery. It was his own detection system, his test of a man's nerve.

"Of course, you know me, gentlemen," he continued humorously. "I think Mr. O'Rear is a liar." He moved his fingers on Michael's arm, like fretting a guitar neck. "He's a liar, out and out," he added. "A man living in the company of three women would claim he's cousin to the Devil himself, or even worse, to old Job Franklin over there. Job, where are you?"

A hand lifted from a table against the wall.

"Here's Job," someone shouted.

"It is, indeed," Garnett replied with dignity. "Not that I can see him without my glasses, but I can tell by the smell that it's Job."

The room exploded in laughter.

"Aw, shit, Doc," Job said easily.

"There's a better word for it, Job," Garnett called back. "It's known as defecation. Now, I know that's high-sounding but it's the mark of an educated man to say 'defecation' instead of 'shit.' You'll not understand this, of course, but that's the difference between a man from Yale and a man from Harvard. I am a man from Harvard, educated in the finer things of life. You are from Yale, which is a condemnation unto itself." He turned to Michael and looked seriously into his face. Michael could tell the doctor had been drinking heavily.

"Mr. O'Rear," Garnett said, "look about you. What do you see?" He swiveled his neck and peered into the audience of the room. "Well, I'll tell you. What you see is the notorious and highly suspect missing link in man's intellectual evolution. Before your very eyes, that's what you see. And hard as I try, I find it impossible to elevate them one iota. I have dedicated my life to that task, and nothing happens. I have read Shakespeare to these men, recited Latin, given lectures on how to hold a teacup the way they do in Boston, and what do I have to show for it? Nothing. But I try, don't I, boys? I try."

"You try, Doc. Damned if you don't," a man answered from a front table.

"And I'll keep trying," the doctor cried with evangelistic fervor. "Now that I've got another educated man with me, I may even succeed. What do you think, Mr. O'Rear?"

Michael took one step forward and studied the men before him in mock seriousness. He said, "Why, I'd say you're bein' a bit harsh with it all. I take some pride in spottin' good men and these seem like good men, all."

Garnett stumbled backward in comical surprise.

"What?" he remarked in horror. "What? You're saying they're capable of learning? Is that what I hear you say, Mr. O'Rear?"

Michael laughed and rocked on his feet. He liked the game.

"That I do," he shouted. "It's a bright lot, unless I've missed my guess."

The doctor bowed graciously.

"Teach them to say 'defecation' and I'll buy you the finest glass of whiskey this condemnable place can offer, Mr. O'Rear," he said.

"Shit, Doc," Job Franklin chortled from his table.

"Job, you will never learn," Garnett replied. "And it's a pity, but, then, you're a pity. Still, there may be others. Are you game for it, Mr. O'Rear?"

"That I am."

Garnett stepped aside and waved his permission for the lesson to begin.

"Now, men, it's easy," Michael said in his rich accent. "The word's 'defecation.' Day-fee-cay-shun. Say it with me, men. Day-fee-cay-shun."

The men answered in unison.

*"Day-fee-cay-shun."*

"Now, put it together, men," urged Michael. "Day-fee-cay-shun. Defecation."

*"Day-fee-cay-shun. Defecation."*

Michael turned to the doctor and bowed from the waist.

"I rest my case, Doctor," he said proudly.

The room vibrated with a wave of celebration. Michael watched the men intensely, studying them. They were like children and the doctor had consented to be their clown, their brilliant jester. It was, thought Michael, the only way Garnett could reach them.

The doctor raised his hands and the room quietened. He paced before them with his head bowed and his arms behind his back. His face was furrowed in serious thought.

"Gentlemen, I am truly pleased with you," he said humbly. He stopped his pacing and turned to them. "When Roosevelt puts us into a fighting war with Adolph Hitler," he continued, "you can march across Germany shouting, 'Watch out Nazi, we're gonna kick the defecation out of you.' Except, in that case it wouldn't be 'defecation,' but 'feces,' but that's another lesson. Still, you will be the smartest soldiers in the entire world and before you return to a hero's welcome and a ticker tape parade down the streets of Yale, you will be speaking five languages and you will be able to waltz like queers and you will know French wine from French whores. Most important, gentlemen, you will be capable of defecating like true continentals. You will defecate only on slop jars with ivory seats. You will insist on perfumed tissues for cleaning yourselves, and you will say 'Excuse me, I must defecate,' when the urge of the bowels hits you. Just knowing you makes me want to weep with pride. But do you really want to know what I think about that demonstration of language you just gave?"

"What, Doc?" Jcb Franklin asked, choking with laughter.

"In a word, Job, it was shit."

# 8

THE TABLES had been shoved into a tight V, fanning out from the corner of the room where Garnett had been sitting since early evening. Michael was at the table with him in a seat of honor at the point of the V. The doctor sat at Michael's right, leaning in his ladderback chair away from the table. His hands were across his lap and he wore his felt hat forward, with the brim over his eyes. Michael could not see the doctor's eyes beneath the lip of the hat, but he knew the doctor was watching him closely as he told his stories.

"Now, lads, that's the truth of it," Michael declared dramatically. "Me and the lady caught in the same doorway, me pushin' and the lady pullin'. It was a sight. A sight, indeed. And this gentleman of the law happens along and shouts out, 'What's the meanin' of this?' And I answers, 'If we go to movin' one way or the other, officer, we're bound to end up bein' engaged to be married.' "

The room was dark with smoke, like a night within a night, and there was the smell of beer and whiskey and men sweating in heavy shirts. The laughter of the men listening to Michael ran up and around him like playful puppies lapping at his feet.

"Well, hell, what happened then?" a man asked eagerly.

"Why, then the lady makes to smack me and when she does, she goes tumblin' out through the door and lands square on the policeman, she does. Bless the man. He was bowled over by her,

her bein' as wide as the Mississippi, and she came to rest astraddle him, like Moby Dick beached."

The men roared at the image and slapped the tops of their tables with their hands. Michael stood and waved for attention.

"So, I go over to him," he cried, "and I say — sweetly, mind you — I say, 'Ah, Officer, could I be helpin' you, now?' And he says — the breath bein' squeezed from him — he says, 'Call the fire department, mon. There's a fifty-pound tit a-crushin' my skull.' "

Michael fell back into his chair, laughing with the men.

"Fifty-pound tit! Goda'mighty," thundered Job. "That sounds like Wanda Harper, don't it, boys? Biggest sack for one tit I ever seen. Hey, Bailey, you ever see that woman?"

The man named Bailey answered, "See her? Lord, I guess. I seen that ol' woman whip a man crazy just slingin' them things around."

There was more laughter and a roll of loud, tumbling voices remembering Wanda Harper. And then the voices quieted down and the men looked again to Michael.

"I tell you, men," Michael began easily, "there's all kinds of women out there. Big women. Skinny women. Short women. Tall women. Sweet women. Mean women. And — and damn mean women." He laughed and added, "That's a fact. I remember one out in California, it was. Good-lookin' woman. Followed me up and down that state like a bloodhound, she did. Seems she thought I'd won her in a wrist-wrestlin' match."

"A what?" Garnett asked. It was the first he had spoken during Michael's storytelling.

"Wrist-wrestlin', Doc," explained Michael. "That was my sport. Even took me a job in a travelin' circus one time, wrist-wrestlin' any man who'd take the dare."

"What was you?" asked Job. "Some kind of cham-peen?" He said the word mockingly.

"I was, Mr. Franklin," replied Michael. "Strong as a horse,

I was. But that was in my younger days and I've lost the touch for it."

"Well, damn," Job said. "Must run in the family."

"What's that?" asked Michael.

"Why, wrist-wrestlin'," Job told him. "Ol' Eli was a wrestler. Wouldn't take seconds to no man. He was always wrestlin' for drinks. Bein' cousins, I reckon you ain't too far kin to be the same kind of man."

Garnett lifted his head and pushed back his hat. His eyes turned to Job and then to Michael. The question was on his face like a tattoo and Michael read it.

"Now, that's a puzzlin' thing," admitted Michael, avoiding the doctor's gaze. "Puzzlin', indeed. Fact is, I'm not clear where the cousin line runs between Eli and me. Never met him. Way it happened that I even know about him goes back to Ireland. It was a thing taught us by my dear mother. When we was just tots, she gave each of us a cousin in America to remember his name and to find, if we ever had the chance. Eli was the cousin's name I had given me. His name and where he lived. I'm shamed to say it, but I've been in America for a long while now, but I've never thought of findin' Eli. Not to a few weeks ago. I was up in Knoxville and I heard a fellow mention the town of Yale and it struck me like a hammer. I'd heard of the place, but couldn't figure out why. And then it all came back, like a spring snapped loose in a pocket watch, and I put it in my mind to look up Eli. It was providence, the luck of the Irish, happenin' up on the farm by accident, and findin' the snake by Sarah."

"Didn't nobody around here know Eli was Irish," the man named Bailey said solemnly. "Could of been, though. Way I remember it, his mama come from somewhere else. Maybe it was Virginia. Died real young."

Michael shrugged. He replied, "Could be that, friend. Bein' little like I was, I never asked about it. I just remembered his name. Eli. I wrote him a letter once, I think. When I was a lad. But I never heard back."

"His name was Elijah," Garnett said. "Like the prophet."

Michael did not answer. He knew the doctor was testing him, prying into his brain with an insight as sharp as an operating instrument.

"Well, Doc, that may've been Eli's real name," a man with a hard, cold face remarked, "but the only time Eli ever come close to a Bible, I reckon, was in some courthouse when he was swearin' to tell the truth."

The man was sitting at a table in front of Michael. He swallowed from his own whiskey and placed the empty glass on top of the quart jar before him and laughed alone at his humor.

"Don't matter, nohow," the man said roughly. He looked up at Michael. "C'mon, Irishman, let's have a go at that wrist-wrestlin'. Me'n you. Best man buys a drink for the other'n."

No one spoke. Michael could feel eyes on him.

"It's a sportin' offer, friend," Michael replied, "but I'm a bit past the prime for it."

"Prime? Hell, man, I'm older by ten years, I reckon," the man declared. "Way you been braggin', I'd say you must be made out of cast iron."

There was a pause, a sudden quietness.

"Braggin'?" questioned Michael. "Ah, friend, if it's braggin' you think I've been doin', I'll ask your forgiveness. I'm a talker, all right, but not for braggin'. That's a different thing."

The man's voice was as cold and hard as his face. He said, "Up around here we call it braggin' if a man can't do what he says he can." He leaned toward Michael and pushed his jar and glass to one side of the table. "Now it's up to you, mister," he added. "You said it. I reckon you got to live up to it, or say out that it was braggin'."

Michael looked at Garnett. Garnett smiled and laced his fingers behind his neck and pushed his head against his hands. Michael returned the smile. He knew the doctor had read the lie of his kinship to Eli Pettit. He did not think the doctor cared. To the doctor, he was a relief, an amusement, and that was more important than the charade of an Irish blood scent in a mother's tale about cousins. Michael thought of the story he had just told the men in the café; it was absurd, but the men had believed him. All except the doctor.

Michael propped his elbows on the table and closed his hands together and rested his chin on his knuckles.

"Friend," he said to the challenger, "you've got a point. I'll go you. Arm to arm, wrist to wrist. Weak as I am, I'll go you."

A mild, approving party cheer fluttered throughout the room. The man grinned and stood and moved his chair to Michael's table, opposite him.

"What would your name be, friend?" asked Michael.

"Teague," the man answered. "The name's Teague." He offered his hand as a greeting and an agreement. Michael accepted.

"It's a fine grip, Mr. Teague," Michael said. "You're a worker, I can tell."

Teague grinned proudly. He said, "Pick the judge, Irishman."

"The doctor'll do fine," replied Michael. He did not look at Garnett.

Garnett laughed cynically. He stood up and leaned on the table, his arms straight, his knuckles down.

"Gentlemen," he said, "I am honored. I have long yearned to participate as an official in an event as noble and athletic as you are about to indulge in. I have even thought of nominating the great township of Yale and the fertile Naheela Valley as a site for the Olympics, and this act of manliness convinces me I am right."

"Aw, hell, Doc, let 'em wrestle," Bailey said.

The doctor grunted an objection; then he said, "Gentlemen, here are the rules: Anybody breaks anybody else's arm, they have to pay for it, but I'll do the setting for half-price." He dropped into his chair and scowled at Bailey.

Michael and Teague pulled their chairs close under the table until its edge pushed into their rib cages. They leaned into the center and placed their right elbows firmly against one another, with their forearms up and their hands spread open. Their left arms rested flat on the table, braced beneath their right arms.

"Are you ready, Mr. Teague?" asked Michael.

"Ready enough," answered Teague.

Their hands touched, thumb to thumb. Michael could feel Teague's strength as his fingers closed over the thumb ridge, and he knew it would not be an easy contest; Teague would hurt him if he could. He shifted his weight in the chair, planting his feet solidly against the plank floor. He looked across the gunsight of his thumb to Teague and smiled. Then he dropped his eyes to Teague's massive arm and his face blinked perceptibly in surprise at the sight of a scar from an old wound that ran in an ugly, white wrinkle from Teague's elbow to his wrist. Teague saw the surprise and answered it.

"Crosscut saw," he said simply. "Never did heal up right."

"Would have if I'd put a stitch or two in it," the doctor remarked.

Teague grinned at Garnett. Garnett had bitched at him for years about the scar.

"Call the start, Doc," Teague said.

Garnett laughed aloud.

"Start," he said.

And the match began. Arm shoving against arm. The clenched hands quivering. Finger tips reddening. Eyes closed. Heads bowed like pawing bulls. The cords of muscles and veins bulging on their necks.

The crowd, standing jammed close to the table, bellowed, but Michael did not hear them. He heard a loud, internal fury crying at the pain in his shoulder and arm, and a demonic anger pounded at his rib cage. He could feel his wrist bending from the vise of Teague's hand and his arm convulsed violently to hold the pressure. He opened his eyes and saw the long scar on Teague's arm, brutally white against the flushed red flesh of the knotted muscle. His mind clicked and a black seizure coated his brain, and his mind could see the arm split apart, seeping with blood, muscle hanging like torn meat, and a giddiness rushed through him. A wide smile trembled onto his face and a laugh like an animal's bray leaped from his throat and drove through the room. His hand tightened in a steel band around Teague's thumb and his fingernails gouged into the flesh of Teague's hand. A great strength was in him and he began to ease Teague's powerful arm down.

"*Goda'mighty,*" someone hissed.

"*Goda'* . . ."

And then the room was silent and the men of Pullen's Café stood frozen by the curling laughter that continued to roll from Michael.

"*Goddam, Teague, get him,*" someone shouted desperately over Michael's shoulder.

Michael's head snapped at the sound. He shook his eyes into focus. He could feel perspiration dripping from his face and the ache returning to his arm. He heard the silence around him. He looked across his hand into Teague's face; it was pale and bewildered and fearing. His brain pounded with the echo of the screaming, and then it cleared and he knew what he must do.

He sucked hard from the thick, hot air and pretended to weaken. His arm relaxed. He pulled Teague's wrist straight and forced his hand to quiver unsteadily, and then he let it collapse in a thump against the table.

"Damn," a voice whispered. Then louder, "Damn!"

The one voice triggered other voices of disbelief.

"*By God, Teague, he almost had you.*"

"*Damned if he didn't.*"

"*Sounded crazy, didn't he?*"

"*Teague's a scrapper, ain't he?*"

"*He is, by God. He is at that.*"

Michael released Teague's hand and dropped his head to the table, across his extended arm. He laughed merrily and rubbed his sweating face over the sleeve of his shirt. Then he pushed up from the table and slumped wearily against his chair.

"You're a man, Mr. Teague," he said with admiration. "Bull-strong, I'll tell you. I'd wager you could make it with the circus tour without a worry."

Teague said nothing. He sat, his limp arm stretched over the table before him, and stared blankly at the tiny nail punctures on the back of his hand. The men around him had heard Michael's crackling, demented laugh, but Teague had felt it and it was like a madness that had swallowed the power of his hand.

"Losin' man buys the drinks," declared Michael. "That was the proposition and I'm buyin' for Mr. Teague." He waved his hand to a man standing behind the crowd. "Mr. Pullen, what-ever his pleasure is," he sang. "But make it a bodied one. He deserves it."

\*     \*     \*

An hour later Michael left Pullen's Café with Garnett.

The doctor had leaned to him and whispered, "Let's go. I've got to make a call and then I'll drive you up to the farm."

Michael had thought to protest, but did not. He recognized an urgency in Garnett's voice and nodded agreement and made a short farewell speech to the crowd, promising to return the following week.

Outside, Garnett and Michael walked quickly and silently across the paved road leading through Yale, along the row of darkened stores and toward a small brick building that stood alone on the bank of the Naheela River. As they approached it, Michael saw the windows were barred with thick steel.

"Jail?" he asked curiously.

"The only one in thirty miles," replied Garnett. He stopped in the street and looked at the reinforced window. There was a weak sheet of light behind it. "Got a customer in there," he added solemnly.

"What's the poor fellow done?" questioned Michael.

Garnett continued walking until he reached the door of the

jail. If he had heard Michael's question, he refused to answer.

"Tell me something," Garnett said, standing before the door of the jail, staring at Michael with his studied, practiced gaze.

"Anythin', Doc. Just ask."

"Why'd you let Teague beat you?" Garnett asked bluntly. "You had him and you knew it. Why'd you do it?"

Michael laughed easily. He said, "Why, Doc, I'm a guest here. You don't come in and make the home people feel like fools. You're a man to understand that."

Garnett nodded. He spat on the street and looked back toward the lights in Pullen's Café.

"I do," he admitted. "But it wouldn't've mattered if somebody hadn't shouted in your ear and snapped you out of whatever fit you were in. What was it? Some kind of hypnosis?"

Yes, thought Michael. The doctor had noticed it, and so had Teague. But Teague did not know what it was; the doctor did, or believed he did.

"You could say that," Michael answered. "I'd call it a circus trick. Nothin' more. Puts the other man off guard for just a minute. Gives you a chance to be turnin' the tide on him." He smiled and searched for the assurance that Garnett believed him. Garnett's face did not change.

"Was it the laughin'?" Michael asked gently. "Was that what it was? Sometimes I do that, I'm told, and I don't even know it myself."

Now Garnett's face changed. It wrinkled into a frown and he sniffed hard and coughed.

"Now that you mention it, I guess so," he remarked dryly. "Sounded like some damn crazy on the loose. I've heard it in the hospitals in Boston. Don't hear it around here, even though there are some crazies. I guess they treat it different and nobody pays much attention to it. It's the best way, I suppose."

Michael leaned close to Garnett. He whispered, "Well, now that you know, I'm grateful for whoever it was that broke it up. I would've felt bad by winnin'."

Garnett pushed his hat back on his head and looked at Michael as he would examine a patient. His eyes narrowed and his lips tightened.

"I won't say anything," he said. "I don't give a damn if you sit up on some fence post and crow every morning, if you know what you're doing yourself." He turned to the door of the jail. "C'mon, let's look at this fellow," he added. He opened the door and walked inside.

# 9

MICHAEL SWEPT the jail with his eyes and memorized it.

The building was made of rock and mortar and heavy timbers, and it was square — perhaps twenty-five feet. In the far right corner from where he stood at the front door, there was a single cell, also square; ten feet, he judged. The steel bars were dark and close, like a cold curtain. There was one small window in the cell, cut high in the back wall. The window was also covered with bars. Across from the cell, in the left corner, was a storeroom, built in the exact dimensions of the cell. The hallway that divided the cell from the storeroom led to a back door that had been nailed closed by a braced framework of two-by-six boards.

The rest of the jail was open. A wooden bench and three ladderback chairs were to the right of the front door. To the left, in front of the storeroom, were a rocker, a desk chair, and a rolltop desk pushed against the inside wall of the storeroom. A gunrack holding two shotguns and a rifle was bolted to the wall beside the rolltop desk. A framed picture of Franklin Roosevelt was on the wall beside the gunrack. And there was one odd piece of furniture: an ancient chifforobe with an ornate facing and round, protruding doors. It was in the corner of the room, to the left of the door. To Michael, the chifforobe seemed out of place in the jail. It belonged in a house, a very fine house.

A deputy whose name was George English slumped sleepily

in a chair, his feet propped comfortably across the shelf of the rolltop desk. He was young, in his early thirties, and impressively tall. His hair was thick and curled in tight, oily knots around his neck, and his face was pockmarked from smallpox.

George smiled happily at the introduction of Michael.

"Heard tell about you workin' on that fence up at the Pettit place," he said. "If I'd of known you'd be over at the café tonight, I'd of walked over."

"And you'd have the sheriff's boot up your ass," Garnett snapped.

George giggled. He said, "Hell, Doc, don't see why this man's got to be treated any different'n anybody else. Shape he's in, he ain't goin' nowhere, even if he could break out. But ain't nobody done that since — " He paused and laughed. "Now, this is somethin', ain't it?" he said. "Last man to break out of here was Eli, best I can remember it, and that was on some damn bet with the old sheriff. Turned hisself in the same day. That's why they nailed up the back door. Anyway, it was Eli, and here comes his own flesh and kin, from what I hear."

"Distant flesh," corrected Michael. "Distant flesh."

"Don't matter. Kin's kin," George said nonchalantly, smiling. He turned to Garnett. "You gonna give him another look, Doc?" he asked.

"Soon as you get up the energy to open the door, George. In your own good time, though. Wouldn't want to rush it."

George grinned again. He said, "Doc, you some kind of smartass, you know that?" He lifted the key ring from the rolltop desk and strolled to the door of the cell and unlocked it.

"Hey, Benton," he called, "you got company. Ol' Doc's back. Had his hands all over some woman up in the hollow and he's gonna give you a smell, boy. Gonna make you forget you locked up in here. Ain't that right, Doc?"

"Shut up, George," Garnett ordered. He stepped inside the cell and walked cautiously to the frail figure cowering like a whipped animal in the deep shadows of the bare room. The man was sitting in the corner on a quilt that had been torn and soiled by years of use. The quilt smelled of urine.

"Goddammit, George," Garnett said angrily, gagging on the odor. "I told you to get this quilt out of here and wash it out in the river."

"Now, Doc, you watch it," George warned. "They come in here pissin' all over the place, it ain't my job to clean up after 'em. Let 'im wallow in it and he'll stop it."

"Dammit, he can't help it," Garnett sighed. "I told you that."

"Help it if he don't want to sleep in it," George said authoritatively.

Garnett shook his head slowly. He was perspiring and he wiped the back of his hand across his forehead. Then he bent forward, toward the still, frightened figure.

"Boy, don't be afraid of me," he said quietly. "I'm not here to hit you."

Michael watched from outside the cell, standing beside George. The figure moved slightly against the rock wall. One hand rose helplessly in front of his face and the face — indistinguishable in the dark — rolled away.

"I'm the doctor," Garnett said. "You know me. I came in earlier. Put some medicine on those cuts. Bandaged you up. You remember me?"

The figure did not move.

"Well, I'm just going to take another look at those bandages. See if they need anything before morning."

Garnett knelt slowly, as if kneeling before something wild and dangerous. He reached for the man, who jerked away instinctively, bashing his head into the rock wall.

"Goddammit," Garnett muttered. "O'Rear, get in here," he commanded.

Michael stepped inside the cell.

"Hold him, but watch his head and chest," instructed the

doctor. "No telling what's broken and what's not. He's scared. Not much older than a boy."

Michael caught the trembling man by the arms, at the shoulders. The body was bones, emaciated and weak. The man froze at Michael's touch.

"Dear God," Michael whispered in surprise. "He must be near to death."

"Not far," replied Garnett. "Pull him out to the light."

Michael eased his arm around the stiff, unmoving man and pulled him gently from the corner of the cell into the light. He looked into the man's face. The doctor was right: He was barely more than a boy. His face had the gaunt look of starvation and it had been savagely beaten.

"Who did it?" Michael asked.

Garnett ignored the question. His fingers moved expertly over the man's body and his eyes squinted in a judgment that Michael recognized as a hard calculation of the degrees of life and death. He could feel the doctor's mind clicking off assets and liabilities, tabulating the mathematical chances of repair and survival, as though the man before him were a machine in need of spare pieces of equipment. Michael was amazed by the doctor's concentration, by his reading touch. What he did was not coldness, Michael thought. Not a meaningless litany in a recital of his practice. It was the physician at work, and his mind raced through the blueprints of the anatomy like an engineer. It was the exercise of a gift — his gift. There was only one thing that was curious about Garnett Cannon, thought Michael: He held his breath as he examined the man. And Michael realized it was not because of the stench of the quilt; it was something the doctor always did, a habit.

Garnett stood suddenly and breathed deeply. "He'll be all right," he said flatly. "Just lay him back down where he is. It'll keep him away from the wall."

"On the floor?" asked Michael.

"On the floor."

Garnett reached and pulled the quilt from beneath the man, wadded it angrily, and threw it against the bars of the cell.

"Let's go," he said to Michael. "I can't stand the smell of piss."

He whirled on his heel and walked to the door of the cell, where George stood blocking the opening.

"Get the hell out of the way, George," he said in an even, steel voice. George stepped aside and Garnett walked to the rolltop desk and leaned against it and glared at the deputy.

"Dammit, Doc," George stammered pitifully, "I don't mean to go bein' shitty, or nothin' like that. It's just that I ain't gonna clean up after a man pissin' on hisself. They ain't never paid me enough for that."

"George," Garnett replied coolly, "if that man dies because you didn't do something you were told to do, you'll be wishing to hell you'd changed his diapers every hour on the hour. Do you hear me?"

George shifted his weight. He lowered his head and looked at the floor.

"When I come in here in the morning, this place will smell like a lye soap factory," Garnett continued. His voice was low and direct and unafraid.

George nodded.

"You heard the sheriff say that nothing on God's earth will happen to that man, and it won't," Garnett added.

"Doc, ain't nothin' gonna happen," George whined desperately.

"All right," Garnett said. "One more thing. Keep it quiet. Nobody knows he's here and we want to keep it that way for the time being, and that's an order." He stared hard at George, then he said to Michael, "Let's go." He turned and walked out of the jail.

"Good to meet you," Michael whispered to George. "Don't worry about the doctor. He's a bit tired."

"Yeah."

"See you at the café one night, I'd guess," Michael added.

"Yeah. Maybe so," George mumbled.

*   *   *

Garnett said nothing as they crossed the street to his car, and Michael did not question him. He had impressed Michael with his authority. He had not bargained with George English; he had issued orders and George had listened and would obey. Michael wondered if anyone ever disobeyed the doctor when he was angry.

The Ford rumbled slowly down the paved highway leading north out of Yale. Garnett drove with both hands on the steering wheel, with his body leaning forward. His face was furrowed in thinking and Michael knew he would speak when he was ready.

A mile outside Yale, Garnett turned left onto the eroded dirt road leading to the Pettit farm. He drove beyond the bridge crossing Deepstep Creek and then pulled the car to the side of the road and turned off the motor.

"Let's stand out and get some air," he said to Michael.

"It's a night for it," replied Michael. "It's one of the things I like about the mountains, more than the sea. You can stand right out in the middle of the mountains."

The two men got out of the car and walked to the front fenders and leaned against them. It was cool. The night was as clear and clean as polished glass.

"Irishman," Garnett said at last, "I'm about to tell you something that nobody knows but me and the sheriff and I expect it to stay among the three of us."

"You have my word," promised Michael. "And it's the word of a gentleman."

Garnett glanced at Michael. His eyes were bright, cold dots in the night. He said, "It had better be." He crossed his arms and looked into the high half-moon, pale gold against the sky.

"That man we just saw — that boy — was beaten by his

daddy," Garnett explained. "Curtis — Curtis Hill, he's the sher-
iff — picked him up this morning. The boy's name is Owen
Benton. They live ten or twelve miles up in the mountain.
Curtis was just by there and stopped in, and found him."

"What'd the boy do?" Michael asked quietly.

"Do?" Garnett replied. He laughed sarcastically. "He was
born Frank Benton's son, that's what he did. Frank's never had
reason for beating his children, at least not in the past few years.
Never saw a man that brutal. Ran off one of his girls — she was
the oldest, I guess — because she spoke to some man in town
one day. Just said 'hello,' but Frank went crazy. Started beating
her right there in the street, calling her a whore, not worth
living." He paused and smiled. "Funny thing," he continued,
"that's what she became. Ran off that night and went to Atlanta
and took to whoring. Heard it from some of my medical friends.
They said she was the best in the business and there's two or
three of them who know whores the way the French know
wines."

"It's a sad thing," Michael said in a sigh. "A man beatin' his
own flesh. It's a madman who'd do such a thing."

Garnett spat on the ground and kicked dirt over the phlegm
with the toe of his shoe. He was thinking of Michael's performance in the café.

"Maybe so," he said. "Maybe it is madness. I don't know. It's
a sickness, at the very least. But you'd have to know Frank. He
wasn't always that way. I remember when he was outgoing and
well, hell, even warm-hearted. He began to change after his wife
died. If you listen to the people around here it's because of his
own father. Seems his father was a preacher of some sort,
started his own cult up in the hills. Had a fair number of people
that believed in him." He laughed and shook his head slowly.
"One of the things he believed in, they say, was raising people
from the dead," he continued. "God knows, I envy that." He
laughed again. "Anyway, they say Frank never believed in any
of it until his wife died and something snapped in him. Grief

can do that. I've seen it. He tried to raise his wife from her coffin and his children dragged him away from the body. Frank got it in his mind that it was the Devil working in the children. He changed after that. Everything they did, he watched, and every chance he's had, he's punished them." He looked at Michael. "Madness, Irishman? Hell, I don't know," he said. "I don't even know what can be done about it. All I know is the boy's in bad shape. We don't even know why Frank did it. I don't think the boy will die, but he's in bad shape."

"The sheriff jailed him to keep him away from his father?" asked Michael.

Garnett's eyes narrowed on Michael. His mouth opened and closed. His head nodded sadly.

"You could say that," he answered. "The boy'd been unconscious for a day. His sister was getting ready to come to town to get us. She's younger by a few years, but I guess she knew."

"What?"

"If the boy had awakened at home, Frank probably would've started the beating all over. It would have killed him."

"Why're you tellin' me about this, me bein' a stranger?" Michael asked.

Garnett laughed. He pulled himself up on the fender of his car, propping his feet against the bumper guard.

"Well, Irishman, maybe it's because you interest me," he replied. "Maybe it's because I think you're one hell of an actor." He paused and removed his hat and placed it on the hood of the car. His thinning hair billowed in the night breeze.

"I want to tell you something," he continued. "I don't believe for one minute that story about you being a cousin to Eli Pettit, but I don't hold you to blame for it. I'd say it was Rachel who made it up, or she wouldn't permit it to be told. But it's all right. As a matter of fact, it's a relief you showed up. Those women have needed a man besides Floyd Crider around. And I don't give a damn if you're bedding down with all three at the same time. I don't pass judgment on those things. I doubt you've touched a one of them, but I don't care. With times as bad as they are and getting worse, I can't blame a man for holding on to some security, no matter where he finds it or how he gets it. But there's some things you should know. First, you'll hear about a great fortune that's hidden somewhere on the farm, some money Eli stole. It's a lie, a myth. I can't tell you why I know that, because there's not a reason. It's just something I feel, and I trust myself. Second, don't worry about Eli returning in the middle of the night and blowing your head off. Eli's dead. I know that, and, again, I can't prove it. I just know it."

Garnett had spoken rapidly, frankly, without fear of sounding foolish. He fingered the brim of his hat with his right hand, waiting for Michael to reply.

"Well, you're not a fool, Doctor," Michael said slowly. "There's no question about it. It's true, the way you see it. I'm not cousin to Eli. It was somethin' Rachel made up when I had the snakebite, like you said. It even shocked me, hearin' it, but it didn't do anyone any harm and I've followed up on it and used it to advantage. It hurts to admit that, but it's the truth, and maybe you're right about a man needin' some security. I've been wanderin' a long time. Havin' a place feels right for a change."

"It's your business," Garnett remarked. "Nobody else knows. Nobody needs to."

"I'm grateful," Michael told him. "There'll be a day when I'll up and leave, but I'd like for it to be easy."

"Had you heard about the money?"

Michael shook his head. "Not a word," he said earnestly. "I'm surprised some of the men didn't bring it up tonight."

"They were too busy being entertained," Garnett answered, laughing. "You're a magnificent liar, you know."

Michael smiled. He said, "I'll take that as a compliment."

"Meant it to be. You'll hear of the money. Somebody's always talking about it. Take it for what it's worth. I still don't believe it."

A silence fell between the two men. A whippoorwill sang its

monotonous flute tune from the black funnel of woods leading to the creek. The air carried the sweet smell of cut timber from high in the mountains.

Then Garnett spoke.

"The real reason I told you about the Benton boy was because I think you can help us," he said. "It occurred to me sitting in Pullen's, listening to you."

"Help? How?"

"For whatever sin I'll be charged with in the hereafter, I have to admit that I'm not only a doctor but also the dutifully elected mayor of Yale," Garnett replied. "That's why George English got an ass chewing and took it. That's why the jail will be clean in the morning. Because I said it and George knows damn well I can make it stick."

"What would I have to do?" asked Michael.

"Well, Irishman, I'd like to put you on the payroll, little as it is, to help keep watch over the boy. Normally, there's nobody at the jail at night and the sheriff's got to put George back on days, and we need somebody. It's that simple. Besides, I've got a feeling you could talk Roosevelt into becoming a Republican and if there's any trouble — like that boy's daddy showing up — you could handle it."

Michael smiled. The doctor knew him well, he thought, but not too well. He walked away from the car a few feet and thought about the proposition.

"Whatever I can do," he finally said. "Besides, it'd make me feel good, earning some money of my own. I spent the last I had tonight."

"It's not much," Garnett warned. "A dollar a day, and you bring your own food. Only advantage you have is getting sick. Won't cost you anything for a cure."

"When do I start?"

"Tomorrow night. You'll meet the sheriff then. You'll like him. He's a decent man. He's up at the Benton place now, trying to make some sense of everything."

"Sense of a beatin'? He'll find none," Michael said.

"Maybe not," Garnett answered softly. He lifted his hat from the hood of the car and placed it on his head. He slipped from the fender and dusted the back of his trousers. "Come on," he said. "I'll take you on home."

"Tell you the truth, Doc, I'd enjoy walkin' the rest of the way," Michael replied pleasantly. "It's a night to drink in, it is."

"Don't blame you," Garnett agreed. "That's the trouble with being rich. First thing you do is buy a car and quit walking." He opened the door to his car and slipped beneath the steering wheel. "I'll see you tomorrow night, around seven," he said. He started the Ford and turned around in the middle of the road and drove away toward Yale.

*    *    *

Michael stood watching the car disappear. Garnett Cannon was not a fool, he thought. Not a fool, at all. He had seen through Michael's ruses and he knew more than anyone. But he was not a danger, either. The doctor was a tired man who drank too much and tried not to care as deeply as he did, and that was a flaw. No, Michael decided. It did not worry him that the doctor knew something about him that others did not.

He began humming and his lips parted and the song sprang from his mouth:

*"I have loved you with poems . . . I have loved you with daisies . . . I have loved you with everything but love . . ."*

He turned quickly in the road, in a mock-military whirl, and he began laughing joyfully as he stepped lightly along the road.

"Michael O'Rear," he said aloud. "You're a man with a job. What a fine settin' it is."

*    *    *

The house was dark and Michael realized it was late, after midnight. He slipped noiselessly across the yard and to the barn. He reached for the latch, opened the barn door, and stepped inside the solid black hull. He closed the door and pulled the latchstring and heard the crosspiece fall softly into place. He stood blinking in the darkness and then he began walking along the barn wall, touching it with his fingers. He reached the partition to his room and turned right with the wall until he touched the closed door, then turned the knob and stepped inside his room and closed the door behind him. The room was as dark as the barn. He pulled a match from his pocket and struck it across the door. The flame sputtered and grew and he touched it to the wick of a candle that he had placed on the iron stove. The pupils of his eyes contracted into dots as the flame blurred his vision. He stretched and looked across the room.

She was standing at the foot of his bed, in the corner of the room, in a blind of shadows. She wore only a nightgown and the candlelight bathed her with a yellow softness. His eyes flashed in surprise, then softened, and he smiled and stepped toward her and opened his arms and she moved hesitantly to him.

"You're sure?" he asked gently as she rolled her hair against his face.

She nodded bravely and slipped her arms around him.

"Unbutton the shirt," he whispered.

Her fingers played across his chest, turning the buttons, pulling the shirt open. He could feel her breath on him and her mouth lightly touching his body.

"I've wanted to find you here, like this," he said quietly. "I've dreamed it. Over and over, I've dreamed it." He lifted her chin with his hand and kissed her easily on the tight line of her lips. "You're not to be afraid," he urged. "Not at all. There's nothin' here but the night. Nothin' else."

She dropped her head to his chest and held him tight.

"Let me see you," he said, sliding the palms of his hands over the back of her gown.

She stepped away from him and raised her arms and he slowly pulled the cotton gown over her head and hands. The eyes of her breasts lifted to him like small fountains and he could see the spasms of her heartbeat pounding in her neck.

"It's bad, what I'm doin'," she whispered.

"Bad? It's like you're praisin' bein' with me," he said. "How can that be bad? No. It's between us. Only us."

She began to cry softly and her body shuddered and she dropped her arms to cover her nakedness.

"Shhhhh," he whispered. "None of that. None of that, sweet Sarah. None of that."

Then he kissed her gently on her forehead.

# 10

OWEN BENTON could not control himself.

He sat limp against the granite wall of the cell, against the coolness of the stone, as the urine oozed from his body and seeped into his clothing, leaving a thick, sickening odor. A rash burned his legs and testicles.

His arms dangled beside him, his wrists resting on the floor and the palms of his hands turned up and opened. His legs were locked straight before him and his head was tilted left and bent forward and his eyes stared unblinking at the dark, damp circle on his trousers. The urine had begun leaking from him after his father struck him on the temple and after he had fainted from the pain.

He had been unconscious for a day when the sheriff arrived at his father's farm, and he had awakened in the cell in panic, intuitively wrapping his knees with his arms and locking his body into a fetal knot. Sitting propped against the granite wall of the cell, Owen felt no pain, no anger, no pity. He felt nothing. His body was awake, but his mind wandered dreamily in the euphoria of memories, of laughing years, of a father with soft gray eyes and soft full lips. And in the narrow corridor of that seeing, he was calm and happy. A fragile smile rested on his swollen face like a sweet sleep.

\*     \*     \*

Curtis Hill sat rigidly in the rocker and stared at Owen through the bars of the cell. Owen looked like a puppet that Curtis had seen in the window of a shop in Atlanta. He would be better off as a puppet, Curtis thought. A puppet with a broken head could have one newly carved; arms and legs were as interchangeable as costumes. A puppet did not have to be force-fed or washed down like an animal. A puppet did not whimper and thrash about when someone approached. Owen did. Owen's body reflexed on touch like some convulsive worship of pain. Christ, it was pitiful. God, yes, Owen would be better off as a body whittled out of wood. He would not drain piss like a cracked pipe.

Curtis was tired and irritated. He had been with Frank Benton for hours, asking about Frank's violence toward his son. He did not understand Frank Benton. He had asked, "Why, Frank? Why?" and Frank had only answered, "Because I seen things you ain't." And maybe he was right. Maybe he had seen things other people could not see. He had accused his daughter of being a whore, and she was — or she had become one. There was a story that his daughter had once mailed Frank a photograph of her in bed with two men, legs circling both and with a laugh of pleasure on her face that could be heard through the envelope. There was no other message; there was no need for one.

He had never arrested Frank for beating his children, Curtis thought. Twice he had stopped beatings in progress — with the girl, Shirley, and the boy, Ray — but both times the abused child had begged him not to hurt Frank. It was sickening: the child, bruised and bleeding, hanging onto Frank's leg, riding the leg like a weight, pulling to hold him, to keep him from being taken away.

Curtis pulled himself angrily from the rocker, stalked to the cell, caught the bars with his hands, and shook the steel door. He knew that deep within him was a longing to kill Frank Benton, to blow his face off his goddam shoulders. It was a horrifying desire. Curtis had once killed a man because he had to. But he had vomited at the sight of the broad, mangled hole in the man's gut and the anguish of it had stayed in his mouth like a thick, slick coating that would not rinse away.

He began to pace the oak floor of the jail office. His arms were crossed over his chest and he could feel the anger churning inside him. He could not let Frank destroy his own son. He had jailed Owen to protect him and yet he knew he could not hold him forever. There would be a time when Owen would return to his father.

He walked to the doorway of the jail. The heavy wooden door was held open with a brick and the hot afternoon air sifted through the tiny squares of the screen door like a fume. He stood in the face of the heat and watched a fly crawl across the screen on its delicate legs. The ache from his encounter with Frank Benton spread over his thick neck and shoulders. The doctor had said he was only tired, that it was nerves. He had told Curtis to drink a half-glass of whiskey and go to bed. He had taken the advice the night before, but he had not slept.

Curtis was glad the doctor knew about the beating of Owen, and he was glad because he had told it freely, and not because the doctor wanted to know.

He flicked at the crawling fly with his finger and the fly fell away on its thin wings and glided to the doorsill. The Irishman also knew, he suddenly remembered. He had met the Irishman the night before and had liked him. He was not certain why Garnett had insisted on hiring the Irishman, but he trusted the decision. One thing for sure: Michael O'Rear had a way with words. If anyone could find his way into the murky recesses of Owen Benton's mind, it would be the Irishman.

Curtis pushed open the screen door and stood outside. He saw Ellis Finch standing in front of Fred Deal's Merchandise Store across the street. Ellis was as still as a pillar. Curtis grinned. Damned lazy Ellis. Standing in the sun would be his only effort all day. No one was as lazy as Ellis, damn his soul. He was a good man, Ellis Finch.

*    *    *

The work at the jail was freedom to Michael. It gave him a pride that he could unfurl like a banner before Rachel and Sarah and Dora. It meant he had been accepted in Yale. Garnett Cannon had ordained it by hiring him, for the people of Yale would not question the doctor. It meant time to trace the map he had in his memory of Eli's farm and time to learn of Eli's habits from the men in Pullen's Café. It did not matter what the doctor had said about Eli's money — that it was a myth, a lie — the men of Pullen's Café believed in it and they joked openly with Michael about stumbling over a buried strongbox. "Right under your nose," they said. "That's the way Eli would've done it. Put it right out, so plain you couldn't find it with a bloodhound."

Michael put aside the work on the fence, with solemn promises to complete it when his duty at the jail was over. He said, "I feel I been lyin' about it, not doin' anythin', but I'll get to it the minute the doctor tells me I've done enough at the jail." The fence could wait, Dora assured him. If the doctor needed him, that was enough. The fence could wait.

He slept late each day, until midafternoon, and at five o'clock he left the farm and walked the three miles into Yale. He stopped first at Pullen's Café, not to drink, but to tell stories and sit with the few old men who seemed to be always there, and who remembered Eli. At seven o'clock he relieved George English at the jail. George did not resent him. There was always a loud, laughing greeting from Michael and a mock inspection of George's work during the day. To George, Michael was refreshing and joyfully alive. Being with Michael, in the few minutes before he left the jail, was the only part of the day he enjoyed.

"Sheriff was by," George would report. "Said he still can't figure out why Frank beat up his boy so bad, but there ain't

nothin' we can do but keep him locked up. Poor bastard. Tell
you the truth, I feel sorry for him."

"It'll take time, George," Michael would reply. "Time's easy
to give. Time's the freest thing on earth."

* * *

Slowly, gradually, Michael began to coax Owen Benton out of
the horror that was closed inside him like a fist.

He did it with the gift of his patience, with the mesmerizing
lull of his voice, with soft Irish melodies, with remembered
poetry of the tent Chautauqua, with conversations he had with
himself like a merry ventriloquist. He did it by caring for
Owen's wounds, by pressing food into Owen's unwilling mouth,
by cooling Owen with sponge baths on his neck and face and
arms. He did it by surrounding Owen with his presence. And
slowly, gradually, Owen's eyes began to wander toward the
voice. The subconscious other person in Owen was emerging
— slowly, cautiously, innocently — and it came to trust the
voice.

Michael saw, and he fed Owen with all of his energy.

* * *

*"The circus? How come I got caught up with the circus? Well,
it was through a buddy of mine, a fellow I'd met not long after
the tent Chautauqua closed down and I was left stranded. He'd
caught on with the circus, cleanin' up after the animals. Smelly
job, but he was Irish and jobs for the Irish in search of the golden
streets of America were few and far between, and shovelin' dung
wasn't as bad as climbin' down in the coal mines, I'll tell you.
No sir. Not half as bad. So, anyway, this buddy of mine talks me
into goin' on the circus with him and we start out tourin'.*

*"Now me, mind you, I'm not for followin' after elephants with
a shovel and broom and I get it in mind to do somethin' else. So
I up and find the circus manager and say to him, 'Hey, I'm the
son of a clown what toured Ireland with the greatest shows in all*

*of Europe.' And he says, 'You are, are you?' And I says, 'I am. My father was called Sad Sean, the Finest Clown in I-re-land.' And he says, 'If your dad worked with the greatest, tell me whatever happened to McKenzie's Magnificent Mammals?' And I says, 'Whatever happened to McKenzie's Magnificent Mammals? Why, every red-blooded circus fellow in the world knows the true story of that. McKenzie run off with the Gorilla Girl and the act went busted.' And he says, 'What Gorilla Girl?' And I says, 'She was half-gorilla and half-girl and when she was makin' love, you didn't know which half was which.' And the bloomin' circus manager was so struck down because he'd been lyin' to me and I lied back even better, that he gave me a job as a barker. And that's how I got started in the circus, Owen. That's the whole of it."*

\* \* \*

Four days after Michael began guarding him at night, Owen finally spoke.

He said, very softly, "Mister, where's my daddy?"

The voice startled Michael. It was as weak and emaciated as Owen's body.

"Your daddy?" he asked gently. "Well, now — " He began walking easily toward the cell. "Well, now, I don't know, Owen," he said. "Not here, though. You don't have to worry about that. There's nobody here but the two of us."

Michael unlocked the steel door and stepped inside the cell. He did not close the door.

"My name's Michael," he said pleasantly. "Michael O'Rear. I work here. In a matter of speakin', that is." He squatted in front of Owen. "Do you know the doctor?" he asked.

Owen nodded.

"Well, he hired me to watch after you at night," Michael said. "I've been stayin' up on the Pettit farm. I'm cousin to Eli." He smiled broadly and leaned close to Owen and whispered, "On the Irish side, in case you're thinkin' I talk a bit different."

Owen pulled himself closer to the wall. He could feel the raw skin where the urine had soaked over his legs. He looked shamefully at his trousers. There was only a small spot on the left pant leg. His mind remembered the blow from his father and the urine flood that gushed from him before he fainted.

"My — my daddy been here?" he asked hesitantly.

Michael shook his head.

"No. No, he's not been around. The sheriff thought it best to keep him away for a time. Seems he struck you good."

"He did," Owen replied simply. "He did. But he don't mean nothin' by it. He don't."

Michael lifted his head and cleared his throat with a cough. He stared through the small barred window of the cell into the dark hole of night. He could hear the gurgling of the Naheela River running a few feet behind the jail. It was past one o'clock, he judged. Pullen's Café had closed and the last human sound had been Teague's lumber truck rattling through town in its awful mechanical pain, and Teague's one defiant yell: "Damn!"

"Such things are hard to understand, Owen," Michael said. "Man or boy, father or son, it's hard. Not that I take to beatin's. I don't. But it's a hard time and bein' a hard time makes men do things they don't understand in the least."

"My daddy don't mean nothin'. He — sometimes he thinks up things and that sets him off. He don't mean nothin'."

Michael stood. He said, "Maybe, but that's enough of that for now. Fact is, you're awake and talkin' and that means you're feelin' better. I can tell. And that'll mean movin' the cot back in the cell. The doctor had it taken out so you wouldn't hurt yourself on it when you was tossin' about, bein' the way you was."

Michael went through the open cell door and crossed the hallway to the storeroom. He returned in a few moments with a small, narrow cot that he placed against a wall in the cell. He had a brown army blanket over his shoulder.

"You'll sleep better the rest of the night," he said. "Bein' on a cot beats the floor. And we'll wash you off some. I'll even bring up a bucket of water from the river. It's cold. Make you feel fresh."

"I been — been messin' up my pants, I reckon," mumbled Owen.

"Not bad," Michael answered cheerfully. "The doctor brought in another pair and I been changin' you out every night. Doc says whatever it was that caused it seems to be healin'. Not much spottin' at all tonight. Just a bit."

Owen watched Michael unfolding the blanket. He said, "Ain't right for a man to be cleanin' up after another man."

Michael laughed. He flipped the blanket open and snapped it in the air and dropped it in a perfect fit over the cot.

"Maybe you're right," he replied. "Maybe so. But I don't exactly see it that way. I could tell you I've done it because the doctor's payin' me a dollar a day — and that'd be reason enough, if you'd done some of the jobs I've done. But the truth is, I've been in somethin' of the same shape myself. Down in Florida it was." He tucked the blanket tight around the cot, smiling. "I'm ashamed to confess it," he continued, "but there was a lady that had me lappin' out of her hand, like a cat on a pan of cream, and me'n her used to go to this special place by the ocean and we'd go at it like some married couple, but it was all arguin', not lovin', and then one day I happened into her at that same place with another man and it was like night'n day. Bless her sweet soul, she knocked me over the head with a steel pipe and they half buried me in the sand and left me for dead. Hadn't been for a kind old man findin' me and takin' care of me, I'd be fertilizin' some palm tree now."

His smile tightened into a bitter curl. He knelt beside Owen.

"And that's why watchin' over you means more than a dollar's wage," he said. "Come on, I'll give you a lift to the cot, but go easy with it. It'll take time to get your legs back. You've been stretched out on that floor for five or six days, I'd guess. Not out, thank God, or you'd be starved away by now. You've just blocked it out, that's all. The mind does that, Doc says. Kind of a built-in medicine."

Owen struggled to pull himself from the wall. He felt at ease with Michael.

"Careful," Michael warned. He caught Owen by his arm and pulled him to his feet. Owen was light, like something hollow, and he stood unsteadily, swaying with the surge of pain that ran in an electric shock over the length of his body.

"It'll take a minute," Michael told him. "Don't worry. I won't let go."

Michael guided him in short, slow steps to the cot and eased him into sitting.

"Take your breath good and deep," he said. "When you get it clear, we'll put you down."

Owen held his hands to his chest. His breathing seemed no deeper than his throat. A hazy filter coated his eyes. He could feel the faint pulse of his heart under the drumskin of his ribs. Dots of purple skittered across the silver of his mind and his intestines crawled inside his abdomen like an uncoiling snake.

"Lie down," Michael said quietly. "It'll be better that way." He put one hand behind Owen's slender neck and stretched him across the blanket on the cot. "That's good. You rest. I'll get the water."

Michael did not lock the door to the cell or the outside door to the jail. He walked briskly to the Naheela River and dipped the bucket into the swirling current and filled it with water. Then he returned to the jail and to Owen's cell. He put the bucket beside Owen's cot and took a clean cloth from the drawer of the chifforobe and soaked it in the water.

"Ah, it's cool, Owen," he said soothingly. "I'd almost swear it came from snow, like the water in the mountains in Colorado." He bathed Owen's face and neck as he talked. "Let me tell you about Colorado. It's as lovely a place as a man could ever hope to see. Land runs flat as a board up to the Rockies — comes out of Kansas that way. And then you get into them mountains and it hurts down to your soul breathin' that air, it's so cold. Water's better. You can take a swallow and it's like a song rushin' through you, tinglin' in your toes and fingers like they'd been frostbit. Comes from the snow that falls in winter and sticks forever in the high places. There's a mountain there — Lookout Mountain, it's called — outside of Denver, and Buffalo Bill Cody's buried at the top of it, near to Heaven as you can be, I'd say."

Michael's voice rubbed gently inside Owen. He closed his eyes and felt the words, like fingertips, on his forehead and temples, and he was at last unafraid.

"How's the water? Cool, is it?"

Owen nodded once. He lay flat on the cot. One arm was across his chest, the other by his side. The cold, damp cloth on his lips and neck made his breathing easier.

"Doc said to wake him if you came around," continued Michael, "but I don't believe I will. Let you get some rest before they start pokin' and askin' questions. No need to rush things, if you're feelin' better." He squeezed the wet cloth over the bucket and unfolded it and draped it over the foot support of the cot. He walked from the cell and returned with a chair.

"You can rest if you want," Michael said, sitting in the chair and leaning against the wall. "Or you can talk, if you'd like that. I'm a good man for listenin', especially for one who's known for doin' the talkin' of a dozen."

"I rested enough, I reckon," replied Owen. He looked at Michael. Michael did not seem a stranger.

"If you could call it restin'," corrected Michael. "I'd say it's been fitful."

Owen said nothing. He touched the scab that had healed over a cut on his lip.

"He didn't mean nothin' by it," Owen mumbled.

"That you said. Did you wrong him in some way?"

Owen turned his head from Michael.

"I'm pryin'," Michael said. "It's a personal thing and it's not right to be pryin'. I'll leave you to sleep." He dropped his chair from the wall and stood.

"It don't matter," Owen told him. He covered his eyes with his hands. He asked, "My daddy didn't say nothin' about it?"

Michael reached into his shirt pocket and withdrew his short pipe packed with tobacco. He struck a match across the floor and held the flame to the bowl and inhaled. The smoke from the burning tobacco rose in a mushroom O above the bowl and drifted in a sheet across the cell.

"Not that I know," he answered. "Doc's not said. Nor the sheriff. From what I know they wanted you here to mend. Don't even know if it's legal, you bein' locked up. There's no charges that I've heard about."

"People in town know I'm here?"

"It'd be a hard thing not to know," Michael replied. "It's a small place and what with the doctor hirin' me for the night work, it got around, but it took some time. No, Owen, there's no secret of it. There's many askin' about you every day. They'll be glad to know you're better."

Owen's face moved in his hands. He said nothing. Michael pulled on the stem of his pipe, filling his mouth with smoke. He wondered why Owen had asked if his father had said anything, and if the townspeople knew something they had not told him. The talk of Owen in Pullen's Café had been restrained, polite, spoken in short, whispered sentences. Michael had believed it was their anger or their awkward expression of sadness; he had believed that Frank Benton had become well known for his abuse of his children, and for being a religious fanatic. But perhaps there was more than a single incident that caused the talk; perhaps there was something lingering in the fixed nodding of the townspeople, and in their too-sudden reserve when Owen Benton was mentioned. Michael could feel the ghost of an uneasy truth, of something more terrible than a father's madness. He sat against the laddered slats of the chair back and the thin overture of a familiar music began to play inside the chambers of his imagination. His teeth closed tight on the pipe, and he waited.

# 11

MICHAEL WAS WEARY as he walked along the road out of Yale. It was morning. The sun was over the trees, above the mountains, riding a line of milk clouds that stretched across the eastern sky like a brush stroke. He had stayed late at the jail, explaining to Curtis Hill and Garnett Cannon what had happened the night before. The doctor had been irritated that his instructions to be awakened had been ignored, but he had not reprimanded Michael. Michael was not George English; at least he made Owen comfortable.

He had been paid six dollars by Garnett for five days' work — with the extra dollar for his caring. "It's worth it just to keep the place from smelling like a slop jar," the doctor said. "Worth more than that. God, yes. It's Friday. Take the night off. Go to Pullen's. Curtis'll be around tonight, anyway. We'll get word to Frank that his boy's conscious, and he'll be around to get him. I don't know when, but we can watch after him tonight."

Michael had tried, but he could not command his instincts to tell the doctor about Owen Benton. For four nights he had watched as Owen's mind sailed in illusions that rested peacefully on his face, while his body jerked in spasms of pain and fear — the mind and body joined like some grotesque Siamese mutation. Michael had attended Owen because the doctor expected it and the doctor was important to his plan. There was nothing unusual about Owen, nothing to suspect. Then Owen had awakened and a signal had flashed in him and Michael had sensed it. It was like a mouse in tall grass scurrying to hide from the hawk's eye. A brown dot there, then not there, imperceptible against the landscape until it moved again.

Patience, Michael told himself. Patience. The mouse would move again.

\*     \*     \*

He crossed the bridge at Deepstep Creek and stopped to rest and he began to trace the winding creek bed in his mind. It wiggled out of the mountains in North Carolina and turned sharply west at the Georgia border. Then it curled east again, like a scrawled C, and slipped around the crown of Eli's farm, through the map of the farm Michael had imprinted on his inner eye, and then it ran in an almost straight line through the Naheela Valley before cutting into the Naheela River above Yale. Michael had come to know Deepstep Creek well. The narrow stream that flowed beside Lester and Mary Caufield's home emptied into Deepstep and Michael had waded that stream into the creek to kill the scent of his presence. He still remembered the numbing cold of the water in the dark March night.

He stooped in the road and picked up a small stone and rolled it in the palm of his hand. It had been a long plotting, he thought. Almost five months of it. He had played it meticulously, expertly, as grandly as the grand theater roles he had performed or watched. And it was no longer only Eli's money that mattered. It was the performance, too. Always had been, perhaps. From the very beginning, with Lester and Mary. Eli's money would be the hire for his performance. One day its hiding place would leap into his mind with the pull of a divining rod. He would find it and then his performance in Yale would be finished and he would leave without anyone in his audience knowing they had been witnesses to a great drama.

He flipped the stone into the creek and stood and stretched

his body in a shaft of sun that shot through the trees. Suddenly he was aware of a wagon rolling toward him on the road, with its uneven sounds of steel and wood and harness and animals. He cupped his hand over his eyes and looked up the road. It was Floyd Crider. His wife, a thick woman whose face was covered by a white sunbonnet, was seated beside him on the wagon seat. He could see the top of Jack's head in the back, where he always sat. He waved to the wagon and waited.

"Good mornin' to you," Michael said cheerfully as Floyd reined the mules to a stop beside him. "You're out early this mornin', Floyd."

"Tryin' to get to town and back before late," replied Floyd. "Wife had some things she needed at the store."

"Good to see you, Mrs. Crider," Michael said. "I know your husband here, and Jack, but I've not had the pleasure of meetin' you. I'm Michael O'Rear."

The woman dipped her head in acknowledgment. Michael could not see her face in the shade of the sunbonnet's peak.

"I forgot you never met," Floyd mumbled. "Her name's Carrie."

"Well, that's a fine name," replied Michael. "Carrie was the name of a lady I worked for in New York City. She was as good as you'd find, and I think a name tells a lot about a person."

The woman said nothing. She stared ahead, at the bridge.

"Now that Mama's passed on, Carrie likes to get out once in a while," Floyd explained slowly. "Got to get some things she needs from down at Deal's."

"I see," Michael said. "I'm just comin' from town myself. I've been helpin' out nights at the jail, keepin' watch over a young fellow named Owen Benton."

Floyd shook his head sadly. He reached for his tobacco pouch in his overall bib.

"Heard tell about Frank beatin' up on the boy," he remarked seriously. "Man ought not do that. Man does that ought to be put in the lockup hisself. Ought not be the boy there. Don't understand it. Frank wadn't always that way." He tapped the tobacco into the trough of a cigarette paper.

Michael agreed: "It's a bad thing. But he's come about. Started talkin' some last night. The doctor said he'd be all right."

"That's good," Floyd said. He licked the edge of the thin cigarette paper and rolled it and sealed it with his fingers. "Always thought he was a good boy," he added.

Michael watched Floyd twist the ends of the cigarette and place it between his lips and light it with a match. The twisted paper danced in the flame, then died away, and the tobacco began to burn.

"Well, now, I'd better be goin' along," Michael said. "It's been a long night."

"Maybe see you later on," Floyd told him. "We'll be droppin' by with a little somethin' Carrie picks up for Sarah."

"Sarah? Why?" asked Michael.

Floyd's face flickered in surprise.

"Ain't they told you?" he asked. "Today's Sarah's birthday."

"Today, it is?"

"That's right. What'll she be now, Carrie? Seventeen? Eighteen?"

"Eighteen," Carrie answered.

"Eighteen," Floyd repeated. "Two years older'n Jack, back there."

"Well, I'm glad you happened along," Michael said. "I'd not have known it otherwise. There'll have to be a celebration tonight, and I'll have to come up with a gift of some sort."

"Uh-huh," muttered Floyd. "Maybe see you later on, then." He clucked to the mules and slapped the rope reins gently across their backs.

"It's good to meet you, Carrie," Michael said as the wagon passed him.

Carrie only nodded.

*   *   *

Michael smiled at the thought: Sarah's birthday. Why had she not told him? Since the night in the barn, before he began staying at the jail, she had visited him once in the middle of the day — boldly, quickly, in a pretense of getting something from the barn. She had wanted to be held and touched, to hear his promise of yearning for her, and then she had bolted from his room in confusion. The change in her had become all too obvious. Around her mother, she was sullen and quiet, and Rachel had watched her closely — not with suspicion, but with bewilderment.

But it was Sarah's birthday and Michael knew immediately what he would do. He had worked his way to center stage in the Pettit home, like a mountain climber inching up a sheer cliff. He was only one grip away from the command he needed. He had taken both Rachel and Sarah, and Dora was yearning — secretly, without knowing — for something as personal as a touch. Yet they had not opened to him; they had not told him of Eli's money. It was sealed in them like a vault, closed hard and locked. He needed one other thing to pull the secret from their mouths, like a hypnotist luring ancient stories from the subconscious. One other scene — superbly played — and they would resign themselves to him.

Sarah's birthday was a perfect opportunity.

*     *     *

He cut runners of a honeysuckle vine from a tangle growing along the road and threaded them into a garland of flowers. Then he walked hurriedly to the house and into the kitchen where Rachel and Sarah were, and he placed the garland on Sarah's head like a crown.

"For the birthday lady," he said, bowing graciously.

Sarah blushed and smiled. She lifted the honeysuckle from her head and offered it to her mother.

"It's yours, Sarah, not mine," Rachel said. "But I think you should thank Michael for it. It's pretty enough to wear to a party."

"And that's what she'll be doin'," Michael replied eagerly. "We'll be havin' a party tonight, just the four of us. A dress-up party, it'll be."

"No," protested Sarah. "We don't do — "

"Don't celebrate birthdays?" asked Michael, interrupting. "Well, we do now. I'm insistin'. Where's Miss Dora?"

"Outside, by the garden," Rachel answered.

"Then we'll have to tell her," Michael said. "We'll need to have a cake. Could you bake it, Rachel? Thick, with plenty of icin'?"

Rachel smiled foolishly. She embraced Sarah.

"Yes," she replied. "Yes. I'll cook three layers, with chocolate icin'. And we will dress up. We haven't done that since — " She paused. "We haven't done that in years," she said. "And you have that new dress Dora made, Sarah. Never even worn it."

"Then it's settled, it is," Michael announced. "I'll get some rest, but I'll be awake in plenty of time to help out."

"What about the jail?" asked Sarah. "You'll be there tonight?"

"I didn't tell you, did I? The boy's better. Started talkin' some and the doc gave me the night off. Couldn't've worked out better. A birthday's worth celebratin'."

"How'd you know it was my birthday?" Sarah asked deliberately.

"Why, Sarah," he said, "how could you ask that? I heard it in town. It's all they're talkin' about. Everybody you see, up and down the street, they're sayin', 'Hey, did you know? Today's Sarah's Pettit's birthday. She's eighteen.' It's big news, I'll tell you."

Sarah looked quickly at her mother. She turned the garland of honeysuckle in her hands, suddenly uncomfortable.

"No, it's not the truth," admitted Michael. "Not at all. The truth is, I heard it from a bluebird down by the creek. He was talkin' to a wren, I believe it was, when a butterfly as yellow as the sun happened by and told all about it."

Sarah remembered what he had said about butterflies. She knew he was speaking to her privately, in code. She wanted to touch him, to hold him.

"And I'd say those birds and that yellow butterfly was Floyd and his family," suggested Rachel. "I saw their wagon go by. I guess you ran into them on the road. They always remember Sarah's birthday."

Michael smiled easily.

"If you want to pin me down," he confessed. "And it's a good thing, too. You ladies are button-lipped about such things."

"A birthday's a day. No need to fuss about it," Rachel said. "We never have."

"But that's wrong, Rachel. Wrong. Wrong as can be," argued Michael. "Every day's new, somethin' special. Every single day the earth turns around. And there's some days more special than others. Bein' born. What's better than that? That's a day for rememberin', not because you reached another year, but because you had to travel through it to get there. That's special."

"Yes," Rachel admitted quietly. Her eyes held his face like hands. "Yes," she repeated.

"So, there'll be a party tonight and there'll be no holdin' back from it," declared Michael. "None. We'll dress to the gills and have a king's feast for supper and a three-layer chocolate cake and we may even do some dancin', like they'd do in Ireland on such an occasion. You ladies start workin' on the festivities. I'll tell Miss Dora on the way to my rest — if there's to be any rest."

\*     \*     \*

The table was crowded with food — the chocolate cake as centerpiece — and the three women sat waiting for Michael. They were dressed as they had promised: in the special dresses that women keep like prizes for a hidden time that seems never to happen. They sat waiting for Michael and stared at one another in amazement. They were participants in a new game that Michael called Party and they did not know the rules. Until now, it had been happy and girlish and the afternoon had been filled with wonder. Now they waited and looked at one another and did not know what to say.

"You sure he heard you call him?" Rachel asked Sarah.

"I told you, Mama. He said he'd be right in."

"Food'll be cold in a minute, he don't come on," said Dora.

They sat, dressed in their elegant dresses, and waited, feeling awkward and misplaced.

"Cold food's no good," mumbled Dora. "No good at all."

"He'll be here, Dora," Rachel said. She stood and walked to the window of the kitchen and looked out. The door to the barn was closed.

"That was a pretty bolt of cloth Carrie brought by," Rachel remarked absently. "She always remembers your birthday."

"Yes'm."

"I remember the night you were born. It was like this," Rachel said. "Lookin' like rain. Dora, do you remember it?"

"All I remember is Mama bein' scared to death," answered Dora. "Said you was too weak to have a baby before its full time."

"Was I early?" Sarah asked with surprise.

Rachel turned from the window. "About two weeks, from the doctor's count, but I always thought he was wrong. Your grandmother worried about everythin'. She was worse than your daddy, and he was bad enough."

"Was — was he mad because I was a girl?"

Rachel laughed playfully. "Mad? Dora, do you think he was mad?"

"I'll have to give Eli that," Dora said. "Only man I ever saw who wanted his first-born to be a girl."

"It was like a parade in here," Rachel remembered, sitting again at the table. "Day after day, your daddy drug people in to take a look at you. He'd stand over your crib like he owned half the world and made everybody who came in hold you, even though he didn't trust them. Kept his own hands spread under theirs in case they dropped you. Used to tell the men they'd been holdin' the prettiest woman they'd ever see, and it was the first and last time they'd ever have the chance to touch you. Said he didn't trust a one of them. Oh, no, Sarah, he wadn't mad because you were a girl. He got exactly what he wanted."

The dim picture of her father focused in Sarah's mind like a photograph yellowed with age. He had been away so often, and for such a long time now, that it was hard to remember his presence — his size, his touch, his voice. When she thought of her father, Sarah thought of the photograph he had mailed her from Chicago. He was sitting in a posed angle on a large rock, a boulder, with his right foot propped against the rock and his hands wrapped around his kneecap. In the background was a canvas as large as a room, painted with a scene of wild horses stampeding across a western plain, chased by Indians wearing feathered headdresses that fluttered like flowers in the wind. In the foreground, angry and powerful, was a single horse, white as powder, rearing up, pawing the chipped canvas sky with its front hooves. Beside the horse was a thorn cactus as tall as a tree. And her father, sitting on the rock, wore an ill-fitting suit with a fancy straw hat tilted smartly down over his forehead. A smile broke across his face like the eternal crackling of a laugh and the light of the camera's flash bounced merrily in his eyes. No one had ever told her, but Sarah knew the scene was rented — the Indians, the great white horse, the suit, the hat; perhaps even the smile. Beyond the borders of the photograph Sarah could sense a line of onlookers, holding their tickets, goading her father into the smile, waiting their turn to have the suit coat pinned to their shape, and she had wondered about the photographs of other fathers, propped on the dressers of other daughters.

\*　　\*　　\*

There was a knocking at the front door, a soft, rhythmic rapping, and it startled the three women sitting at the table. They did not move. The knocking fell again, louder. Rachel stood and pressed her hands over the apron that covered her dress, smoothing it to her body. She walked into the living room and to the door.

"Who is it?" she asked.

"It's a gentleman come callin', in the proper way, at the front door," Michael boomed from the outside. "It's my understandin' there's a party waitin' for company."

Rachel smiled at the game. She motioned for Sarah and Dora to remain seated, then tossed her head emphatically and pulled her body erect and opened the door.

"Mr. O'Rear?" she said in mock sophistication. "We've been expectin' you. Please come in."

Michael stepped proudly through the door and raised his arms and did a dance spin to the middle of the living room.

"Ladies, how do you like it?" he bellowed.

He was dressed entirely in green. In a forest-green suit that was slightly too tight. In a bright green shirt with an open collar. A green paper shamrock was pinned to the lapel of his coat. And a green handkerchief covered something in his right hand.

"It's my Saint Paddy's Day suit," he announced before anyone replied. "Green from top to toe, and in places you can't even see. Bought it for a parade in New York City and it's been with me since, packed away in the bottom of my knapsack."

He turned again, strutting around the room.

"I know how you feel, awestruck like you are," he continued. "Seein' a true Irishman for the first time, in his own true colors. It's little wonder that you can't speak. First time I put eyes on this fine garment, I was the same. Stood there like a statue, I did. The salesman had to kick me in the shins to bring me around. Why, I've worn this in some Saint Paddy's parades and had people paralyzed in their tracks by the sight of it. They'd bring a wagon along and load them up like blocks of wood, and sure enough there'd be a story in the newspapers about that fellow O'Rear and his green suit."

He stopped at Rachel's side and offered her his left arm and then marched officiously into the kitchen with Rachel beside him.

"Sarah, birthday-girl Sarah — no — birthday-woman Sarah — tell me what you think of this wonderful sight before you," he said happily.

Sarah looked at him carefully and a smile eased into her face.

"Don't be timid now. Try hard. The words will spill out of you if you let them," he added. "What do you think of this handsome green sight?"

"You — you look like — like a — a tree," Sarah answered.

There was nothing funny in what Sarah said, but Michael threw back his head and roared with laughter. His whole body shook and he pulled away from Rachel's hand and leaned against the wall. The three women looked curiously at one another and then began to laugh awkwardly with Michael, and then the laughter grew until it pealed uncontrollably in giggles and loud bursts, subsiding and building again, until they were spent.

"I don't know what's funny," Sarah said innocently.

"Nothin's funny. It's the celebratin'," Michael replied. "So I look like a tree, I do? Well, I've been called worse, for sure. In fact, a tree's a fine thing to be called. There's lots you can do with a tree. Reason I'm standin' here with my hand covered like a bloomin' magician's is due to a tree." He leaned to Sarah and kissed her on the forehead. He could feel her push against his lips. "It's your birthday present, Sarah. Made it with my own hands, I did. Go on, now. Take away the handkerchief."

Sarah stared at the green handkerchief folded over the object in his hand. She reached timidly and pulled the handkerchief away and her eyes widened as she saw the gift he held. It was a woodcarving of a girl on her knees, bending backward, letting her long hair fall free to the ground. Her elbows were pointed up and her hands were cupped behind her head and her fingers pushed into her hair like combs. Her delicate wood face seemed caught in a seizure of ecstasy, her lips slightly parted, as though the last touch of the knife blade had been unbearably sensual.

"It's — it's beautiful," whispered Rachel. "Dora — "

Dora did not answer. She was numbed by the figure in Michael's hand.

"It's beautiful," Rachel said again.

Michael offered the carving to Sarah and Sarah accepted it hesitantly, holding it carefully in the cradle of her hand. She turned it slowly, memorizing it and the moment of receiving it.

"I've been workin' on it for weeks, now," Michael said proudly. "I got the idea for it the first time I saw you, Sarah, sittin' on the edge of the woods, watchin' the cows." He laughed. "It's a way of relaxin' with me, workin' with a knife," he added. "Two things I know I can do. Make paper flowers and carve wood. There're those who've said I've a genius for the knife, and there're times when I'm holdin' one, I think they're right. But that's my favorite of all the carvin's, Sarah. And it's right for you. A girl, risin' up out of bein' a child and becomin' a woman, and that's what you're doin'."

Sarah could feel the blood rushing through her throat, under the tight fitting of her dress collar. She looked up at Michael and held his eyes with hers. She did not care if her mother or Dora saw how she felt.

"Thank you," she said in a small voice. She slipped from her chair. "I want to put it up. On my dresser."

"Well, do it quick," Dora said. "Supper's gettin' cold."

"That it is," Michael declared, picking across the table with his eyes. "And it'd be a pity to let it go to waste. Ah, ladies, you've outdone yourselves. There's enough here to feed the county, and before I go and completely forget my manners, I've got to say how lovely you look. All of you. Why, you'd be courted royally in New York City, and by the richest of men there. If I look like a tree, Sarah, the three of you look like flowers. Lilies bloomin'. Or daisies. Yes, that's it, daisies. Like white velvet petals with soft yellow eyes. I've a song about daisies. Made it up myself. Later on, I'll sing it." He turned to Sarah. "Now, do as Dora says," he told her. "Run along and put up your gift and put on your crown of honeysuckle, if it's not too drooped, and let's be for havin' a party."

Sarah left the kitchen and went into her room. She sat on the edge of her bed and rubbed the carving of the girl with her fingers and thought of her night with Michael. She could feel him against her, invisibly pushing, bruising her with a tender pain. His fingers fed her and filled her and her body rose weakly to him, obeying his touch. She could feel the hot, volcanic stream splattering across her in heavy pearl drops and the sighing of his body as he dropped over her like a blanket.

"Sarah!" It was Rachel.

"Comin'," she answered. She placed the carving on her dressing table and picked up the garland of honeysuckle with its withered blossoms and placed it on her head. She went quickly back into the kitchen. "I'm sorry," she apologized. "I was just lookin' at it."

"You can look at it later, all you want," scolded Dora. "It's time to eat."

*　　*　　*

A drizzling rain began during the birthday supper, falling from a thin, rolling sheet of clouds that had been cast like a net out of the black heart of a thunderstorm that roared through the North Carolina mountains. The lightning of the storm flickered dully and its thunder echoed like the fighting of a distant war. And as it rained, the wind lifted, cooling the house.

"There'd be those who'd say rain puts a damper on a party," observed Michael. "I'd say it makes it cozy." He laughed. "Now that's a word I like: cozy. Not the kind of word a man says, but it's a good one. Means a lot, if you're not afraid of usin' it. What d'you think, Miss Dora? Does the rain make a party cozy?"

Dora felt a flush of embarrassment in her face. She replied, "Rain's needed. It's been dry."

"Miss Dora," chided Michael, "that's not the question. How does it make you feel? Cozy? Wet? Like you'd be drownin' if it keeps fallin'? How?"

Dora flipped away the question with her hand. She began to stack the dishes on the table before her.

"What about you, Rachel?" Michael asked softly. "How does the rain make you feel? Do you like it?" His eyes followed her, as teasing as his voice.

Rachel met his eyes. "Yes," she said simply. "Yes, it makes me feel cozy." Yes, she thought. Why are you asking me? You know. You must know. She stood at the table. "We'd better get the dishes washed," she added.

"Not after a birthday supper," protested Michael. "They can wait for a while. We've got a party to carry on."

"We always wash after supper," Sarah told him.

"Well, tonight's not always, Sarah," argued Michael. "To-night's a party. And to show you I'm a sportin' man, I'll even volunteer to help out later. Me and Rachel, we'll wash them. Rachel, are you willin'? Is that a fair enough bargain?"

Rachel looked at the dishes she held in her hands, and then to Dora, then to Sarah.

"Yes," she said. "It'd be worth it just seein' you in soapsuds up to your elbows. And you'll do the washin'. I'll dry and put up."

"And I'll watch," Dora added. "Wish I had me a camera."

"It's settled then," thundered Michael. "Come along, ladies, it's dancin' time."

\*  \*  \*

Michael stood in the middle of the living room, turning slowly on his heel, nodding.

"Now, ladies, since you've been good enough to elect me

parliamentarian of this event, this is what we have to do," he announced. "Move all the furniture along that wall." He gestured with a sweep of his hand. "We'll put the radio in the corner and light some candles for the mantel. Wouldn't you like that? Candles? Sarah? Rachel?"

"Candles, yes," replied Rachel. She stood beside Sarah in the doorway of the kitchen.

"Candles it'll be then," Michael responded. "Miss Dora, you'll be in charge of the candle-lightin' ceremony. And we'll need music. Sarah, you'll find us somethin' on the radio, and if the battery's weak, you'll be hummin' for us all night. Rachel, lend me a hand with the furniture."

The room was prepared as Michael commanded, with laughing and playing, with Michael's voice riding throughout the room like a ringmaster building suspense for a great show. The finger flames from the candles made amber pools, like hearts, on the scrubbed wood walls, and the rearranged furniture opened the room like a hallway. It was, Michael pronounced, the equal of any ballroom east of St. Louis, and he had been a guest in all of them. It was a room that was warm and inviting, he said. A room where you'd gladly tip the waiter a handsome sum for a table.

But there was a storm and static and the only sound from the radio was a crackling like a fire. It was not a problem, Michael concluded. Not a problem as long as there were people with willing voices that could be tuned, as fine as a violin, to the proper song. "We'll do it that way," he determined. "All sing out like we was a London, England, choir, and since I'm the only gentleman present, I'll take turns dancin' with every lady on the premise." Sarah first, he said. Sarah first because it was her birthday and it did not matter that she protested she had never before danced. "You'll learn," vowed Michael. "You'll learn. It's a matter of your feet listenin' to what your heart tells them. And, besides, I'm the man and the man does the pushin' and shovin' when it comes to dancin'.

You go where I push and shove and you'll be dancin'.' "

The song, decided Michael after deliberation, would be "Jeannie." That was it. "There'll be no hagglin' now. That's a song an Irishman would've been proud of writin'. 'Jeannie, with the Light Brown Hair.' Listen to it. Sounds Irish, it does. May have been. Stephen Foster. Could have been Irish. Someday I'll ask some of my music friends. Come on, now, everybody, on the count of three. One, two, three . . ."

And they began. Softly, haltingly, until Michael stopped them.

"Is that singin'?" he bellowed. "Why, I've heard many a chicken more excited over the layin' of an egg. Now, sing it out. It's a party, not a bloomin' wake."

They began again and Michael's strong baritone-tenor opened over the three women like an umbrella. And as he sang, he extended his hand to Sarah and pulled her into the middle of the room and began to dance with her in wide, strong steps. Sarah stumbled awkwardly after him, but she was not embarrassed; she was with him, holding him, and he was playing with her, tenderly, comically, and her whole body was happy.

And then it was Rachel's dance. A slow, polite dance, hands and arms touching but with distance between them — distance that Sarah watched with confused jealousy. Michael and Rachel sang "Beautiful Dreamer" as Sarah and Dora's small voices struggled to follow them, and Rachel felt she was alone with him, holding him.

The dance ended and Michael bowed theatrically and escorted Rachel back to her chair. Then he turned to Dora.

"Miss Dora," he said earnestly, "I have heard it mentioned in Yale that you are the dance queen of the Naheela Valley. There are men who have smiles frozen in their faces like a carvin' in granite when the talk of a dance comes up and the name of Dora Rice is said. I have been told — in secret, of course — that even in cakewalks you used to put to shame every other lady in the hills. So, it'd be an honor if you'd permit this hobbled old man a short dance."

Dora's eyes widened as she stared at him. Her mouth was opened in disbelief. She twisted in the armchair to look at Rachel.

"It's the truth, Miss Dora," Michael continued. "That's what I've heard."

"Well, you've been listenin' to some of them drunks in Pullen's," snorted Dora. "I don't remember the last time I tried dancin' and I ain't about to try it now."

Sarah giggled behind her hands.

"Miss Dora, you're hurtin' my feelin's," pleaded Michael.

"Go on, Dora, dance," Rachel urged. "You know he's actin' the fool, but what he don't know is how you used to dance. I remember it."

"See," Michael said. "See. I knew you did."

"She was as good as anybody," added Rachel. "I remember when I was little and they used to have street dances in Yale. Dora would dance the night away."

"That was a long time ago," Dora said simply.

"Time? Time's nothin', Miss Dora," argued Michael. "Look at me. It's been a year or two since I saw twenty, and I'm still a fool, like Rachel said. One of the worse things a person can do is quit bein' a fool."

"Dora — "

"No, Rachel," Dora snapped. "I ain't gonna dance."

Michael stepped away and surveyed the three women. He began to hum a lively Irish tune and his feet began tapping lightly across the floor. The hum grew into a trumpet sound blaring from his lips and his feet stamped harder, faster, like a pounding drumbeat.

"What's that?" Sarah called above the trumpet and feet.

"Irish jig," answered Michael, picking up the rhythm.

"Don't look like no jig to me," Dora said. "Looks like cloggin'."

Michael did not stop. He bounced happily about the room, his shoulders and arms swinging free, his legs driving like pistons.

"It's a jig," he shouted between music stops. "And it's somethin' you can't do, Miss Dora. I'd bet a week's worth of wood-cuttin' on it."

"Call it what you want, it ain't nothin' but cloggin'," Dora shouted over the noise. "I know cloggin' when I see it."

"Then, let's see you do it," roared Michael. He passed before her and grabbed her hand and pulled her to her feet. Then he backed away, facing her. His feet slowed to a soft, sweeping tap-shuffle, playing the floor like an instrument.

"Come on, Miss Dora," he teased. "Let's see it."

"Go on, Dora," Rachel urged.

"Please, Aunt Dora. Please," Sarah squealed, applauding.

Michael lifted the pace. He was breathing hard and his face had reddened. He began a rhythmic finger-snapping to the tune that squeezed through his lips, and Rachel and Sarah picked it up. He moved closer to Dora, motioning to her with his arms.

Dora began tapping her right foot, finding the beat. Then she stepped into a spirited toe-heel tap and she whirled over the floor and circled Michael. Her face was somber as her mind raced to remember the steps, and as she skipped over the floor, Michael stopped dancing and stared in astonishment. Rachel and Sarah had picked up the beat with their staccato clapping and they were laughing happily.

Any of them would tell me, Michael thought as he watched Dora. His plan for the party had worked. Any of them would tell him gladly. He need only ask. And there was time to ask.

"She's dancin'," Michael thundered. "Miss Dora's dancin'. By God, we've got us a party now. We've got us a party."

# 12

THE PARTY had lasted long — until after midnight, after the rain had been swept away in the wind — and Michael had gone to the barn and waited for the visitor he knew would arrive. It had been Sarah's birthday and he had seen the woman step forward and the shyness of the girl fall away from her like a discarded garment. He knew she would come, and he had waited and taken her quickly and then dismissed her. Then he had fallen into an easy sleep.

He was still asleep when the 1936 Chevrolet with SHERIFF lettered on the front doors arrived at the Pettit farm on Saturday morning.

George English waited solemnly and fretfully inside the barn room as Michael quickly dressed. George had said the sheriff and the doctor needed him. He did not say why. He knew, but he did not say, and Michael realized that George had been bound to a threatening pledge to remain silent.

As they rode back into Yale, speeding over the top-slick dirt road and then down the narrow paved highway, Michael sensed a fear, or perhaps an anger, building in George. It was not the game of law and order that George often enjoyed playing as he sat at the rolltop desk of the jail, imagining heroic episodes of legendary bravery. George was not a brave man, except in his illusions, which had become, in their own way, real. No, thought Michael, this was not a game. Whatever it was, whatever awaited him in Yale, was serious, and George English felt caged by it.

*   *   *

Michael saw the men, gathered in front of Fred Deal's Merchandise Store across the street from the jail. He knew the scene immediately: It was a judgment crowd, silently standing, waiting, wondering. He recognized many of the men from his visits to Pullen's Café. Especially the older men. He did not see Teague or Bailey or Job or the sawmill workers, who would arrive later, nearer evening. Michael knew the crowd and their mood. Crowds like this had followed him for years, yelping and spitting anger from their diseased tongues like a spray of dragon fire. He knew them from inside their souls and their guts. He knew the impregnable shields of their single-mindedness. He knew their generals and their followers — could pick them out at a glance.

"Any trouble yet?" he asked George.

"The sheriff'll tell you what you need to know," George mumbled.

Michael swiveled in his car seat to face George. He said, "Dammit, man, I don't need to know what's wrong to see that's a thinkin' crowd. What I want to know, and I want to know it now, is if there's been any trouble yet."

George shook his head. He was surprised by the ice in Michael's voice. Michael had been a jester.

"Nothin' yet," George replied. He flipped his head toward the crowd of men. "They ain't moved since I left to come get you."

George braked the car to a stop in front of the jail. He got out quickly and went inside without looking across the street. Michael sat and waited. He could see the doctor watching him through the door of the jail. He opened the door of the car and slipped out of the seat and stood and stretched. He waved broadly to the men standing in front of Deal's store and strolled lazily inside the jail.

Garnett Cannon nodded to him.

"Doc. Sheriff," Michael said in greeting. He looked beyond Curtis Hill. He could see Owen through the bars of the cell, sitting on the cot, his head bowed into his hands. The tension in the room was almost material.

Michael did not ask why he had been summoned. He knew he would be told. Instead, he said, "The boy all right?"

"He's better," answered Garnett. "All right? Hell, no. He won't be for days, if then." His voice was sharp and bitter. He paced the office, looking out the window at the men gathered across the street. "Sit down," he finally said to Michael. "We'd better explain some things."

Michael sat in the chair beside the door. He crossed his arms and waited. Garnett motioned to Curtis, and the sheriff shuffled nervously where he stood.

"The boy's daddy — Frank — he come in early this mornin', right after sunup," Curtis began. "Said he'd come for the boy. Said the boy had to pay for his crimes, and he'd do the punishin', since it was his own flesh."

"Crimes?" asked Michael. "What crimes?"

Curtis bowed his head and thought through his words. He was uncomfortable around the doctor, Michael realized.

"A little while back, maybe three months or longer, there was a young couple livin' up the valley a few miles, and they was killed," Curtis answered slowly. "Murdered. Both had their throats cut in bed. Frank said it was his boy that done it."

A shiver ran through Michael. A sharp, needle pain began to throb inside him. He could see Lester Caufield falling from the bed. He felt the warm spurt of blood lap across his arm. He heard Mary Caufield's cry and felt her limp, thin body.

"Did you hear him?" Garnett asked.

"I did," answered Michael softly. His mouth was dry. His palms began to perspire. The nausea swept through him like a heat wave and then it was gone and a chilling, exhilarating coolness filled him and he could hear the echo of applause from a blackened arena.

"Frank said he's seen it," Curtis continued. "Said he'd tried to beat the truth out of his boy, but Owen wouldn't own up to it."

Michael did not move from the chair. He looked across the jail to where Owen sat.

"Did he?" he asked. "Did he see it?"

"For God's sake, Irishman, you'd have to know the man," Garnett replied irritably. "He saw it in his mind, like some goddam picture show. The boy was talking about leaving home, going to Chattanooga to work, where his uncle lives. That was all. He told Frank that he'd been thinking about it since the Caufields were killed, because he'd talked to Lester about it and Lester was thinking of moving there, too. It was just a comment, just something he said, but it was enough for Frank. He began to have a vision of his boy killing the Caufields. It's all in his mind. I suppose it's the thought of another child leaving home, and after what happened to his daughter, well, hell."

"Where is the boy's father now?" Michael wanted to know.

"He left," answered Curtis. "Went ridin' off a few minutes before you showed up. Said he'd be back later. The boy kept sayin' he wanted to talk to you. That's why I had George come up and bring you in."

"And the crowd?" Michael said. "You expectin' trouble from them?"

Garnett shrugged. He paced the room. His hands were stuffed deep into the pockets of his coat. He kicked at the rocker, then sat in it and leaned back and rubbed his temples with his knuckles.

"It comes down to this," he said at last. "There's not one shred of evidence in what Frank says, but that's not going to matter very much. There're a lot of people in this community who were blood-related to Lester and Mary Caufield; that's who they were, if I didn't say."

"You did," Michael replied.

"Well, hell, they weren't more than twenty," Garnett continued. "If that old. Anyway, they're old-line family. That house belonged to Lester's grandfather. Everybody knew them, and liked them. Even George is first cousin to the girl. Saw her grow up from a baby. Had to help take her body out of the place. This thing that Frank's telling will fill out in their heads like yeast. The boy's damned any way you look at it. Turn him loose and Frank'll probably kill him; keep him here and it'll seem like he's guilty and God only knows what'll happen then."

"Frank could be right," George blurted suddenly. "By God, he was right enough about that girl of his."

Curtis sighed. He shook his head sadly and said, "George, you sonofabitch, you know damn good and well that girl didn't start whorin' until after she'd run away from home. God-a'mighty, you were here. You almost arrested Frank that day he was beatin' her out in the street. Now, I know how you feel about Mary. Everybody around here feels the same, but this is a boy's life we're talkin' about, not some damn sack of oats."

"But what if he's right?" argued George. "Nobody never thought about it bein' anybody from around here. It could have been like Frank says."

Garnett rocked forward in his chair. He touched the fingertips of his hands together. Michael watched him carefully. He could sense the words forming in the doctor's mind like crystals. George English's anxiety was a matter of the memory of his mutilated cousin and a revived lust for vengeance raging in his mind. It was necessary to have George understand, to believe that Frank Benton was wrong.

"George," Garnett said patiently, "you know that boy. You know he wouldn't kill anybody. Now, I'd like to see the bastard who murdered Lester and Mary hanging from his balls with his heart cut out, but it's not Owen. It's not. You let those people out there even halfway believe Frank's right and you've as much as executed that boy yourself. Besides, dammit, you know the law. You know you've got to have some evidence, and you know you don't." He paused and rubbed his hands across his mouth and slumped back into the chair and looked at George. "But if reason won't work, George, let me put it to you this way: If I hear of you spreading any kind of gossip about this, I'll personally have you arrested for obstructing justice and I promise you that you will lose your job and if I have to bring in a lawyer from Atlanta, I'll see to it that you serve time." He paused again. "Do you understand me?" he asked quietly.

George nodded.

"Good," Garnett mumbled. "I'll tell you this: What happens here depends eighty percent on you. Believe me."

George walked away and peered out the door. He was breathing hard and the perspiration dripped from his hair down his neck and into his shirt, staining it with lines that looked like claw marks.

"One question," Michael said. "Why's it not been talked? I've not heard it since I've been here."

There was a pause. Garnett smiled wearily. He waved a hand in the direction of Curtis.

"It's private," Curtis answered slowly. "People around here keep such things to themselves. It's their way." Then he added, almost to himself, "It's best that way."

"You'll learn it, Irishman, if you stay around," Garnett said. "I have. Still don't understand it, but, by God, I've learned it. And, believe me, it's the truth." He thought for a moment, then added, "Maybe Curtis is right; maybe it is best."

Yes, thought Michael. That was why no one had spoken of the Caufields. He had often wondered why, had been tempted to lead a conversation to it, but it would have been too risky. The death of the Caufields was part of the silence that he had seen in the stark, secretive faces in Pullen's Café, and in Floyd Crider's shyness, and in Dora's suspicious glare when he arrived at the farm. They would not talk of the Caufields because it was private, a tragedy that belonged only to them.

"Leave the boy with me," Michael said, standing. "Go outside, anywhere you like, but not around the jail."

"That's a lot of men across the street," warned Curtis.

"Men you know," replied Michael. "And right now they're just curious. Nothin' more."

"Maybe so," Garnett said, "but they know what Frank said. He made sure of that. Went up and down the street ravin' like a fool before he ever got to the jail. Seemed like he wanted to raise an audience."

Michael smiled. "Now, I understand why they're out there, Doc," he remarked casually. "If I'd heard such, I'd be curious, too. Wouldn't you?"

Garnett pulled himself from the rocker. "I guess," he mumbled. "God, yes. Why wouldn't I? Maybe we'll go over and talk to them, Curtis. Maybe that's what we should do. Right now. Not leave it hanging."

"I would," agreed Michael. "They know everythin' you know, but they're over there and you're in here, and that's a far distance to cross over."

Curtis thought of the men huddled across the street. Michael was right. There *was* a distance, a space separating their waiting and the uncertainty of what he would do.

"We'll be close by," Curtis said to Michael.

\*     \*     \*

Michael took the key from the rolltop desk and unlocked the heavy steel door and stepped inside the cell. Owen was still sitting on the side of the cot, his elbows resting on his knees, his face dipped into the bowl of his hands.

"Did you have breakfast?" Michael asked.

"Some," Owen answered softly.

"Good," Michael said. He sat in the chair in the cell. "That's good," he repeated. "Shows you're gettin' back some strength."

Owen dropped his hands between his legs and clamped together his fingers. Michael saw that he had been crying.

"Don't pay attention to all that's goin' on here," he said. "It's just talk. Too many people angry about somethin' they can't put their finger on. That's all."

Owen did not move.

"It was bad, was it?" asked Michael. He packed his pipe with tobacco and tried not to look at Owen.

Owen's voice quivered. "Daddy — Daddy said I'd done that," he stammered. "But I didn't. I didn't do what he said."

"No, Owen, you didn't. Your daddy's wrong. That's the first thing you have to do; you have to say he's wrong. He'd have his pound of flesh. You have to say that over and over to yourself. Say it so you'll believe it."

Owen stared at his fingers. "He's my daddy," he said pleadingly. "He's my daddy."

"Well, now, Owen, think about that," replied Michael. He lit his pipe and drew smoke from the stem and blew a gray ring swirling across the cell. "You think about that," he repeated. "That man who was in here today, accusin' you of murderin' some poor people, is somebody besides your own father. He's another man. Changed over by some blindin' sight that's built up inside him like a sickness. That's not your father. I'd say your father — the father you're rememberin' — was a carin' man, carin' and gentle. Am I right?"

Owen did not answer. He whimpered weakly and began to cry.

"Don't be ashamed of the feelin'," Michael said quietly. "It's a way to hold it all up, to keep it from crushin' in on you like a stone. I know about that, Owen. I've been in the same place. Seems like there's no room for breathin', but there is."

"I didn't kill nobody," Owen sobbed. "Not Lester and Mary. Lester and me — Lester and me, we was friends. We went to school together when we was little. We was talkin' about goin' to work together in Chattanooga. I wouldn't kill Lester and Mary."

Michael drew smoke from his pipe and listened as the hurt

broke open in Owen Benton and poured from him. He was such a small person, thought Michael. Brittle. Frail. And he was being sacrificed for a crime he did not commit. Michael shifted uncomfortably in his chair, thinking. What was it about Owen that had made him curious, that had attracted his attention on the night Owen first spoke? Destiny, he thought. But what destiny? A sense of remorse shot through Michael. Owen was his substitute, his stand-in, and he had been delivered to Michael in the disguise of fate. Nothing could save him from the role. The doctor could heal him, but the doctor could not save him. It was destiny.

"There'll be nothin' come of it, Owen," he said. "I promise that. You didn't kill anybody. I know it. I know it to be true." Owen did not see the quick smile that wandered into Michael's face like an amusement.

"My daddy'll come back. He'll come back. Like he said he would."

Michael touched Owen's shoulder with his fingers and gently pushed him up into a straight sitting position. He said, "Owen, do you trust me?"

Owen nodded hesitantly.

"I know there's no reason to, me bein' a stranger, but I'm askin' you to," Michael continued. "I've been all over, and I've seen many tight spots like this. I'm askin' you to trust me and not say what I tell you to the doctor or the sheriff or anybody, and I promise you there's nothin' goin' to come of it, nothin'll happen to you. If I must, I'll steal you away from here and take you to someplace that's safe."

Owen struggled to stand, but could not. He sank back on the cot, and a shudder, like a chill, whipped through him and he wrapped his arms around his body and began to sway.

"I'm not sayin' it'd be easy, leavin' home," Michael whispered. "It never is, no matter what. But sometimes it's best. And you don't have to be like your sister. Yes, I know about her; the doctor told me before. There's lots of people leave

home, tear away from their families, and go on their own." He
sucked on his pipe and spit the smoke from his mouth. "I did
it," he added. "And it was much the same with me as it is with
you, exceptin' it was my mother who did the evil." He twisted
in his chair and his voice tightened. "They say she was taken
with fits and didn't know she had the madness, but when you're
a lad and you feel it across your back, you don't know about
fits."

Owen stopped his swaying and listened to Michael. A muscle
in his jaw twitched. He seemed far away. "My mama died," he
said calmly. He added, "Before Elizabeth left home. Elizabeth,
she's my sister."

"They never told me," replied Michael. "But it's as good she
did, before seein' this. She'd be burdened by it. My own good
father was."

They sat quietly. The dim memories swimming in Michael no
longer seemed certain. He did not know if they were real or if
he had invented them as a touchstone, as some trail of crumbs
to lead him back through the maze of his wanderings. There
had been times — totally unexpected — when the living ghost
had leaped out of him and streaked through a dark hole of
history and wrapped itself in a silky cocoon around a single
idyllic moment older than all of his senses. He did not know
what formless jelly-drop of life was bubbling in the cocoon, but
it had no stories to tell him. In its bliss, it was the essence of
a sinless promise, and he had longed to peel it open and slip into
its thick, quivering plasm and be born in its peace.

"I can't go back home," Owen said, breaking the silence. "I
know what'd happen. He don't mean it, but he won't never
believe I didn't do what he sees in his mind."

"Then you'll not go. I'll see to it."

"But there's the others."

"Your brother and sisters?" guessed Michael. "You're worried about them?"

Owen nodded.

"I can't help them," he mumbled. "I can't do it no more. Somebody else'll have to do it."

"They will," Michael assured him. "You know the people here. They'll step in and do what's to be done. You'll see."

Again they were quiet. And the music began inside Michael, a delicate, reedy melody. There were lights on an empty stage and the floor of the stage glistened under the lights in an oily brilliance. The audience waited.

"I won't say nothin' to the sheriff, or the doctor, or nobody," Owen promised.

"Not a word?"

"Nothin'."

"You're a trustin' man, Owen. I'll tell them we spoke of your innocence. That's all. That'll be enough."

Owen looked at Michael. His eyes, which were small blue buttons in his face, were dull and lifeless. He said in a whine, "I didn't do nothin'. What my daddy said was wrong."

"I know it, Owen. I know it."

Michael's eyes narrowed and he lifted his head to the window of the cell. The mumbling audience quietened.

"I know it," he repeated absently.

# 13

MICHAEL CROSSED THE STREET from the jail to the men huddled beneath an awning hanging from Fred Deal's Merchandise Store. He was relaxed. On another morning, he would have been jovial and called the men into a standing circle around him to play them for their smiles. There, around him, in their sideway postures, they would have listened to his impish stories and begged with their mumbling for his favor. On another morning, he would have juggled them as nimbly as brightly colored balls.

The doctor was with them, and the sheriff and George. They watched him cross the street, wondering what he had been told, what he knew that would add to their curiosity.

"Gentlemen," Michael said somberly as he approached them.

A few voices muttered a return greeting.

"The boy all right?" Garnett asked.

"Upset some, but he's all right," answered Michael.

"Me'n George'll go back over," Curtis remarked. He stepped away from the crowd of men and walked briskly across the street. George followed, his head bowed.

"I hate to confess it, but I was sleepin' like a baby when George drove up for me," Michael said idly, "and I've not had so much as a cup of coffee the whole mornin'. Anybody wants to get out of the heat, I'd like the company for breakfast at the café."

Garnett and the men followed Michael into Pullen's Café.
They sat at tables surrounding Michael and Garnett and drank
coffee as Michael ate. No one spoke. They sat and watched
Michael as they would watch the movement of a storm. All of
them knew Michael would tell them. And Michael knew they
were waiting.

He did not speak until he had finished his breakfast and
pushed the plate away from him. Then he said, "I know you're
wonderin' about the boy. And it's right that you do. He grew
up here and he's been accused of a harsh thing by his own
father. That's enough to make anybody take notice."

He sipped from his coffee and let his eyes circle the faces of
the men sitting around him. They were eager but their eagerness did not show. It was as though some discipline of caution
had been born in them. They yearned to know what he would
tell them, but none of them could ask for him to say it.

"Well, I know it's not my place," he continued, "but there's
times when a man speaks his mind, no matter where he is or
who he is. Far as I'm concerned, now's such a time." He pulled
close to the table and propped his elbows and brushed at his
face with his hands.

"I tried to tell them the boy didn't do anything," Garnett
said. "Maybe they'd believe you, if you said it."

The men remained silent, waiting.

"Well, now, maybe the boy did do it," Michael replied casually. "Maybe it happened like his daddy said he saw it."

"God Almighty," whispered Garnett in surprise. "What're
you saying?"

Michael looked over his hands at Garnett.

"Maybe Owen did it," he repeated. "The mind's a funny
thing, Doc. The mind can see things that eyes couldn't see in
a million years."

"He's right," exclaimed someone in a deep bass voice. "I
heard tell of such things."

Michael turned to the voice. He dropped his hands on the
table and leaned forward.

"I said *maybe,* friend," he replied evenly. "And maybe I could jump off that mountain out there and fly. Or maybe I could lift the doc's car and carry it down the street on my back. Maybe a lot of things, and maybe that boy's a murderer. But you'll not have me sayin' it. Far as I'm concerned that boy's done nothin'. Only wrong he ever did was bein' born to a man what 'sees' things and then takes it out on his own flesh. Fact is, it's not as good a tale to say he did nothin', now is it? Here we're sittin', a group of good men, and we're willin' to believe the worst because it makes us feel better, and damned be to him that's to suffer from it. No, friend, Owen Benton didn't kill anybody. He's not yet a man and what fight he's had in him, his own father's taken out with the whip."

He stared at the man who had broken the silence of the onlookers, who had heard of the power of visions and believed in them. The man was old, with old, tanned skin that folded like scars into the eroded furrows of his cheeks. He breathed through dry lips and his front teeth were missing. His eyes were wide and puffed and covered with a watery film that pooled in the corners like thick tears. He had the face of a man with a child's mind who is the fool of tricks played for amusement.

"I don't mean it harsh, friend," Michael added quietly. "It's just that I've seen many a man jump on a shadow and not know where his feet would be landin'. It'd be a sad thing to believe in the boy's guilt without knowin' the truth of the matter, and I'm not one to put stock in what a man tells me about some dream he's had."

"I — I never said Owen done it," the man stammered. "But I heard tell of them — them things. Man told me about it." He paused and looked frantically about him. He leaned back in his chair and dropped his head. "I never said — " he mumbled.

"Nobody said you did, Azel," interrupted Garnett. "What the Irishman's telling you and everybody else is what I've been trying to say: That boy needs help, not doubting."

"What'd the boy say about it?" asked another man.

Michael's eyes stayed on the man Garnett had called Azel as

he answered the question: "He denied doin' it. Only thing he's worried about is the younger ones, if his father gets it in his mind to start beatin' on them."

"Kin'll take 'em," the man said simply. "I heard tell Frank's brother over in Chattanooga offered as much a year or so ago. Frank ain't been right since his wife passed on and he couldn't raise her up."

Michael broke his locked stare on Azel. He toyed with the coffee cup before him. The feel of the audience around him had slipped away and he waited for someone to speak.

"You want, I'll take you back to the farm," Garnett said at last. He sounded tired.

"No," replied Michael. "I'll wait. I want to see a man who'd do what he's done to his own son. If he's comin' back, I want to see him."

"He'll be back. He said he will, he will. I know Frank." It was another voice from another man.

*   *   *

Frank Benton returned to Yale before noon. He was driving a model A Ford with a rusting roof. He carried a shotgun in his lap, with its barrel protruding through the opened window. A girl, perhaps fifteen, was with him, sitting low in the car.

He drove to the jail and parked and sat in the car holding the shotgun. Across the street the crowd of men had again clustered under the awning of Fred Deal's Merchandise Store, like wasps on a nest. They watched as the girl slipped from the car and walked in small, frightened steps to the jail. The girl was thin. She held her shoulders high and pinched and her elbows were tight by her sides. Her hair was uncombed. Her face was turned to Frank, to her father, as she walked, and she begged with her eyes to be called back.

"Goddammit," one of the men at Fred Deal's store muttered angrily.

Curtis was alone inside the jail. He watched at the window

as the girl inched across the distance separating the jail from the car. He saw Frank, holding the shotgun, sitting erect in the car, staring stoically at the jail. It was Frank's show of war, he thought; the girl first, like a dove of peace, and then the raised gun of violence.

"Damn," Curtis whispered.

The girl stopped in front of the screen door leading into the jail. Her hands were clasped at her sides to the worn cotton dress. She breathed in short, shallow gulps. Curtis walked to the door and pushed it open.

"Come on in," he said. "Shirley. That's your name? Shirley?"

The girl mumbled, "Yessir." She looked quickly to her father and stepped inside the jail.

"No reason to be afraid of nothin'," Curtis assured her. "Nothin' in here's gonna hurt you. You here to see Owen?"

"Yes — yessir."

"He's right over here," replied Curtis. He walked to the cell and unlocked the door and swung it open. "Go on in," he added. "I ain't goin' to lock it." He walked away to the window and stood with his back turned to the cell.

Owen sat forward on the side of the cot and watched his sister. Her eyes darted like a confused bird over the box space of the cell, over the thick steel bars and the high, small window, and the fear of its inescapable weight made her suddenly gasp. She was like his mother had been, thought Owen. She was timid and quiet and obedient, and she would suffer whatever she must.

"It's all right," Owen said gently. "They ain't gonna lock you up."

Shirley looked at her brother. He seemed changed. Older. Someone different.

"Daddy said to come on," she said.

"He whip you?" asked Owen.

She shook her head.

"He will," Owen said.

"He said to come on," she repeated.

"I ain't never goin' with him," Owen said quietly. "He ain't never goin' to beat on me no more."

Shirley stepped backward to the door of the cell.

"He's got the gun," she said. "He said he'd take you, you don't come on."

There was no change of emotion in Owen's face. He shook his head slowly. "Don't matter," he mumbled. "Don't matter none."

"I got to go," Shirley said. "He told me to come on back."

"He whip anybody?"

"Ray, some. Not much."

Owen nodded.

"He said you done somethin' bad," she blurted.

"I didn't do nothin'," Owen replied patiently. "He's seein' things, like it was a dream. Like he's done before. Like he done when he thought he was talkin' to Mama all them nights after she died."

"I got to go, Owen." She stepped cautiously out of the cell.

"Shirley."

She stopped and looked back at him. She was beginning to cry.

"Nothin'," he said. "Watch after Ray. He hurts easy."

She turned and walked quickly across the jail and through the screen door. At the window, Curtis watched as she pulled herself into the car with her father. Frank spoke to her and she shook her head and Frank opened the door of the car and stepped onto the pavement.

"Dammit," Curtis hissed. He automatically touched the pistol holstered at his side. "Owen," he called, "get in the storeroom. Now."

He did not turn from the window but he heard Owen's movement and the door of the storeroom open and close. He stepped to the side of the front door, in the room's shadow, and watched Frank beside the car, cradling the shotgun. He could see the men across the street breaking from their bundled group and spreading along the sidewalk. Someone — he did not know who — bolted in a half-run toward Pullen's Café, where Garnett waited with Michael. He thought about his decision to send George home; it was a mistake. Frank moved a step away from his car and faced the door of the jail.

"I come for my boy," Frank called. "Let him out."

"Go home, Frank," answered Curtis. "Owen's stayin' here."

"I have to, I'll take him and God be on my side," Frank replied, raising his voice.

Curtis stepped to the door and pushed it slightly open. He pulled his pistol from its holster and let it dangle in his hand by his side.

"Frank," he said in a low, hard voice, "you point that shotgun and you could get yourself killed. Now, you put it up and get in your car and go on home. I'm holdin' the boy."

"He's my flesh. I'll do what's to be done," Frank stormed. "Don't need no law of man to do it for me. God's law's enough." He shifted the shotgun in his hand.

"Frank, I mean it," warned Curtis. "It ain't God's law to do what you done to that boy." He thumbed the hammer of his pistol and the sharp metal click stopped Frank abruptly.

"I ain't never killed but one man," Curtis said quietly, "and he made me do it. I didn't like it, but I done it." He paused and raised the pistol to his waist. "I have to do it again, by God, I will, Frank," he added.

"You got no cause to hold him," Frank replied angrily.

"For God's sake, Frank, you never even thought about Owen killin' the Caufields until he mentioned goin' away to work," Curtis snapped. "It's that that's botherin' you. You're seein' things that ain't so."

"Let him out," Frank replied. "I mean it. I know what I got to do."

Curtis did not answer. Beyond Frank, he saw Garnett and

Michael crossing the street from Pullen's Café, and a light flush of relief ran through him.

"He's got a gun, Doc," someone yelled from the line of men in front of Deal's Merchandise Store.

Frank whirled and raised the barrel of the shotgun in the air. He stood with his back against his car.

"Stay where you are, Doc," he growled. "It ain't got nothin' to do with you."

Garnett and Michael stopped in the middle of the street. Garnett tugged at the tip of his hat and glared at Frank.

"I come for my boy and I aim to take him with me," Frank thundered.

"You're going to get killed if you don't put away that gun," Garnett answered calmly. "You know damn well you can't come in here in front of a whole town and take somebody out of jail."

"He's got one of the girls with him," Curtis called from the jail. "She's in the car."

Garnett removed his hat and rolled his forearm across his face in a nervous, aggravated motion. He cursed Frank Benton silently.

"For God's sake, Frank," he pleaded. "What do you want?"

"The boy's got to be punished for what he done," Frank intoned.

"Done? What's he done?" It was Michael. He took one step forward in the street. His hands were pressed against his hips. His voice was relaxed and pleasant and a smile rested easily in his face. He could see the surprise of his unexpected presence trip in Frank Benton's body like a hidden trap.

Frank shifted the gun in his hand and lowered its barrel to the ground.

"He's done what I said," he insisted coldly.

"Well, now, I've heard about that," Michael said, nonchalantly toeing the pavement with the point of his shoe. "Even talked to Owen about it." He turned his eyes to Frank. "Seems he disagrees," he added.

Frank stared suspiciously at Michael. His fingers curled around the ridged handgrip of the shotgun and his thumb circled nervously over the smooth steel crown of the hammer. He had never met Michael, but he knew instantly that Michael was the man Owen had insisted on seeing earlier. A stranger, Curtis Hill had explained. Hired to stay nights at the jail. Kin to Eli Pettit.

"Tell you the truth, Mr. Benton, that's a fine boy you've got," Michael continued. "Hard to believe he could've done what you're sayin'."

"He done it," Frank said. "I know my own flesh."

"Is there proof of it?" asked Michael. "More'n just your own sure word?"

"Ain't no proof needed," Frank answered defiantly. "I know it. That's enough."

Michael nodded thoughtfully. He looked over his shoulder to the doctor and then turned back to Frank. He rubbed his hand over the stubble of whiskers on his face.

"Well, seems like there's a little problem here," he said. "Unless I'm wrong, the sheriff's decided to keep Owen for a while longer. At least until he heals up. Is that right, Sheriff?"

Curtis stepped through the door of the jail onto the sidewalk. The pistol was still raised in his hand, cocked for firing.

"The boy stays," he replied. "We'll find out if he's done what you say."

"You got no right to hold him," Frank shouted. "Not against his will, and stayin's not his will, 'less you got him scared."

"Frank, you damn fool, ain't nobody got that boy scared but you," Curtis growled. "Now you leave him alone and go on home."

"It ain't right keepin' him," bellowed Frank. He moved angrily away from the car into the middle of the street, facing the line of onlookers standing in front of Deal's store. "Hear what

I'm sayin," he shouted. "My boy's bein' kept in jail against his will. I know. I talked to him this mornin'. He said he'd come home. It ain't right, keepin' him."

The crowd of men stood motionless. They were spectators to a dangerous sport and they knew it. They knew also they were jurors to an open court, hearing arguments of an awful illusion or an awful truth.

"Against his will, is it?" Michael said in a strong voice. "Now that's a hard thing to say, considerin' the circumstances. But if you think it, I'd say we put it to Owen. How would that suit, Mr. Benton? Bring Owen out and ask him about it. If he's bein' held against his will, let him say it straight. How would that be?"

Frank turned slowly to Michael. He held the shotgun like a stick in his right hand. His lips trembled.

"I mean it," Michael added, walking slowly toward Frank. "Put it out in the open, before all these people. Let it be said, so there's no doubtin' it in anybody's mind." He stopped a few feet from Frank and stared deep into his confused face. "Sheriff," he called without moving his eyes, "bring him out. Nothin'll happen to him. Mr. Benton's not here for killin'." His voice softened. "Are you now, Mr. Benton?" he asked. "You're not here for killin'?"

Frank shook his head.

"I just come for my boy," he answered weakly.

"Bring him out, Sheriff," Michael said. His eyes covered Frank Benton's face like a target, narrowing on an unguarded pinspot of fear in Frank's confused mind.

Curtis lowered his pistol and backed into the doorway of the jail. He stood for a moment watching the frozen confrontation between Michael and Frank, and he realized that he was in awe of the Irishman. If there had been any threat in Frank, the Irishman had removed it as cleanly as an amputation, leaving Frank to stand dumb and harmless before him.

Curtis turned and walked to the storeroom and opened the

door. Owen was sitting on the floor in the corner of the room.

"Owen," he said, "you heard what's goin' on?"

"Some," Owen replied. "Can't make out everythin' bein' said through the walls."

"Your daddy said we was holdin' you against your will. Said you was ready to go home, but we'd put fear in you."

"I ain't goin'," Owen said.

"The Irishman wants me to bring you outside so you can say it. Wants everybody watchin' out there to know it. I think he's right."

"My daddy still out there?"

Curtis nodded.

"He got his gun?"

"He ain't gonna use it," Curtis answered. "I'll be beside you."

"You want me to do it?"

"I do. More'n anythin', for the people standin' around. There's some out there that'd believe anythin' and what happened to Lester and Mary ain't easy to put out of the mind."

Owen dropped his eyes to the pistol in Curtis's hand and Curtis could feel his fingers twitch on the handgrip. He pushed the barrel quickly back into its holster.

"I didn't do what my daddy said," Owen mumbled. "I didn't do it. I just told him me'n Lester had talked about goin' to work in Chattanooga, since the jobs around here was scarce. Told him I could live with my uncle and send back money to help out. I didn't do what he said."

"I know that, Owen."

*   *   *

The men who had been waiting since early morning for the return of Frank Benton began to move cautiously from the sidewalk into the street. None of them had seen Owen since he had been in jail and there was a need in them to examine him, both for the beating Frank had inflicted and for the aura of guilt or innocence they expected to see, or sense. They did not speak among themselves; they did not need to. They would look and listen and later they would decide. It was that simple and it did not matter if ballots were ever cast against Owen; nothing would sway what they saw and heard at that moment.

The screen door to the jail opened and Curtis stepped outside. His hand was poised above the butt of his holstered pistol. He stood holding open the door with his left hand, and his eyes swept across the men in the street, across Frank and Michael to Garnett Cannon.

"Doc, you got anythin' to say about this?" he asked.

Garnett moved beside Michael. He looked at Frank and then at Shirley, huddled in the passenger seat of the car. He would never understand these people, he thought. Never.

"Bring him out," he said.

The only sound as Owen appeared in the doorway was a high, frightened whimper from Shirley. She sank suddenly in the car seat and covered her face with her hands. The men in the street were as still as photographs as they watched Owen standing close to the sheriff — part boy, part man, quivering like some hunted and trapped thing displayed in a carnival tent.

"There's nothin' to be afraid of, Owen," Michael called gently. "There's a question you need to answer. That's all."

Owen did not move. His head was bowed. His arms were crossed over his chest.

"Your father says you're bein' held here against your own free will," continued Michael. "Says you'll be wantin' to go home. Is that true? Are you wantin' to go home?"

Owen raised his head slowly and looked at his father. His father seemed ravaged by madness. Owen shook his head and his body swayed. He muttered, "No."

"Boy — " Frank said helplessly.

Owen stepped backward, into the sheriff. He shook his head again.

"You heard him, Frank. Go on home," Curtis advised.

Frank looked at Owen and started to speak, but did not. He moved in a daze past Michael and Garnett to his car. He opened the door and slipped inside, placing the shotgun beside him.

"You're doin' the right thing," Michael said. He walked to the car and leaned down to the window and whispered, "I'm askin' you to think about it. When I was talkin' to Owen he was worried that you'd start beatin' on the little ones, like the girl there. I wouldn't be doin' that."

Frank stared hard at Michael. He switched on the motor of his car and the motor roared noisily.

"Don't be doin' it, Mr. Benton," Michael warned, smiling.

"Raisin' my own's my duty," Frank replied nervously, pulling his eyes away from Michael.

"It is. Indeed it is," Michael said. "But if you take the whip to the first one of them, I'll kill you. There'll be another cut throat. Think on that, Mr. Benton. I'll kill you and never think a minute about it." He smiled and winked at Frank. "I've done it before and I can do it again," he added merrily.

The only person who heard Michael threaten Frank Benton was Shirley. She looked past her father into Michael's smiling face and a great fear drove deep into her.

# 14

THE MEN OF YALE sat in Pullen's Café into the night and early morning and saluted Michael's stand before Frank Benton with their drinking and their attention and their loosened praise. But there was a giddiness, a wonder, in their words.

*"He could have had his head blowed off."*

*"Could have, damned right."*

*"Ol' Frank looked crazy-like in the face. You see it?"*

*"Like he was took. Wild in the eyes."*

*"Got it from his daddy, I reckon, but, by God, he wadn't that way growin' up. It just come on him."*

*"Happened after his wife passed. I heard tell he tried to raise her, like his daddy used to try to do."*

*"By God, the Irishman didn't flinch none."*

*"Not a hair."*

*"Ask me, it was callin' the boy out that done it."*

*"Ain't no question. Throwed Frank off."*

*"Looked to me like Frank wanted Curtis to shoot him."*

*"Curtis would've done it. I seen that Miller fellow after Curtis shot him. Blowed a hole in him the size of a door."*

*"Boy looked like he'd been beat bad."*

*"He was tellin' the truth. He ain't done nothin', like the Irishman said."*

*"See how the Irishman just stood there, smilin', like it was all a big joke?"*

*"Looked kind of crazy hisself, you ask me."*

Michael listened to the murmuring swirling about him, from
Teague and Bailey and Job, and from men he had never before
seen but who had been summoned from their homes by the air
of rumor and celebration. He sat at a table against the wall,
leaning back on the two rear chair legs, accepting the babble
around him like an amused hero. The doctor sat close beside
him and served him as an emissary who inspected the offerings
of awe from the men who squeezed their way through the
crowded room to acknowledge him. The doctor was tired from
the weight of the day and the ungiving pressure of his years, and
he had been drinking heavily. He was clinging to Michael and
Michael could feel him tugging for recognition.

"It was the doc who showed nerve," Michael said again and
again, feeding Garnett's need. "It was the doc who stepped up
first and had the say."

And Garnett waved with his hat at Michael's words, waved
with a beckoning motion that fanned the praise, like air, into
his flushed face.

In the night's frenzy Michael became certain of one thing:
When he needed them — if he needed them — the doctor and
the men of Pullen's Café would listen to him and believe. When
he needed them he would push his words into the fertile heat
of their brains, and his words would swell and sprout and grow
wild in the fields of their imaginations. They would listen to him
and they would believe.

He breathed deeply of the thick room air and accepted a
drink thrust into his hand by the doctor. He smiled cockily. The
three women would tell him of Eli's fortune, if he asked them.
Sarah, especially. If Sarah knew. It would be that easy. Yet
there was something about Owen that he could not put aside.
There was a role for Owen to play in all of it. He shifted
restlessly in his chair, scrubbing his shoulders into the chair
back. And then a chill ran into his shoulders and up his neck
and trembled in his lips.

"What's the matter, Irishman?" Garnett asked.

"Not a thing, Doc. Not a thing."

Michael swallowed from the whiskey. He was content.

*     *     *

In his bed, in the colorless night of his barn room, Michael felt the energy of Pullen's Café seeping away in an aura of pale gray, and the ceiling above him separated ethereally in his mind into the wide mouth of a great stage. He saw the players gathered silently behind bastard flats in the dim wings, poised shyly like museum mannequins in drab costumes. Principals and walk-ons, their roles painted on their faces with dabs of rouge and thick lines of black pencil. And center stage, bowed in the cross arrows of a white light, Owen Benton waited, lifting his head in the slow mime of a final scene. A quick exhilaration, like a sweet pain, tickled across Michael's body. The time was very near; he could sense it. He wondered where he would go when he left, what he would do. He closed his eyes and the stage in the ceiling above him faded away.

*     *     *

At lunch on Sunday, Michael related the story of Frank Benton to Rachel and Sarah and Dora. He told it as a bystander would tell it. He did not talk of his own role in the drama.

"It's a sad thing to see," he said. "Sad to see a man accuse his own flesh of such crimes. There's stories about that Frank's father believed he could raise the dead and there's some kind of ghost inside Frank, like a worm inside his head, swallowin' up his good senses."

"I remember when his daddy was alive," Dora said. "He started a church up in the hills, had a half-dozen families goin' regular and there was talk about him tryin' to raise the dead. Some said he used to use the children for a layin' on of the hands on the dead. Frank would've been one of them, I guess. Seems to me, everybody moved away after Frank's daddy died. Frank was the only one who stayed. He's got a brother over in Chattanooga."

"So they said," Michael agreed. "There's talk of sendin' him word, so he can come for the smaller ones in the family. Seems Frank's been beatin' on them ever since his wife died and he couldn't bring her back."

"I'd heard that from Floyd," Rachel said. "I wish somebody'd take the younger ones. But maybe it's all over now. Maybe he'll leave the boy alone."

Michael nodded thoughtfully.

"Maybe," he replied. "But I've got a feelin' we've not seen the last of this. I've a feelin' we've all missed seein' somethin' plain as day, right in front of our noses."

"What?" asked Sarah.

"Sarah, child, I don't know," answered Michael. "It could be nothin'. There's somethin' you'd need to know about the Irish to understand what I'm sayin'. We've a habit of payin' attention to our own imaginations as much as to the fact of the matter." He pushed away from the table and stood. "Now, if you'll be excusin' me, I think I'll spend some time on the fence. Way it's goin', Miss Dora, I'll be retirin' to a ripe old age before I get that wire strung."

Dora blushed and looked away.

"Don't work on the fence," begged Rachel. "It's Sunday. You're bound to be tired. Rest."

"Believe it or not, doin' a little work's what I need, Rachel. Just to shake off the cobwebs. Work's good for makin' a man think things out."

He stepped to the door and turned back to the three women.

"There's somethin' more to happen," he said. "I can feel it."

*   *   *

In the following week the tension that had been released in Pullen's Café began to build again and a premonition of fear rested over Yale like a gloom. Curtis stayed at the jail each day with George and into the night with Michael, guarding Owen. And when he was not with his patients, Garnett was also there, playing listless games of checkers with Curtis or George, or, late at night, walking with Michael and Owen outside the jail, by the river, to assure that Owen exercised his healing body. Curtis, Garnett, George, the townspeople who stood at their street windows — all were waiting for Frank Benton to reappear. But nothing happened, and on Saturday afternoon, a week following Frank's challenge for Owen, Curtis drove to the Benton farm. He returned at night and called Garnett and Michael outside the jail. Frank was sitting inside his home, Curtis reported, holding a Bible in his lap, staring blankly into the fireplace.

"Expectin' some kind of sign, I reckon," Curtis said. "He wouldn't say nothin' to me. The girl — Shirley — told me he'd been that way. Hadn't said hardly a word."

"Has he taken the whip to any of them?" asked Michael.

Curtis shook his head.

"Looked to me like he was sick," he replied.

"Maybe I'd better go up there tomorrow and check on him," Garnett mumbled wearily. "Could be his whole behavior's caused by something physical. A tumor, maybe. Pressure gets on the brain, it can play havoc."

"I'll go with you," Curtis said. He looked solemnly at Garnett. "You hear me, Doc," he added quietly. "Don't you go near that place unless I'm with you."

Garnett laughed. He pushed his hat back off his forehead.

"It's damn good to be worried about," he said. "Tomorrow, then. Town'll be closed. Won't attract as much attention."

Curtis nodded agreement.

"You'll need to be here, Irishman," Garnett added. "Hate to say it, but I don't want to leave George alone with the boy, the way George feels."

"I'll be here," Michael promised.

*　　*　　*

It was one o'clock in the morning when the sheriff left the jail. Michael stood outside in the cool August air and watched him

drive away. The moon was at quarter, with its underbelly spoon
of gold precariously balancing the shadowy bubble of the full
globe like a cosmic trick. He could hear the monotonous swirl
of the Naheela River and the night cries of night creatures. He
looked down the street toward Pullen's Café and saw Teague's
truck and, through the windows of the café, a dull light. Soon
Teague would stumble out of the café with his friends. They
would be drunk and would pile comically into the truck and
roar away into the mountains, and John Pullen would close his
café-tavern and slowly climb the outside steps of the building
to his living quarters upstairs. Michael thought of John Pullen,
whose entire life was linked by a set of stairs between his sleeping and working. He tried to remember the sound of John
Pullen's voice, but could not; he could not remember ever
hearing John Pullen speak.

He went inside the jail and locked the heavy wooden door
with its slip-bar. He walked to the cell where Owen slept on his
cot. The rhythms of his body quickened and pumped through
him in harmony and he knew it was time for the tragedian to
awaken and accept his role.

"Owen," he said quietly. "Owen, wake up."

Owen stirred on the cot.

"Owen, wake up," Michael repeated. "We need to talk."

Owen lifted his head and peered sleepily toward Michael.

"What's wrong?" he asked.

"Shhhhh, quietly," Michael replied. "We need to talk."

Owen sat on the cot, pulling his legs beneath him. He looked
around the jail, confused. The only light was from a table lamp
on the rolltop desk.

"What's the matter?" he whispered.

Michael lifted his hand for silence. He removed the key from
the desk and opened the steel door to the cell and pulled the
chair in the cell close beside Owen's cot. Owen watched him
carefully.

"You remember when we talked before?" began Michael. "I asked for your trust. You remember that, Owen?"

"Yes," Owen replied. "I remember it."

"Now's the time for it. Do you still mean it?"

"Yes."

"There's talk," Michael said.

"Talk? What kind of talk?

"About a trial."

Owen's face opened in fear.

"It's bein' kept quiet," Michael added quickly. "Nobody knows about it but the sheriff and the doctor and me. The sheriff went up to talk to your father. Seems there's somebody — I don't know his name — claimin' he saw you up near that farm the day that young couple was murdered."

"I — I wadn't," Owen stammered. "The sheriff asked me about that. Asked me where I was. I was at home. I told him that."

Michael waved down Owen's protest with his hands. He pulled the chair closer to Owen and leaned to him.

"I know it's the truth you're tellin'," he whispered. "But the sheriff's caught between what he believes and his duty as a peace officer. You're not supposed to know about it, and I'd have my tongue ripped out for sayin' it, but the sheriff and the doctor are plannin' on goin' back tomorrow for some more questions, to ask your family to try and remember where you might've been durin' that time. And they'll be lookin' over your things for a knife."

Owen began to shake his head. He tried to speak but there was no sound in him.

"You're not to be afraid," Michael assured him. "We'll work it out. I've made you my own promise that nothin'll happen, and I'm a man of my word, as I'm hopin' you know." He paused and rubbed his hands together. Then he said, "Answer me somethin', Owen. Is there a knife? Somewhere in your things, is there a knife?"

Owen nodded slowly. "My — my pocket knife," he said weakly. "Used to be my daddy's. He give it to me when he got him a new one."

Michael leaned heavily against the back of the chair. He stared at his hands as if in deep thought.

"I was afraid of it," he said. "And that could be enough, along with somebody's lyin', to make a case. It could, at that, and that's the damnin' part of it. Everybody's got a knife, who's a man. For God's sake, I've got a knife, long as a sword and sharp as a Turk's razor. Keep it with me everywhere I go, strapped to my side or my leg." He pulled up the right leg of his trousers. The sheath of the long hunting knife was tied to the calf of his leg by a strip of canvas, with its point tucked into his sock. "A knife's a thing a man needs, off in the woods, travelin' about," he added. He pulled the knife free and held it up for Owen to see. Its fine cutting edge caught the dull light of the table lamp on the rolltop desk and flashed in Owen's widened eyes like a silver scratch.

Michael rolled the knife once in his hand, as he would play with a toy, and slipped it back into its sheath. He said, "But it'll not matter much, if there's wildfire gossip when it gets out. There'll be people willin' to believe anythin' told by anybody."

"I didn't do nothin'. I didn't," Owen mumbled.

"True. You did not," Michael said. He touched Owen's arm. "I know it, in my heart. And that's why I'm takin' you away with me, as my travelin' partner." He squeezed Owen's arm. "You'll like it, Owen, believe me. We'll follow the circus and I'll show you sights your mind's eye could never see. Buildin's as high as these mountains, people as fancy as lace. Ah, Owen, it'll be a wonder for you, a true wonder."

Owen said nothing. He bowed his head and crossed his arms tight against his body.

"Owen," Michael said gently, "I'm runnin' off with my stories again, not mindin' what you'd be feelin'. It's like I said before, leavin's not easy. It never is. Sometimes you have to do it. You have to take it on yourself to put aside all those things that's been a part of you, cut it off like an arm, and go on livin' the best way you can. But leavin's not the endin'. It's the beginnin'. People can't see that. They may not like what they've lived in, or the way they've lived, but it's what they know, and bad as it may be, it's a warm tit to be pullin' on, even if there's a dry bag at the nipple. Take you: You stay here and face the threat of a murderer's trial and they could put you to death for somethin' you've never done. Or, worse, you could live with all the chains of your surroundin's hangin' on you forever. And that I can't let you do. Not and live right with myself."

Owen sat very still, his head down, thinking. Then he said, "When we goin'?"

"Tonight. Now."

Owen looked up with surprise.

"How?" he asked. "We — we just walk out?"

Michael shook his head.

"It'd be too risky that way," he answered. "We'll stage it — like it was a play we were doin'. You makin' off, leavin' me lookin' dumbstruck by what happened, and then I'll put them that search for you on the wrong track and we'll meet up in a day or so and go off in the opposite way."

"What if they don't believe you?" Owen asked. His voice trembled.

"I'm trustin' they will, Owen," answered Michael. "I'm trustin' they will. Mind you, it's not somethin' I like doin', the kind way I've been treated here, but I'm the only one to do it, me bein' a stranger. The sheriff would do the same if he could, but he's born to this place; he can't. The doctor would — I'm sure of it — but he's put in too many years carin' for all the people around and he's needed, no matter how he feels. And that leaves me, a stranger, and much as I dislike it, I've seen too much wrong done in the name of the law to take the chance with any man's life."

"What — what are we gonna do?"

Michael again leaned close to Owen and spoke in a whisper. "I'll take you outside, to stretch your legs like we've been doin' with the doc — the sheriff'll go along with that — and then you'll take off and I'll jump in the river and say you pushed me in and started runnin' off south, into the woods. But it'll not be south you'll be goin'; it'll be north."

"It'll make me show up like I done what they said," Owen whined.

"It will, yes. For the time bein'. When we're clear away, someplace like Chicago, I'll write the doctor and explain the truth, tell him it was my doin'. More'n likely he'll understand, though it's a chance we'll be takin'. But you won't be dead, Owen, and that's the chance you're takin' now."

Owen nodded. He looked around the cell. He rose from the cot and moved absently to the cell bars. He stood, with his arms still crossed tight to his body, and leaned his forehead against the cold steel of the bars.

"Owen, you tell me no and I'll drop it," Michael said evenly. "Maybe I'm wrong about it all. Maybe there's nothin' to it. Maybe I'm thinkin' of too many other times. It's you that has to give the answer."

Owen rolled his head against the bars.

"No," he replied. "I'll do what you say. It don't matter. Not no more."

*　　*　　*

They moved quietly outside, staying in the shadows beside the jail, until they reached the cluster of scrub trees growing on the bank of the river. They sat beside the river under the trees and listened to the lusty bellowing of treefrogs and the shrieking of crickets and to the rushing of water. After a few minutes, they heard laughter and then the roar of Teague's truck sputtering out of town, and then there was quiet.

"It's time," Michael whispered. He reached for his leg and

pulled his knife from its sheath. "Take this," he said. "You may be needin' it."

Owen looked at the knife in horror.

"Take it," Michael said bluntly. "They'll not know, and you'll be needin' it." He shoved the knife into Owen's hand.

"Now this is what you're to do," Michael continued. "Follow by the river, goin' north. Cut off by the creek road, leadin' up by the Pettit place. There's a patch of small pines nearby the road cuttin' up to the house, with a big rock in the center. I've put a sack of things there — provisions — in case I'd ever be needin' to leave quick. I change out the food every few days when the ladies are busy, just to be sure. It's under some limbs and pine straw. Take it with you."

"Where'm I goin'?" Owen asked nervously.

Michael moved closer to Owen and stared deep into his face.

"A place where they'll never look, and I know it'll make you a bit queasy, but it's the best place around," he said.

"Where?"

"That old house, where the young couple lived."

"That — ?"

"That house," Michael repeated firmly. "It's been closed up. I took a walk up there not long back and looked it over. You can pry out a board on the back door and get in."

"I — I can't go there," Owen stuttered. "Not where they was killed."

"Dammit, man, it's the best place," Michael insisted. "Believe me, I've been around these things before. I know what they're bound to do."

"I ain't — I — "

"What?"

"I ain't never been in a killin' house."

"It's the place," Michael said. "You stay there, hid, and I'll come for you in a day or two, and then we'll make our way out, after I've got things goin' the other way."

Owen breathed hard. His heart was pounding. He wanted to run, to be in the cell, protected, but he was afraid.

"Listen. Listen, Owen," Michael said gently. "It'll only be for a short time. And there's nothin' there. Nothin'. Just a place where you'll not be found. Now go. Be gone, and keep out of sight. I'll give you time to clear town before I give the signal."

Owen stumbled backward in his crouched position. He looked quizzically at Michael.

"Go!" Michael hissed.

Owen turned and slipped away, along the river, behind the row of buildings. Michael sat on the ground and watched until he disappeared, then he stood and began humming. He strolled to the river and waded into the cold water. He shuddered at the chill, then rolled his body beneath the water. The water covered him like ice and he lifted his head from its surface and gulped the night air. He swam to the shoreline and waded to the river bank. His body jerked with cold and he began to massage his arms with his hands. He stretched and shook his body like an animal. He opened his mouth and lifted his face to the sky and let the water run into his lips. It was time, he thought. It was working, all of it. Timed perfectly. He smiled broadly.

*   *   *

The doctor's house was on a knoll at the end of town. It was a majestic frame house, painted white like a great shell. There were four brick columns across the front porch and the shrubbery that surrounded the home like a fur wrapping was trimmed to a sculptured perfection.

Michael stood in the driveway and studied the house. A thought amused him: The doctor had never invited him into his house. He wondered if the doctor had ever been married. No one had ever mentioned a wife. Probably not, he decided. The doctor was the kind of man who would take whores like a prescription medicine.

Time, Michael thought. It was time.

He broke into a run and bounded up the front steps and began beating heavily on the front door.

"Doc, wake up," he yelled. "Wake up."

He continued pounding on the door as he saw lights pop on in the house. He could hear the doctor stumbling through rooms.

The door opened suddenly and Garnett stood in the doorway. He had pulled a tattered robe around him and his face was red.

"Goddammit, what's the matter?" he snapped. "You're tearing the door off its hinges."

Then the doctor's eyes focused on Michael, dripping with water, shaking uncontrollably.

"God Almighty, what happened?" he said in astonishment.

"The — the boy got away," Michael stammered. "He — he shoved me in the river and run off."

"Jesus Christ."

"He went south, out of town."

"God Almighty," Garnett muttered. "Come in. Come in," he added quickly. "Get out of the cold."

"Doc, I — " Michael swallowed the words and kicked hard against the doorjamb.

"What's the matter?"

"Doc, he — he got my knife."

"Jesus Christ. Jesus."

# 15

THE TELEPHONE MESSAGE from Garnett was blunt, a simple command, and Curtis had asked no questions, though he knew immediately the trouble was Owen Benton. In thirty minutes he was standing in Garnett's kitchen listening, as Michael, stripped of his wet clothes and wrapped in a blanket, sat at the kitchen table and retold the story of Owen's escape.

Owen had awakened and complained of cramps in his legs and asked to walk for a few minutes outside the cell. He had been alert and more talkative than before, saying again and again how grateful he was for the care he'd been given, and then he had asked to walk beside the river, as he had done on other nights with the doctor. The night air had revived him even more and he had spoken of his sister in Atlanta, the sister named Elizabeth. He talked of how he had missed her, how they had been close, and how he yearned to see her again. And then he had asked Michael to cut him a twig from the cottonwood tree to chew on, to clean his teeth, and when Michael had pulled his knife, Owen had rushed him, striking him in the chest with his shoulder, making him drop the knife, and pushing him into the river.

"I saw him grabbin' up the knife when I plunged in," Michael reported regretfully. "And off he runs, like a deer, straight down the road and into the woods. And there I'm thrashin' about in the water, freezin', feelin' the Devil's own fool. It was my fault, Curtis, and I'll take the full blame for it. I trusted him. I truly trusted him."

"You wadn't the only one," Curtis replied. "Nobody on earth could've made me believe that boy'd up and run. Nobody. I kind of thought Frank might've come back and talked him into leavin'. I been expectin' that. I reckon I was wrong."

Garnett poured a half-glass of whiskey from a jar and shoved it across the table to Michael.

"Drink this," he ordered. He pushed more wood into the furnace of the kitchen stove and pulled the chairs draped with Michael's clothes close to the rising heat.

"One thing I don't want," Garnett said. "I don't want a bunch of crazy damn fools after that boy. First thing people'll be thinking is that Frank was right, that the boy did that killing. And this running off may not be that at all. It just may be that he was scared. By God, I'd be. I'd be terrified if I knew I'd been accused of murder."

"But he got the knife, Doc," argued Curtis.

"So what? It fell, he picked it up. That's a natural reaction, if you ask me. What's that supposed to prove?"

"Maybe nothin' in court," answered Curtis, "but it could mean a lot to people around here."

"And that's why you're not to say anything about it," the doctor countered. "We make that known and somebody'll kill him on the spot."

"Maybe you're right."

"Well, goddam, Curtis, thanks for the confidence," Garnett said incredulously. "There's no right or wrong in this. There's just no reason to inflame people, that's all. Now, where do you think he's headed? Back to his home?"

"I don't know," Curtis mumbled.

"I'd be doubtin' it," replied Michael. He stood and circled the table to stand close to the fire in the stove. He could sense Curtis and Garnett watching him intently.

"I'd say he'd be off to where his sister lives," continued

Michael. "He'd not be goin' home, not the way he was talkin'. I'd say he'd go where he thought he could get some protection, him not havin' much experience outside the home."

The sheriff nodded agreement.

"Well, by God, it'll be a trick if he can get to Atlanta on foot with men after him," Garnett said.

"And why is that?" asked Michael. His voice was edged in nervous surprise.

"Why? There's only two roads out these mountains, and you have to take one of the two no matter if you're headed for the next continent," answered Garnett. "Going over the mountains wouldn't work. Some of those hills are about as straight up and down as a fall to Hell."

"That don't mean much," Curtis replied slowly. "He knows them woods, Doc. Them people know ways of gettin' around they don't even tell one another about."

The doctor smiled. He had been gently reminded that he was an outsider.

"Just find him," Garnett said. "And do it with as few people as possible." He paused, then added, "And try to keep from killing the boy."

Curtis pulled his hat into a snug fit on the crown of his head.

"We'll do it," he mumbled. "I'll go get Tolly Wakefield and let him get up two or three more men. Don't see how the boy could've got too far. He wasn't that strong." He turned and left the room and the house, and Michael and Garnett listened until his car left the driveway.

"Curtis is a strange man," the doctor sighed. "He won't sleep a minute until Owen's found, but you'll never hear him complain."

"I'll join up with him as soon as my clothes are dry," Michael said.

"No. I'll take you home."

"But Owen got away from me. I could at least help find him."

"Irishman, let me tell you something," replied Garnett.

"You're just like me in one way: You weren't born here. There's some things they do by themselves, and you wait and see what happens. Believe me, the future of that boy is out of your hands now."

\* \* \*

Owen dropped to his knees in the cover of the island of trees below the Pettit house, breathing hard, trembling, cowering at the sudden, scurrying sounds around him. His face twitched. He realized that he held the knife in his hand. His palm perspired around the handle of the knife and he threw it on the ground and stared at it. He could not remember carrying the knife as he ran. He wiped the palm of his hand across his trousers, then cautiously picked up the knife and slipped it into his belt.

Since he had left Michael at the jail, he had not stopped running, and now he was spent. His lungs ached and his eyes burned. He did not know if he was at the right place, where Michael had said the provisions would be hidden. He wondered what time it was. It was dark but he could feel morning rushing like an army over the eastern hills, pursuing him with its dangerous light. In the deep black forest above the Pettit house, he heard an owl. The voice of the owl was an omen, was it not? He remembered stories of the ancient, demented Indian, the last of his people, who spoke to the owls as if they were his brothers. The Indian had wandered the woods at night, hooting, chasing after sounds like echoes, and weeping for the sad messages he had heard from those secretive, seeing birds. It was part of the lore of the mountains that the Indian had died and had been swept away on the wings of owls, which had buried him in the nest of a tall beech tree. A woodsman had found the bones in the nest, as soft and white as chalk, covered with feathers. There were those who believed, for all those years, that the Indian was still alive in the voice of the owls.

Owen was afraid, more afraid than he had ever been. Afraid

of the owl and the night and the house where he must hide. He crawled on his hands and knees to the center of the island of trees. The rock was there, as Michael had promised. It was the size of a wagon body and dull white in the bare light of the quarter-moon. He stood and made his way quietly behind the rock. He saw a mound of limbs covered with pine straw and he began carefully to uncover the camouflage. The sack was there and he opened it and found that it contained a blanket and biscuits and potatoes. The food was fresh and he wondered about Michael's story of replenishing the supplies: Was it true, what he had said, or had he planned the night of the escape? Owen tied the top of the sack securely into a knot and lifted it over his shoulder. He knew he could not rest; he had four miles to go before the house, perhaps six. He could travel the road by night, but if he waited until sunrise he would have to slip through the woods and it would be risky, even on a Sunday morning. He stepped quickly into the road. He heard the owl, far off. He looked once at the Pettit house. It was a blot, a silhouette, against the skirt of the woods.

The blue steel of morning was beginning to seep over the mountains as he passed hurriedly by Floyd Crider's house. He heard a dog bark and another answer and he broke into a steady run until he was far from the house. He wondered if the dogs had awakened Floyd.

He was hurting inside. His nose had begun to bleed and he wiped at it absently with the sleeve of his shirt. He tried to set the distance to the farmhouse where Lester and Mary Caufield had been murdered. He had been to the house once with his father, when he was very young, before his father had begun to punish them for their unknown sins. The house had then belonged to a man named Alton King, who was Lester's grandfather and who had outlived three wives and six of his ten children. Owen remembered the story he had heard from his father about Alton King. His third wife was only thirteen when he married her, more child than woman, and she still played with dolls. To please her, Alton King, who was nearing seventy, had built a dollhouse for her in the backyard — a dollhouse with doll rooms and doll furniture. In the daytime, when Alton was in the fields working, she would play in her dollhouse, and at night she would be his wife. The girl had died at fifteen in labor. The child was stillborn.

Suddenly, Owen felt the seizure of a chill.

He stopped in the road and looked around him. To his left, above him, was the house. He could hear the water-song of the stream that ran into Deepstep Creek and the soft crush of sand as he turned slowly in the track of the road. He imagined that he heard a wind, but there was no wind, only the early yawning of the day as it unfolded like the sleepy opening of an eye. He took two steps and stopped. He thought of Lester Caufield. They had been friends. They had talked of going away to work together. Lester was always laughing. Always.

The house seemed to grow larger as Owen approached it. It was gray and silent. There was a look of waste about it, like any abandoned thing. He looked at the windows that had been coated with the frost of cobwebs. Under one window, at the front of the house, there was a windowbox containing one dead flower stalk.

He circled the back of the house to the porch stoop, and mounted the steps. The board that had been nailed across the screen door was loose — Michael, he thought — and he pried it off easily. He stood at the door, his hands poised inches away from the smooth knob of mountain laurel. The house seemed to resist him, to warn him. He knew it had been cleared and boarded quickly by men who were frightened and he knew it was a house no one would ever live in again. It would decay like a buried thing and the roof would fall around its chimneys and people traveling along the road would not stop to look at it, but would rush past as though skirting an evil that could never be put to rest. It was a house of murder and a house of murder was an ominous place, with screams that had been driven into the walls like hidden nails.

He touched the knob and opened the screen door and then turned the handle of the wooden door. It was unlocked. Owen opened it and stepped inside the kitchen. The room was empty and he could feel his breathing and his heartbeat echoing, thundering in his temples. He moved slowly into the house, his arms outstretched before him, groping blindly. The house was the same as the house he had lived in all his life, the same as dozens of other houses in the mountains: the kitchen, the sideroom off the kitchen, the living room with its brick fireplace, the bedrooms along the back of the house.

He slipped numbly through the doorways of the rooms, a dull hypnotic lured by a voice outside his mind. His body felt leaden. His vision was blurred. He could sense an obscure presence, like sleep, choking his brain and he shook his head to clear the trance. His eyes narrowed and focused and he realized in horror that he was standing in the bedroom where Lester and Mary had been murdered. His eyes were fixed on the single piece of furniture still in the house — the frame of the bed. He felt the ice of fear crawling over his skin, under his shirt, and his mind flashed to a scene that he had heard described the day after Lester and Mary had been discovered, before the people of the valley quit speaking of the murder: Lester on the floor, his head hinged back, his throat open like a wide mouth, and Mary, her face covered with one pillow and her naked body lifted under the lower back by the other pillow, her legs bent at the knees and spread, as though stopped in the middle of a leap.

"God," he muttered. He tried to tear his eyes from the bed frame, but could not.

He heard a flitting, scratching noise in the corner of the room and he jerked the knife from his belt and whirled to the sound. The light of the coming morning poured through the window in a silver fog and he saw a field mouse dive into a crack in the wall, and he heard the mouse race inside the wall.

He began to tremble. He sank weakly to his knees and caught the knife in both hands and held it tight to his abdomen. A painful guttural cry rose in him, turning shrill in his mouth, and he began jabbing the knife into the hard oak wood of the floor.

\* \* \*

At sunrise, Garnett and Michael left Yale to drive to the Pettit house. They rode in silence until they crossed the bridge at Deepstep Creek and then Michael asked, "Will they find him, Doc?"

Garnett shrugged and twisted his hands on the steering wheel of the car.

"I don't know," he confessed. "There's a good chance. Curtis did what I thought he would. He has only those four men, but I know them. They live in the woods. Come out maybe once or twice a year and then only to Yale. You'd never find one of them in Pullen's, that's for sure. If they do any drinking, they drink their own and they do it alone, or with each other."

"Would they have any idea where the boy'll likely be found?"

"They know it better than a pack of bloodhounds," answered Garnett. "There's one of them — Tolly Wakefield, the one Curtis mentioned last night — who could go off and live in those woods and never lift a hand at planting a seed. Only man I know who could feed you a seven-course meal of nothing but berries and find every damn one of them within a half-mile radius."

Michael smiled. The doctor was easily awed, he thought.

"The boy. Will they harm him?" he asked.

Garnett shook his head. He said, "Not likely. Not unless he forces it. Even then I doubt it. The one that worries me is George. It's a good thing Curtis left him at the jail, but no matter what I say to him now, or what Curtis says, George feels justified in being angry. He thinks he was right all along. He won't keep quiet about this. He'll have it all over the valley before sunset, but, God knows, as much as I hate to say it, I understand the poor bastard. One thing I've learned, Irishman — these people may be simple, but they're noble in their own way. They damn well may kill one another, and they do if they feel vengeance, but they'd never do some of the things you and I have seen. I remember a boy in Boston, when I was studying medicine. He was brutalized by another man. Sodomy. Well, by God, that wouldn't happen here. Never. You'd find a man like that pinned to a tree, drying out like a rabbit skin."

"I'd say you're right," replied Michael.

"Damn right I am."

Garnett thought for a moment, then laughed softly. He said, "Tolly once killed a bear with a woodaxe, and that's not one of the tall tales you always hear. It's the truth. He was cutting wood one day when this bear appeared out of nowhere, standing on its hind legs, ready to rip him apart. Tolly had a piece of wood in one hand and the axe in the other. He threw the wood at the bear — just tossed it like a ball — and when the bear reached to catch it with its front paws, Tolly drove the axe a half-foot into its heart."

"My God," Michael whispered in amazement.

"They're not ordinary men, Irishman. Not at all. We're ordinary. You and me."

"I'd believe it," Michael agreed. He shifted uncomfortably in his seat and began to drum his fingers on the dashboard of the car.

"What's bothering you, Irishman?" asked Garnett. "You've been uncommonly quiet for the last couple of hours."

Michael laughed wearily.

"Nothin' important, I don't suppose," he said. "Just thinkin' about the boy. Some of the things he said in the last few nights, when the two of us would sit around talkin'."

"Such as?"

"Well, like — like his talkin' about Eli."

"Eli?"

"True," answered Michael. "Surprised me, too. But you've got to remember, Doc, you're the only one who knows the facts of that. To a man, everybody else believes I'm kin to Eli. And the boy especially. Said I even reminded him of Eli. Said he remembered Eli comin' around when he was little, and how alike we was, tellin' outlandish stories."

"Well, by God, there's some truth in that," exclaimed Garnett. "You could've come from the same belly, if that's a measure of it."

Michael laughed again. He rolled his head against the back of the car seat. He knew he must be careful what he said to the doctor.

"Anyway," he continued, "Owen got onto the money Eli was supposed to have buried somewhere on the farm."

"There is no money," Garnett said firmly.

"Maybe not, Doc, but you'd never prove it by the men in town. I've heard many a jest about it."

"I told you you would. It's a good story."

"It is, indeed," agreed Michael. "But the boy seemed preoccupied by it. Kept sayin' I should be lookin' for it in different places, like it was a game he was playin' in his head. Like a lad on a treasure hunt."

Garnett frowned. He mumbled, "Sounds funny, coming from him."

"I thought the same," Michael said. "He told me once that he'd be off to Europe if he had that money. Asked a lot about Ireland. Said we ought to go there together."

"Seems strange," Garnett replied.

"It was. Him goin' through what he'd suffered. I'd try changin' the subject, but he'd guide me back to it, askin' if I'd looked under the house, or in the chimney, or in the loft of the barn."

"You wouldn't think it'd ever cross his mind."

"No, you wouldn't. Not in the least."

"What'd you tell him, Irishman?"

"About what?"

"The money," Garnett said, smiling. "Where you'd looked. You have looked?"

Michael broke into a tired laugh.

"Looked?" he said in mock seriousness. "Doc, I've torn the place apart. Looked everywhere any kind of sane man would've hid such a grand prize, but it must've been that Eli was a genius of sorts."

Garnett turned the car into the road leading to the Pettit house. He motioned with his hand to the blue ribbon of smoke rising from the kitchen chimney. The smile was still on his face. His eyes sparkled.

"There's your money, Irishman, burning away, cooking bacon," he said lightly. "That's the kind of genius Eli was. There's not any money. Never has been."

"Did you ever think there was, Doc? Ever? When it was first mentioned?"

Garnett thought for a moment, then replied, "Maybe. Maybe. Eli was a persuasive man and there were times when he had me believing him. But I've never seen any evidence of the money, and it's been a long time. That's why people want to believe it so bad, because they still haven't seen it. It's like anything, Michael; people believe what fascinates them. Owen must've been fascinated by it. Hell, he's been dirt poor all his life, like everybody else up here. Who wouldn't want something like that? The only thing I've ever wanted so bad it hurt was a woman I met in Boston. Most beautiful creature I've ever seen, but bound up in that damn straitjacket of convention. She was Catholic and I wasn't and, God, what a waste it was — and I don't mean that against the Catholics, because I know that's your persuasion; it was just a goddam waste. No matter how much I wanted her — and I would've given up everything; tried to, in fact — I couldn't have her. So, I know how they feel. It's a dream, Irishman, but you don't know it's a dream because it seems so damn real, and you find yourself saying, 'It's got to be real; I can touch it. It's got to be real.' But it's not, Irishman. It's not."

Garnett stopped the car in front of the house. He sat staring through the windshield, remembering. He could see the girl again, turning her face as he leaned to kiss her. He could hear her voice saying no and he could see the ice in her eyes.

"Doc?"

"Yeah," Garnett said. He wiped at a small necklace of perspiration under his chin.

"That why you came here?" Michael asked softly.

Garnett leaned against the seat and smiled.

"I don't know," he answered. "Maybe. I don't know, Irishman. I've been here too long to remember."

# 16

IT WAS LATE AFTERNOON when Michael approached the house through the cover of trees. He moved noiselessly, stopping and waiting, watching the house for the prey he knew was there, trapped in the pit of its walls. He was rested and calm. A smile of amusement was on his face. Closing on the house was a game and he played it well, without haste or error, and he was exceedingly proud of his skill. He wondered if Curtis Hill's small band of woodsmen, led by the bear-killing Tolly Wakefield, could ever track him.

He was near the back of the house, beside the barn. He could see the board had been removed from the screen door, but he could not see into the darkened windows. If Owen was watching, he was deep in one of the rooms, away from the windows. But Owen would not be watching. Owen would be hiding.

He sprinted in a crouch to the porch stoop and pressed his ear to the outside planking of the house and listened, but could hear nothing. He pulled himself onto the stoop and quietly opened the doors to the house and stepped inside, closing the doors behind him.

"Owen," he whispered. "Owen, it's me. Michael. Where are you?"

He heard a noise from the living room — a small, wordless voice — and stepped through the kitchen doorway into the room.

"Owen?"

Owen sat huddled in a corner of the room, against the wall, holding the sack of provisions under his left arm and the long steel knife in his right hand. The point of the knife rested loosely against his chest, over his heart.

"Owen, boy, be careful of that knife," Michael warned. "You jerk once and it'll split you open like a melon. I keep it sharp."

Owen pulled the knife away from his chest and let it drop to the floor. He rolled his face away from Michael and Michael could see that he had not slept, that he had fallen into the corner of the room hours earlier and had not moved.

"It's all right now," Michael said gently. He crossed the room and knelt before Owen. "There's nothin' to be afraid of. I'm here, like I promised, and we'll be gone soon. Did you eat? I've brought along some fresh food. Chicken. The ladies served it to me in my room in the barn and I put it away." He fumbled in his pocket for the chicken, wrapped in paper, and handed it to Owen. "Come on, now, eat. You'll be needin' your strength. We'll leave soon. Tomorrow night, and you'll need to be able to travel hard for a day or so."

Owen nibbled at the chicken. He did not look at Michael.

"That's better," Michael said, coaxing Owen to eat. "Better'n cold bread and potatoes, though I've made many a meal with less. A man can live off dirt or tree bark if he has to, and I've had to more times than I like to remember." He sat on the floor beside Owen and picked up the knife and slipped it into the sheath strapped to his leg.

"When it gets dark, you'll be needin' to get out to the stream by the house and get some water," he continued. "It'd be risky now, this close to the road. I wouldn't expect travelers, but it's a chance not to be taken."

"I saw where they was killed," Owen said weakly. "There's blood drops on the floor."

Michael nodded gravely. "I know," he replied quietly. "I saw them, too. When I came in before, I saw them. Made me a bit queasy at first, too, Owen. But it's nothin' but spots. Nothin' but that."

"People'll be thinkin' I done it now. People'll think I run away because I done it."

"Some, maybe, but not all. Not the doctor, or the sheriff. I was with them all night. They don't believe it, and it won't matter what the others think. We'll be off and gone and I'll write back later, like I promised, and then everybody'll know it was me who got you out, and not somethin' you'd done on your own."

"I can't stay here no more," Owen whispered. "I — I can't do it."

"Not stay?" Michael said, astonished. "Of course you can. You must. The time's too close, now. Too close. What's there to be afraid of, anyway?"

"The — the house," Owen stammered.

"The house? It's made of wood and nails and stone. It's a place. Nothin' more. There's nothin' here to fear, not flesh, not blood drops, not ghosts. Nothin'. What you're fearin' is yourself, Owen. Yourself. And you're more man than that."

Owen struggled to stand. He clutched the sack in his hands and walked to the side of the window and looked out.

"This mornin' I could hear Lester talkin', like he did the last time we was together," he said in a whisper. "I was in the room, right after I'd come in, and I could hear him, and then I was in here and I wanted to run away, but I couldn't."

"And it's good you didn't," Michael told him. "There'll be people lookin' for you even with the hunt goin' on down south. When I told Rachel and Sarah and Dora about last night, they kept lookin' out the windows, like they expected to see you come walkin' up."

"What'd they say?" Owen asked, turning to Michael.

"They thought it sad, Owen. They thought it sad what'd happened to you. But none of them said you'd done the killin' of that young couple. Dora said she hoped you'd make it away, that they didn't catch you."

"Who's out lookin' for me?"

Michael stood and pulled the leg of his trousers over the knife. He said, "The sheriff got up some men. I didn't know them. One's named Tolly somethin'."

"Tolly Wakefield?" Owen asked in surprise.

"That's the name. Why?"

"I know him. He knows the woods better'n anybody. He was the one that did all the lookin' when they found Lester and Mary."

"He did?" Michael asked curiously. "And did he find anythin'?"

Owen shook his head. "Don't know," he replied softly. "Nobody talked much about it. They never found nobody." He glanced nervously out of the window. "They got Tolly Wakefield lookin', he'll know I didn't go south," he added.

"By that time, we'll be gone," Michael declared. "We'll be out of sight. Tomorrow night we'll leave. That'll give me time to get up my things and — "

"Tonight," Owen begged. "Let's go tonight."

"No," Michael said, shaking his head. "Tonight's too early. It'd get out I'm gone and there'd be people swingin' up this way, lookin', if I'm not around. They'd think somethin'. Tomorrow I'll go into town and talk to the doctor and be seen and they'll not be thinkin' of me when I tell them I'll be restin' for a day or so."

Owen dropped his head and looked at the sack of provisions that he still held in his hands. He turned the sack absently, touching it with his fingers.

"How we — how we leavin'?" he asked Michael.

"We'll wait until late, after midnight. You'll come by the Pettit house, to the barn. The ladies'll be asleep and there's no dog, and I'll put my things together and you'll help me take them out. We'll strike out over the mountain behind the house — straight over it, the way I come in — and we'll be in North Carolina. Then we'll cut west, over to Nashville. We'll do it slow, goin' the woods. By the time we make Nashville, we'll be full-bearded and nobody'll be expectin' us."

Owen stared at Michael.

"I know what you're thinkin'," Michael added quickly. "It'd be faster by the road, and it would, but it's not fast we're after; it's safe. The longer we take, travelin' the woods, the less chance we'll have of bein' found out. There's been many a man stroll out of trouble while his buddies were hangin' by their necks for runnin'. Nobody suspects a walkin' man, Owen. Nobody."

"I don't care," Owen answered. "It don't matter." He walked to the door of the bedroom where Lester and Mary Caufield had been murdered and stared inside at the bed frame.

"Go look at it, Owen," Michael said easily. "Go on. Walk on in. Take a look at it. There's nothin' there but a bed frame and some brown dots on the floor. Go look at it." He crossed the room to Owen and stood beside him.

Owen's eyes widened and he breathed in a quick, shallow panting. He did not move when Michael caught him by the arm.

"Come on, Owen, let's look at it together," Michael insisted. "The two of us. There's nothin' there and I'll prove it. Nothin'." He pushed Owen into the room and guided him to the bed frame.

"Look at it, Owen. Look at it," Michael urged. "What'd you see? Faces. Brown eyes starin' back at you? Are you hearin' any voices now?" He released Owen and stepped back. "Wait a minute," he whispered in shock. "Was that someone speakin'? Did you hear it, Owen?" He turned in a full, bold spin in the middle of the room. "Are you there?" he called. "Are you here, Lester Caufield? If you are, speak up. Say it out loud, like a man." He laughed sharply, then turned back to Owen. "See, Owen, there's nobody here. There's nothin' but a bed frame and it's not said a word." He stepped to the frame and pushed against it with his hands. "If you had a mattress, you could sleep on it, and it'd do nothin' but hold you up."

Owen looked at Michael in disbelief. He stumbled backward in the doorway, then turned and bolted from the room. Michael heard him in the kitchen, vomiting. He looked once around the bedroom, to the blood stains on the floor, then strolled leisurely into the kitchen. Owen leaned against the wall near the door, bent at the waist.

"Owen, lad, I didn't mean to put fear in you," Michael said softly. "I had to show you — there's no ghosts here. In your whole life, you've not done a thing to anger man or spirit. And you can't be fearin' somethin' you've not angered. You've a life ahead of you. You have to live it like a man."

Owen turned from him, into the wall. His head was lowered and his eyes closed.

"I'm leavin' now," Michael said. "I'll not worry about you. I know what it is that you're feelin'. But I know what you are inside. You're a man. Tomorrow night, you'll be at the barn. There's a window there, on the lot side. It's the only window. You tap twice and I'll answer. But make it late. Give the good ladies time to be sound asleep."

Owen did not reply.

"Do you understand what I've said, Owen?" asked Michael.

Owen nodded.

"If there's a change, I'll be back here before sunset. But I don't expect it."

Owen nodded again.

"In a week, you'll put it out of your mind," Michael said evenly. "It'll be like it never happened. None of it." He stepped to the door of the kitchen and opened it. "It's a lovely day," he added lightly. "Ah, it is. A good time to be travelin', Owen." He stepped through the door and closed it behind him. He stood for a moment on the stoop and stretched. The afternoon sun was wedged like an orange ball in a V along the shoulder of the mountains, and the shadows of the trees fell long and dark across the narrow slipper of the land bar behind the house. It *was* a good time to travel, he thought. His mind flashed to

the men who had gathered with Curtis Hill to begin the search
for Owen. He suddenly wished they were tracking him. It
would be fine sport to match skills with such men. He jumped
sprightly from the stoop and jogged easily into the cover of
trees.

*　　*　　*

It was early night when Michael returned to the Pettit farm. He
ate a full meal that Rachel had kept in the warmer oven of the
kitchen stove, and explained his unannounced disappearance of
the afternoon. To wander the hills, he said. Just as a precaution.
Not that he believed Owen would be in the area, but he felt
responsible and needed to do something.

"Just a way of walkin' off worry," he explained. "I've been
that way as long as I remember. Maybe it's why I've been a
wanderer. Maybe I've been walkin' off worry all my life."

"Where'd you go?" Dora asked, pouring coffee for Michael.

"Go? Around," Michael answered. "I was up near the Crider
place. Thought to stop in and speak to Floyd about what'd
happened, but I didn't see any sign of people and it bein' Sunday, it struck me they might be off visitin'."

"They were," Sarah said. "They came by here for a few
minutes."

Michael was surprised. "Indeed?" he replied. "By here? And
whatever for?"

"They get out some since Mama Ada died," Rachel told him.
"They'd heard about Owen this mornin' at church, and I suppose Floyd wanted to hear you tell it. He didn't say much. They
left after a few minutes."

Michael's face furrowed in thought.

"I should've gone by earlier," he mumbled. "Floyd not knowin' which way Owen went, he'll be worried."

"Floyd'd worry about his own shadow," Dora insisted. "He
was sayin' the dogs woke him up in the middle of the night, last
night. Said he reckoned it could've been somebody goin' up the
road, but he couldn't see nothin'."

"Must've been an animal," Michael said.

"We told Floyd which way Owen went," Rachel explained.

"What'd he say?"

"What he always says," replied Dora. "Nothin'. He just kind of nodded and stood there. You could make more sense out of one of them fence posts you been puttin' up."

"He did say somethin'," Sarah corrected quietly, looking at Michael. "He said he was glad you were here with us. Said it was right to have a man around." She paused. "I'm glad, too," she added.

"Well, I'm glad I'm here, too," Michael declared, slapping his hand on the table. "So, ladies, that's what I'm goin' to be — around. Tomorrow I'll go into town for a spell and tell the doctor they'll have to find somebody else to be a jailer. I've got a responsibility here and I'll not shirk it."

"We can watch after ourselves," Rachel said.

Michael pushed away from the table. He stretched and reclined in the chair, folding his hands across his stomach. He looked teasingly at Rachel.

"Can you now?" he said.

"If we have to," she replied.

Michael tossed his head and laughed easily.

"And I'd believe it," he exclaimed. "From what I've seen, the three of you could fight off the Devil himself. But I'd still feel more at ease bein' around."

"And I would, too," Sarah said bluntly.

"Then it's settled," Michael remarked. He pulled himself from the chair. "And, now, ladies, I feel full and lazy and I want to walk about before puttin' myself to bed. How about it, Rachel? A short walk down the road and back. It's a pleasant night out. Just cool enough."

The invitation surprised Rachel. She looked quickly to Dora and Sarah.

"Ah, I've said it wrong," Michael added softly. "My mind's muddled a bit. No offense." He looked at Sarah.

"It's up to Mama," Sarah said coolly. "She can go if she wants to."

"Go on," Dora urged. "We'll clean up in the kitchen. You like walkin' and you've been inside for days."

"No, it's all right," Michael insisted. "It's not the thing for a man to say, under the circumstances. I forget where I am and I get carried away. Let's all go."

"No," Dora said emphatically. "Me and Sarah'll clean up the kitchen." She pushed at Rachel with her hands. "Go on, Rachel. Don't you know the man's restless? He needs to be pacin'."

"That I am, Miss Dora," Michael agreed, smiling. "I've been walkin' every blessed night into town and my feet seem to want to go it on their own. I'd like the company, Rachel, if it's all right."

"I'll get a shawl," Rachel replied reluctantly.

Sarah turned from the table and began work at the kitchen counter.

*　　*　　*

Outside, Michael packed his pipe and lit it, and the sweet smell of tobacco filled Rachel's breathing as she walked beside him on the road leading from the house. She said nothing to him. She crossed her arms in a hug against her breasts and walked slowly, in his pace. She could hear his quiet drawing on the pipestem and the spewing of the burning tobacco.

They were well away from the house when he spoke.

"I think Sarah's upset about us walkin'," he said.

"She's been moody lately," Rachel answered.

"I've missed you," he told her calmly. "Could you tell it?"

Rachel did not answer.

"You've been removin' yourself," he added. "Why's that?"

"I did somethin' wrong," she said evenly. "I shouldn't've."

"I could feel you when I was dancin' with you, and it was like the night in the barn."

Rachel stopped walking. She looked back toward the house. "We'd better go back," she said.

Michael tapped the loose ashes from the bowl of his pipe and swept the night around him with his eyes.

"I didn't mean to say somethin' wrong," he told her. "Fact is, I took a chance gettin' you away from the others." He looked into her face. "I've got to tell you somethin'," he added, "and it's somethin' I don't like doin'."

His voice was like a touch. She could see the pinpoint of a brilliant light in the dark pit of his eyes.

"What is it?" she asked.

"It has to do with Owen."

"Owen? Why?"

"Because of some of the things he'd been sayin' to me," answered Michael. "I told the doctor about it, but I need to tell you, too."

"What is it?"

"It's about Eli."

"Eli?"

Michael began walking again and Rachel followed beside him.

"It's about the money Eli stole and hid out," he said at last.

She smiled slightly.

"There's no money, Michael. That's just a story," she said. "It was Eli's braggin'."

"And I believe you," he replied. "I've heard tell of it since goin' into Yale that first night, and I've never thought twice of it. It's a good tale, good for drinkin' men. Nothin' more."

"Then why does it mean anythin'?" she asked.

"Because Owen believed it," he answered. "He told me he'd find a way of gettin' at the money. Said he'd make you tell."

"How?"

Michael stopped walking and shrugged. He drew on the pipe and a string of smoke snapped like a whip from the bowl.

"How?" she repeated.

"Well, one way, he said he'd take a knife to Sarah's throat until you told where Eli put it."

Rachel's eyes widened in surprise. She looked quickly toward the house, then back to Michael.

"Owen?" she asked. "Owen said that?"

Michael nodded affirmatively.

"I let it pass," he confessed, "because I thought he wasn't bein' himself, that he'd been hurt in the beatin' and his mind was wanderin'. And I still think it's so. I still think it, but I can't let it go without tellin' you about it."

"I can't believe it," Rachel whispered. "Owen?"

"I don't think there's any need to worry. I just wanted to make sure. If there was a chance — any chance at all — that the story of Eli's money was true, then we'd need to take care."

Rachel turned from him. She pulled the shawl tight around her shoulders and began to walk ahead of him, near the opening into the main road.

"It's not true, is it, Rachel?" Michael asked quietly.

She shook her head.

"I mean, I'd understand if you didn't want to say anythin', since it's been all these years and nobody's ever heard you speak of the money."

She stopped walking and looked again at Michael. She could see an eagerness twitching in his face.

"You don't believe me, do you?" she asked simply. "There's no money. If there was, I'd tell you. Eli put out that story just to cause some talk, then he up and left and everybody believed it."

He reached for her and caught her gently by the arms and stepped close to her. He could feel her stiffen and pull against his hands.

"Rachel, you could be hidin' a gold mine, and it wouldn't matter to me," he whispered painfully. "I'm not a man after money. If I was, I'd have torn up the place long ago. It's not that that keeps me here. It's the feelin' that I belong. I belong here, with you. I just don't want anythin' to happen to you, or Sarah or Dora."

She tried to pull away from him, but he held on to her.

"Don't be pushin' me aside when I know you don't want to," he said. "What d'you think it's been like for me? I've been achin' just to touch you. Nights at the jail, when the boy was sleepin', I'd think about you and the hurt was more'n I could bear. If I'd thought mentionin' the money would drive you away, I'd never have done it."

"It — it didn't," she stammered. "It's — it's just wrong."

"It's not wrong," he argued quietly. "It's right, because we both feel it." He pulled her into the dark hull of the limbs of a chinaberry tree beside the road.

"Don't," she whined softly. She tried to move from him.

He slipped his hands over her crossed arms, rubbing his palms over the nipples of her breasts. She trembled, but she did not move.

"I want to hold you," he murmured. "I want to pull you near me and press myself into you, and feel the fit of your body on me."

"Please, don't — "

"It's dark. There's nobody watchin'. Nobody."

He lifted her face with his hand and cupped it and kissed her. He could feel her mouth part and the moist heat of her lips pressing against him, and his hand circled eagerly over her breasts and he could feel the thunder of her heartbeat.

# 17

IT WAS A SINGLE STEP that Tolly Wakefield heard. Not the step of an animal or the fluttering of a bird in dry leaves. It was the step of a man, a single, heavy step, and then silence. Tolly's mind snapped like a trap. The sound was above him in the dense underbrush of mountain laurel that rolled off the side of Yale Mountain, and whoever was there could see him easily. He had not tried to hide as he searched for Owen; he wanted to be seen, to prove that he was not an enemy. He knew Owen would be careless in his escape. Owen would have followed the flat hem of the mountains, along the narrow paths of animal trails that were imperceptible to most woodsmen. Tolly read their invisible braille with his fingers, and his fingers understood what his eyes could not tell him. Owen would have followed these trails like a map, not because he saw them, but because his senses would have led him along them until he became tired and stopped to rest. Tolly knew if Owen had disappeared into the mountains south of Yale, as the sheriff had said, he would be found, and he did not want Owen to be afraid of him.

But Tolly knew instinctively that it was not Owen who had taken the step above him. There had been no sign of Owen. Nothing. And Owen would have left signs. He would be weak and confused. Whoever was above him was not.

The echo of the step was still in his mind when he turned quickly and began running up the hill toward the sound. He saw a movement, a flash of brown, and knew he had surprised whoever had taken the step. He could hear someone running and he stopped and dropped into a crouch and peered through the brush, but he could see nothing. There was only the sound of running, but it was not wild and thrashing; it was easy and sure, almost teasing. Tolly cursed bitterly. He was tired and knew it. For two days he had zigzagged the mountains, bent at the waist, moving in a walking trot as steady as a runner, his eyes darting like a bird's eyes, reading the woods in words that he understood better than anyone. And now he was tired and there was someone in the woods with him, but not Owen. His mind, his senses, told him that it was not Owen, and he felt as though someone was taunting him.

He stood and moved slowly through the tangle of the undergrowth, his eyes scanning the ground carefully. Beside a thin white oak, he saw it: a footprint, pushed deep into the leaves. He knelt and studied the print. It was large and had pushed the leaves aside as though the man had stood for a long time, waiting. In front of the print was a sharp hole, perhaps two inches deep. Tolly's eyes tightened into a puzzled frown. He touched the hole with his fingers. Something bothered him, something remote and disturbing, but he did not know why.

A bluejay chattered angrily in the top of a beech tree fifty yards away and Tolly lifted his head and stared at the tree. A squirrel sprang from a limb to the trunk of the tree and flattened itself in a camouflage. Tolly strained to listen, but he could hear only the bluejay. It was enough. The man who had taken the step and then run away was waiting for him at the beech tree.

Tolly eased into a sitting position. It was past midafternoon and the shadows on the eastern side of Yale Mountain were deepening. He watched the bluejay and traced his own location in his mind. There were no pines, only hardwood, and it would be impossible to move through the fallen leaves of the hardwoods without being heard. He wondered if the man waiting at the beech knew that, had planned it that way. A half-hour earlier he had been in a forest of pines. A half-hour earlier he could have moved on the man without a sound. But he knew the woods. The mountain turned into a natural wall, like a collar, and the land below it spread open in a perfect oval, covered in thick grass. A stream tumbled out of the mountain, over a rock bed, and curled out of the palm of the oval valley and emptied into the Naheela River miles away. Tolly had hunted deer in the valley. If he could get above the beech tree, the man who was hidden there would be forced into the open plain. He wondered again who the man was. It was not Owen; he was sure of it.

"Dammit," he muttered. He pushed from the ground and began a sprint up the side of the hill, above the beech, thrashing loudly through the undergrowth. He heard the bluejay scream at the noise and dive screeching from its perch. Suddenly, he was out of the brush and into timber and he ran harder until the beech was directly below him. Then he stopped and waited and watched the tree. He was breathing in long, deep gulps, and he could feel the perspiration rolling from his face. He began to move cautiously down the hill, kicking leaves as he walked. He saw the movement, a brown blur, drop from behind the beech and roll and then he saw the man spring to his feet and run easily toward the grass field in the oval opening. "Dammit," Tolly said again. He turned left and ran along the crown of the hill that formed the base ridge of the mountain, keeping the man below him. From the shadows and distance, he could not tell who the man was, but at least he knew it was not Owen. The man was taller and heavier and older, and he was not afraid: He did not look back as he ran.

The man dashed suddenly out of the edge of the woods and into the field of grass, running away from Tolly, toward a small knoll that rose in a terrace that separated the field from the stream. Tolly could see the man clearly, but still he did not know him. The man carried something in his hand that looked like a long rifle, and for the first time Tolly felt the queasiness of danger. He watched as the man ran smoothly over the ridge of the knoll and disappeared from sight on the other side, just above the bank of the stream. Then it became clear to him: The man wanted him to think that he had taken to the stream and would follow downstream until he reached the protection of the pines. It was a game, he thought, a goddam game, and he would not be led into it like a child. He scanned the knoll carefully, but he could see nothing. The man was there, watching for him; he knew that. He knew also that he had the cover of the trees and that he was too far away to be heard. "The sonofabitch," he muttered. He turned back and moved up the hill to his left, squatting and slipping behind the wall of trees. He knew how the stream came from the mountain, slithering over its rock bed like a string of ice. High on the hill, at the top of a waterfall, the trees cupped open and a flat ledge jutted over the straight drop like a platform. The entire valley was visible from the ledge and it would be easy to see the open stream until it disappeared into the pit of trees at the southern end. He had watched deer feeding in the valley from the ledge and once had seen a bear and her cubs playing in the stream. The man who made the footstep, the man who was playing a game of hide-and-seek with him, would not go south as he wanted Tolly to believe; he would go upstream, into the mountain. And Tolly would be waiting for him.

Tolly reached the ledge quickly and stood hidden beside an ash tree and looked down on the stream that split the valley in a straight line. The man was easy to find. He was a brown dot hidden in the grass that grew along the bank of the stream. He moved cautiously toward the mountain, toward Tolly, stopping every few feet to peer downstream. He was deliberate, Tolly thought. Patient and deliberate and practiced. He wondered if the man had a gun.

It was fifteen minutes before the man worked his way to the foot of the mountain and scurried quickly from the grass into

the trees and out of sight. Tolly's senses tensed. He was now the
hunter and the game was his to play. He slipped quietly from
the ledge and began to move downhill, delicately, like an animal
gliding through a pool of shadows. The stream poured past him
in its swirling music and he could feel the air cooling, with a
fine spray mist leaping off the rock bed. His eyes focused on the
banks of the stream; he knew he would find his man near water.

The man was no more than ten feet away when Tolly saw
him. He was sitting on a bed of moss, with his back to Tolly,
resting. Tolly looked at him closely: It was the Irishman. A
great, shuddering anger coursed through Tolly. Goddammit,
he thought. He wanted the Irishman to turn on him, to challenge him.

Tolly stepped from behind the oak that covered him. He was
in a slight crouch.

"Mister," he said in a growl.

Michael whirled at the sound. He scrambled to his feet and
faced Tolly. His mouth was open in surprise.

"Stay where you are," Tolly warned.

"My God, man, you've scared away half my life," Michael
replied weakly.

Tolly stared at him. He saw the walking stick that Michael
held loosely in his hands, with the carving of a face on the knob.
He knew there was no gun to fear.

"What're you doin' out here?" he asked evenly.

Michael ignored the question.

"I remember you," he said. "You'd be Tolly Wakefield. The
sheriff introduced us yesterday mornin'. I'm Michael O'Rear."

"What're you doin' here?" Tolly asked again.

"Why, lookin' for the boy," Michael answered in astonishment. "The same as you."

"You been followin' me," Tolly said coldly.

"Followin' you? Why, man, I've been chased by some fellow
who rushed me back in the woods and I made it to the fields
and up to here, scared to death I'd wind up a corpse."

"You're a liar," Tolly replied calmly. "That was me in the woods and you know it."

Michael slumped to his knee on the moss, leaning against his walking stick. He wiped his face across the sleeve of his shirt and shook his head wearily. He looked back to Tolly.

"If it was you," he said earnestly, "then you've a right to think that. But I swear on the holy head of God that I didn't see who it was, but there was all that crashin' about and it put the fear in me and I ran, and that's the truth of it."

Tolly said nothing. He stared hard into Michael's face.

"For God's sake, man, that's the way it happened," Michael exclaimed in exasperation. "Maybe I shouldn't be out here, and I promised the doctor I'd stay away, but I couldn't help it. The boy was in my care. I let him get away."

"Go home," Tolly said.

Michael stood. He breathed deeply and stretched his back. "I will," he replied. "Indeed, I will. I guess the good doctor was right. I'm doin' nothin' but interferin'."

"You see anybody else, don't run," Tolly advised bluntly. "Some of the others have got guns. You run, they'll kill you."

"Don't be worryin' about that," Michael said. "I'll stand as still as Lot's wife." He turned to leave, then stopped and looked back at Tolly. "Tell me," he said, "if that was you down in the woods, how'd you get up here?"

"I been here before," Tolly answered simply.

Michael smiled and nodded and began to stride down the mountain. He felt good. Tolly Wakefield had surprised him, but that did not matter. He had followed Tolly for more than an hour before letting Tolly find him. That was victory enough. He was as good as the best of Curtis Hill's men.

*   *   *

Tolly slowed his pace down the mountain. There was no reason to hurry. It was after sundown and he knew the sheriff and the other men had already met in the field where the sheriff's car had been parked. They would not have waited for him because they knew his habits: If he wanted to follow the hunt for Owen into the night, he would. Tolly did as he wished, when he wished, and he did it alone. He preferred being alone. It was safe. With people, there was always a bargain, always compromise, always someone with tender feelings souring around a wound that had been pricked by an innocent word. The sheriff and the other men would have left him in the woods, without any effort to find him, because they understood him.

The night air washed over Tolly and he stopped and lifted his face toward the sky like a listening deer. The air swept around his neck and cooled him. He stepped from the trees into the road leading to Yale and stood quietly on the gravel edge of the pavement. He was very close to Hollings Bridge, which crossed the Naheela River off the heel of Yale Mountain. He pulled his pocket watch from the bib of his overalls and popped a match on the thick nail of his thumb. He held the match over the face of the watch. It was ten minutes after nine. He was a mile from Yale, two miles from his house. On another night, he would not have hesitated; he would have gone home. But on this night, he had to see the sheriff. He flipped the match to the pavement and watched it darken. He pulled a hard biscuit from the pocket of his denim jacket and bit into it and chewed slowly. Then he turned in the road and began to walk in a long stride toward Yale.

\*    \*    \*

At the outer rim of the town, Tolly stopped and studied the street. He could see a line of cars parked in front of Pullen's Café and he realized that it was Monday night. For a moment, standing there, he had been distracted, deceived by time. How long had he searched for Owen? Two days. Two days without a sign, except for the Irishman. There had been no cars at Pullen's on Sunday night, for on Sunday night John Pullen did not permit drinking.

He knew why the men were there: The news of Owen's escape had spread into the hills like a hissing flame, fanned by George English's venomous anger. He had known early — on Sunday morning — that George would not be silent about Owen. George had needed a mob audience and he had ordered one with his careless talk. Tolly did not want to see George. George had blamed him for not finding the trail of the killer of Lester and Mary Caufield months earlier and the tension between them had grown. But Tolly knew the men of the Naheela Valley believed he would find Owen, and they were waiting for him at Pullen's.

He did not want to risk being seen and slipped behind the hedge of trees growing along the bank of the Naheela River and approached the jail from the back. He remembered the barred back door. It would mean going in the front, in the light, and there might be men watching from Pullen's Café. He stood at the cell window, thinking. Inside, he heard the muted voices of the sheriff and the doctor and, he thought, George. The men in Pullen's might see him, but that couldn't be helped. He had come to speak to the sheriff and he would. He walked quickly around the corner of the building to the front door and opened it. He stepped inside and pushed the door closed behind him. The sheriff was sitting in a chair at the rolltop desk. The doctor was in the rocker. George paced the floor angrily. They turned in unison to Tolly and stared at him.

"Tolly," Curtis said, rising from his chair. "I didn't expect to be seein' you. You find him?"

Tolly shook his head. He removed his felt hat and turned it slowly in his hands. His eyes settled on George.

"You see anything?" Garnett asked eagerly. "Any sign of him?"

"Nothin'," Tolly answered. He looked from George to Garnett. "He ain't out there," he added.

"What the hell does that mean?" demanded George. "What kind of stupid goddam thing to say is that?"

Tolly's head snapped back. His eyes narrowed on George and his lips trembled.

"He ain't out there," he answered deliberately, slowly. "Like I said."

Curtis felt the anger building in Tolly. It was cold, and Curtis remembered what a man — a stranger — had once told him: There were two kinds of anger; one was hot, one was cold. The one to fear was the cold. He stepped between Tolly and George.

"George," he said, "you been ravin' like a dog all day, and I'm tired of it. Now, you shut up or get out and I mean it. You been holdin' a grudge against Tolly since that killin' and it's time you put it away." He turned to Tolly. "Don't pay him no attention," he added. "He's been up at Pullen's."

George's face flushed. He glared at Curtis but did not speak. He whirled unevenly on his heel and walked to the cell and leaned against the bars.

"Now, what'd you mean, Tolly?" Curtis asked. "He ain't out there?"

"He didn't go south," replied Tolly. His voice was heavy and tense.

"Then where?" Garnett said.

"North, I reckon. Goin' north'll be easier. Not as many houses that way."

"How do you know he didn't go south?" Garnett asked.

"Because I do," Tolly answered bluntly. "The boy ain't old enough not to leave some sign."

Garnett leaned forward in the rocker. He shook his head thoughtfully and wiped across his mouth with his hand.

"But the Irishman told us Owen went south," he protested. "He came back into town this morning. We walked the direction the boy ran. He said he watched Owen until he was out of sight."

"He was out in the woods," Tolly said.

"Who?" Garnett asked. "The Irishman?"

Tolly nodded.

"He was followin' me," he said.

"Well, dammit, I told him to go home," Garnett said.

"Why was he followin' you, Tolly?" Curtis asked.

"I don't know. He was. He said he wadn't, but he was. Said he was lookin' for the boy."

"Now, goddammit, Tolly, maybe he was," Garnett said. "He's been worried about the boy, feels responsible for what happened."

Tolly pulled the felt hat back on his head, tight over his brow.

"Maybe the boy hid out and circled back to throw us off," he remarked. "I don't know."

"Then we'll look north," Curtis replied. "In the mornin'. You can bed down here if you want to, Tolly."

Tolly shook away the offer. He said, "I'll go on up the road a piece. There's a couple of places I'll look tonight. Maybe he ain't far, if he was weak." He reached for the door.

"Hey, Tolly, he ain't no bear, is he?" George barked defiantly. "He ain't out there thrashin' around, plain as day. That's it, ain't it? And you ain't no goddam bloodhound, like we should've had before when you couldn't find nothin'. That's it, ain't it? You can't find him and you're sayin' he ain't out there."

"Shut up, George," Curtis snapped. He stepped in front of Tolly.

"Why, hell's bells, Tolly's right," George crowed. He spit out an acid laugh. "Don't know why none of us never thought about it. Owen did just that. Turned back, struttin' right through the middle of town, leadin' a band. You got it, Tolly. You got it right on the head, you asshole."

Curtis felt the rush before it began. He reached to grab Tolly, but Tolly's left arm lashed out and shoved him stumbling across the room into the chifforobe. He saw George pushing himself from the cell bars as Tolly moved over to him in one stride, like a cloud. George's right hand dropped instinctively for the pistol at his side, but never reached it. Tolly caught him by the wrist and twisted it viciously and Curtis heard a bone snap like a dry stick. George screamed and fell to his knees, tucking his head into his shoulder. Tolly held to the splintered wrist and raised his right hand, with the palm opened and cupped. The hand dropped across George's face in a splattering slap of flesh on flesh and George fell forward like a slaughtered animal. He rolled on the floor, on his back. His body convulsed once in a violent heaving and his eyes wandered dully across the ceiling of the jail. A trickle of blood oozed from his nose and left ear.

"God Almighty, Tolly," Garnett whispered in shock. He had not moved from the rocker. The swiftness of the attack had immobilized him. It had taken no more than four seconds.

Tolly stood over George like a tree. He looked calmly at Garnett and then Curtis.

"Hope I didn't hurt you none, Curtis," he said matter-of-factly. "He pushed me too far." He stepped across George and walked to the door. "I'll meet you up at the bridge across Deepstep in the mornin'," he added. He opened the door and stood for a moment staring at the cars parked in front of Pullen's Café, and then he was gone.

# 18

MICHAEL LAY on his back across his bed, his legs crossed at the ankles, and counted time in a silent, monotonous ticking that clicked in his mind like a precisioned march. His eyes were closed and he rested peacefully in the silky cradle between sleep and exhilaration. It was a calm that he loved, that intoxicated him like a sweet wine. He was not like other men, he thought. Other men would be tense and fearful, praying for courage. He was at ease.

He moved his head on the feather pillow and opened his eyes and looked out the window cut into the side of the barn. He could see nothing but a single dim star, like a phosphorous spot smeared on the pane. It was late. Eleven, he imagined. The time was nearing. Soon Owen would be tapping at the window like a timid beggar. He closed his eyes again and began humming the melody of his song, and the words floated on clouds in his mind: *"I have loved you with poems . . . I have loved you with daisies . . . I have loved you with everything but love . . ."* He smiled at the euphoric giddiness rising in him and he could feel the blood flooding to his loins. He thought of Rachel. Soft. And fierce. And afraid. Yes, above all, afraid. And, also, helpless. He remembered her from the walk of the night before. Touching her, feeling her pull away from him with her weak protest. But she had opened her arms in wings and gathered him to her and he had felt the spasms of that gathering beating inside her. It had happened quickly and she had suddenly been embarrassed. He had held her and kissed her lightly on the eyes and then had led her back to the house. That morning, at breakfast, she had looked at him secretly and her eyes had smiled and he knew her embarrassment was gone.

She had told him there was no money, no hidden treasures. It was all a story, she had said, one of Eli's harmless lies. But he knew different. Yes, and she would tell him. What he was about to do would bring her closer and she would open her secrets to him as willingly as she had opened her legs. He smiled again and moved his locked hands behind his head. But what if there was no money? He thought. What if Rachel had told the truth, that it was nothing more than a boasting legend left by Eli, the mocking epitaph of a wanderer? He shrugged as if answering the question for a stranger. Would it really matter? He was content. The search — if it was a search at all — had become as intriguing as the prize.

*     *     *

Tolly Wakefield paused on the bridge crossing Deepstep Creek. He could take the road to the house where the Caufields had lived and died, or he could go through the woods. It was shorter by the woods, though there was a hill to climb and he was tired. Still, it was shorter by the woods, and somehow the distance, and the time to travel it, mattered to Tolly. He wanted to rest, but he could not dismiss the house from his mind. It gnawed at him, aggravated him. There was a picture in his mind of Owen at the house and he wondered why it was there and why he could not push it aside. The Caufield house was the only empty house north of Yale. No one would ever think of Owen hiding there, in the place where murder had been committed. He was a boy. Just a boy. He could not have the courage to go to the Caufield house. Yet Tolly felt it: Owen was at the house.

He turned on the bridge and crossed it and he could hear the sound of his footsteps echoing against the creek banks beneath the bridge. He could feel a chill tightening the muscles in his shoulders and neck. Owen would not go to the house by his own choice, he thought. He would never do that.

Tolly stepped quickly from the road and began his climb up the hill, measuring a straight line to the Caufield house.

*     *     *

Owen could not judge the time. He had watched the lights blink out in the Pettit house and had waited across the road, squatting in the darkness of a water oak at the edge of the field, until time had no meaning for him. He had stared at the rising moon and the stars that seemed to chase it like small, proud warriors, and he had tried to plot the time, but could not. Only the moon and its chasing stars seemed to move; not time, nor the earth around him, nor space. He had not slept in two days, or if he had, he could not remember it. He was numb and confused. The only thing his mind could hear was Michael's voice, like a whisper deep in his skull. The voice was his master. It repeated his instructions like a litany, a sweet propaganda that would deliver him safely to the life of a new person in a new world. Owen had never wanted to leave, but he did not know how to stay. He did not know how to disobey the voice that was deep in his skull.

A star broke apart millions of miles away and sizzled across the universe and died in a single fiery drop beyond the hills above the Pettit house. Owen's eyes widened and focused on the house. He stood, pulling himself up by the trunk of the oak. There was a dull pain in his neck and he rubbed it gently with both hands. He lifted the sack of provisions that Michael had hidden. He had waited long enough. He walked hesitantly out of the field and crossed the road a hundred yards from the turnoff to the house. He knew he could circle wide and be hidden by the stand of sassafras trees that grew along the house road, and he could reach the barn easily. His neck ached. The pain drove into his spine and his mind flashed to his mother patiently massaging his back after he had fallen from a tree. He had been ten years old and she had made a lotion out of bark and had rubbed it into his muscles. Her hands had been as warm as the lotion. She had told him stories as she tended him — giddy stories that were private — and they had healed him as quickly as the lotion. His mother's face formed in his mind and then vanished and he found himself standing at the lot fence that looped around the back of the barn from the stables. He saw the mule under the umbrella of a persimmon tree in the barn lot, and the cows rooted into the ground on their great bellies. The cows turned their heads to him like bored onlookers. He caught the fence with his left hand and crept slowly along it, bent forward, his head swiveling from the house to the barn and to the house again. He saw the window in the side of the barn. It looked odd, being there, an out-of-place remedy for the boarder inside. He slipped close to the barn, dragging his shoulder along the slatted planking. Then he was beneath the window and he rose cautiously to full height. His heart was racing, driving the blood into his temples like a storm. He tapped the window lightly with his fingers. Once. Then again. And suddenly there was a face, smiling, pressed against the pane, a round pocket of hollow shadows in the lifeless light of the weak moon. The face mouthed "Wait" and disappeared. Owen dropped to his knees, close against the barn.

*　　*　　*

Michael opened the barn door carefully and studied the darkened house. There would be no chance that anyone would be awake, but he would not be a bumbler, giving away himself by a careless step. He closed his eyes and read the script of his plan a final time in his memory. He could hear the dying mumbling of the Chautauqua audience and the restless shifting in their seats as they braced to watch and listen. He felt a rush of excitement speeding through him like heat. He breathed deeply in an exercise of calming his eagerness, and then he stepped out of the barn — from the wings of his stage — and walked hurriedly to where Owen waited beneath the window.

"Owen," he whispered gladly, kneeling beside Owen and grasping him by the shoulders. "I knew you'd come. I been waitin', hopin' you'd not change your mind and leave me to go off alone. But I knew you wouldn't. I knew it."

"I — I didn't know what time it was," Owen stammered.

"Close to midnight. Couldn't be better."

"Are — are you ready?"

"I am. Got everythin' packed away in my knapsack," Michael answered. He turned Owen toward the north. "Look at that night," he exclaimed in a hushed voice. "It's a night for travelin'. Two hours from now, we'll be lost up near North Carolina, and you'll feel the weight of it all droppin' off you like water. Come on, let's go inside and get the things."

Owen crouched down and followed Michael along the front of the barn to the door. Michael pulled Owen inside and eased the door closed. There was no light in the barn and Michael struck a match and gestured for Owen to follow him to his room. In the room, he lit a candle on the floor beside his bed. Owen stood in the middle of the room, holding his sack, waiting.

"Don't worry none about the light," Michael whispered, crossing the room and closing the door leading into the barn. "The window's away from the house and it's not enough to show through anyway." He caught Owen by the shoulders and smiled broadly. "Didn't I tell you?" he said. "There was nothin' in that house to frighten you. Nothin'. And you're here as proof of it."

"When — when we leavin'?" Owen asked.

"In a few minutes. Give you time to catch up to yourself. Come on, sit down."

Michael led Owen to the chair and gently pushed him into it, then he stepped to the bed and sat on the edge of it.

"Here's my belongin's," he said proudly, patting the stuffed knapsack beside the bed. "Got the whole of my life in it, and like I told you in the jail, it's not worth much. Just some things I've gathered along the way."

Owen stared at the knapsack.

"Got plenty for both," Michael continued. "I been puttin' away food for a couple of days, and we'll have enough, what with the things we find in the woods. And we can take our time, Owen, lad. I was in town today. Told the doctor how you'd run off south. Even showed him the way you went. There'll be nobody chasin' after us."

"You see Tolly Wakefield?" Owen asked quietly.

"They was out, all of them. The doctor said they'd been in the night before and lit out again this mornin'. Said they'd looked the ridges and along the river and were goin' over Yale Mountain today."

"We better go," Owen said suddenly.

Michael stood and walked around the room. He said cheerfully, "It's a good room I'm leavin', Owen. A good room. I need to drink in the memory of it." He turned in the middle of the room. "I used to do this when I was on the circuit, Owen," he added. "After every show, every place we'd pack up and leave, I'd go to the stage and walk it, keepin' the memory of it in my own way."

Owen sat stiffly in the chair, staring at Michael as though hypnotized.

"I told you about my actin' days, didn't I, Owen?"

Owen did not answer.

"Ah, it was a good time," Michael continued easily. "I was good at it. Yes, I was. No place in the world like a stage. You can be anythin' you want on a stage. There's all kinds of plays, Owen, all kinds. Once I played Iago." He looked at Owen and smiled. "Iago, Owen, Iago. It's from Shakespeare, from a play called *Othello*. I could hear the handclappin' for a week. You know what it's like? It's — it's like hearin' them tiny bamboo sticks tapping together in the wind. The Chinese wind chime, that's what. Music, but not music. Clacking little sounds. Ah, it's somethin', Owen. It's somethin'."

"We better go," Owen said again.

"We will," Michael replied. "In a minute." He walked to the bed and sat on it. He clucked his tongue against the roof of his mouth. "The newspapers said I'd been the best Iago ever, Owen. Said Iago was the best role out of all of Shakespeare, and I'd done it better than anybody they'd ever seen." The smile faded. "I used to have that clippin'," he said. "I lost it."

Owen moved in his chair and the chair legs scraped like a yelp on the barn floor. He looked at Michael. Michael was staring into the ceiling and into the distance of another time. Then his eyes closed and he stood beside the bed and bowed gracefully before Owen. A smile locked across his face. He dropped his head suddenly, like a weight, and his arms spread in wings at his sides. He turned the palms of his hands up. The applause of his remembered audience fell around him like flung roses, and the song of their cheers rang in a deafening crescendo. Then his audience faded, dropped from the sight and hearing of his mind, and the seizure of his memory disappeared. He rose slowly, his body stiffening at his waist. His hands came together in front of his chest and he looked at Owen.

"It's a thing to remember," he whispered. "It is."

"It's — it's late," Owen said.

Michael nodded.

"We'll be goin'. In a minute," he mumbled. "In a minute." He stared into the light of the candle and the bronze tip of the flame blazed in his eyes. "It's been a long time since I thought about that play," he said softly. "There's a role you could've played, Owen. Cassio. He was wronged. Like you." He turned to Owen and laughed easily. "It's true. Be damned if it's not."

Owen shifted again in his chair. He pulled the sack of provisions in his lap. He tried to avoid Michael's eyes.

"Did you kill that young couple, Owen?" Michael asked evenly. "Did you?"

"N-n-n — no," Owen stammered.

"I know it, Owen. You were wronged, like Cassio."

"I didn't do nothin'."

Michael took a step forward. He stood over Owen and stared calmly at him.

"Them men that's lookin' for you, they'd be heroes if they found you," he said. "They would. The whole town's waitin'. They're takin' bets on who it'll be. Man that finds you, he'll get the treatment, he will. Drinks on the house. Him tellin' about it, over and over. People slappin' him on the back, sayin' how he made up for that young couple bein' knifed. You know that, Owen? Do you know that?"

"I didn't — didn't kill nobody."

Michael shook his head sadly. He clucked his tongue.

"But you come in here, wavin' the knife, sayin' you'd be splittin' the throat of those good women asleep in the house if you didn't get Eli's money."

"No — no, I didn't." Owen's voice was a whine.

"You shouldn't've done that, Owen. Not with all the help I've been to you."

"No. No — "

Michael reached for the knife sheathed at his leg.

"All this time I been trustin' you, Owen. Never dreamin' you'd be turnin' on me."

Owen's face trembled. The sack of provisions slipped from his hands and fell to the floor. He stood up from the chair and began to back away toward the door.

"Here, Owen, here's your knife," Michael whispered. He tossed the knife at Owen's feet, against the door. "Now you've got me helpless, and there's nothin' I can do but look for somethin' to defend myself with." He whirled and scrambled across the room. His voice became higher and his accent thickened: "Me lookin' frantic-like for somethin', not knowin' what to do, beggin' 'Don't kill me, Owen, don't kill me.' " He stopped at the foot of the bed and reached to the floor and turned back to Owen. "And luck would have it — blind Irish luck — but I find a pitchfork I'd been mendin'." He held the pitchfork before him.

Owen stood frozen against the door. His heart quivered. His tongue felt wadded in his mouth. His arms raised helplessly, automatically, above his head. His right foot touched the knife on the floor.

"Yes," Michael began to whisper. "Yes, yes, yes." He could feel the perspiration oozing from his palms. The music began faintly in his mind and he could see vague dots of faces in his audience, people squirming, shoving against the space separating them from the power of his presence.

"Plea — please," Owen begged.

Michael stepped into the full light of the candle. He held the pitchfork before him, like a lance.

"I'd like to be helpin' you," he said soothingly. "I'd like to, but what could I do? You comin' in here like this, wavin' your knife — likely the one that's cut the throat of that young couple — vowin' to do in them poor ladies asleep in the house. You shouldn't've done that, Owen. Makin' me do this."

Owen's face turned to the door. He closed his eyes and locked his trembling knees and pushed up on his toes.

Michael was breathing hard. He heard his audience gasp, heard their great collective "No!", heard the concert of their horror spilling in panic as they grabbed one another like victims of an executioner's gun. The music soared in him and the searing eye of an imagined spotlight covered him with its heat. He raised the pitchfork and leaped across the floor, driving it hard into Owen's throat, pinning him against the door.

Owen's eyes snapped open in surprise. His tongue rolled in his opened mouth and a stream of blood spurted over his lips and down his chin and dripped across his chest. The face of his mother flew into the silver shell of his mind. He felt her fingers on him. His head swiveled back against the door and he died.

Michael stood, pushing with his weight against the pitchfork. Through the handle he could feel Owen's body convulse and then relax as his life left him. A blinding white heat sliced through Michael's brain like a whiplash and he shook his head to clear it. Then he stepped tentatively away. The pitchfork held Owen to the door like a limp bundle.

Michael stared at the dead man before him. The room was quiet. There was no audience. No music. No light. No sound. He closed his eyes to bring his audience back before him, to hear their applause. There was nothing.

He reached for the knife on the floor beside Owen. A drop of blood had splattered like a thick raindrop across the handle. He wiped the handle dry on the left sleeve of his shirt.

He turned from the body and walked to the bed and methodically smoothed the bedcovering. He then sat on the edge of the bed and took his knife and cut a thin line in his flannel shirt, above the left elbow. He pulled the tip of the blade across his arm, leaving a small slit, like a clean scratch.

He looked across the room at Owen as the blood seeped down his arm and into his shirt. A sudden confusion pumped in him: Why had he killed Owen? Was it because of Eli's money? Or was it something in his imagination? Owen was part of a drama that had been written for him from the moment he saw the house where Lester and Mary Caufield lived, and he could not change it. Yes, he thought, that was why. He had killed Owen because it was predestined; it was beyond his control.

He stood at the bed and crossed the room and gently opened the door with Owen's body on it. He walked rapidly through the barn, across the yard, and to the house. He stood at the front door kneading his arm, forcing the blood to flow. He lifted his face and listened again for his audience. He could hear nothing. He began kicking at the door with his shoe.

"Rachel, Rachel," he screamed. "For God's sake, Rachel, open the door. I think I've killed the boy."

\* \* \*

At the house where Lester and Mary Caufield had been murdered, Tolly Wakefield knelt in the corner of the dark, bare living room and held the bones of the chicken that Owen had eaten. He sniffed the bones as a dog would sniff them and then he walked outside the house and stood on the stoop of the back porch. He had been right about the house and Owen. He could feel a chill, like the presence of an apparition, on his face. But it was not the ghost of Lester or Mary Caufield.

Owen Benton was dead. Tolly could feel it.

# 19

TOLLY SAW THE LIGHTS of the Pettit house from a half-mile away, on the road leading back to Deepstep Creek. The lights were two small orange spots on a level line in front of the house. He looked at his pocket watch. It was three o'clock. He had decided against returning to the bridge at Deepstep Creek through the woods; he had no reason to hurry, and the road was easier walked, if longer. He stared at the lights in the house and his head began to ache again with the premonition of Owen's death.

"Dammit," he muttered.

He reached the house quickly. Through the front window, he saw Michael sitting forward in a chair, his head bowed. Rachel and Dora, wearing heavy gowns, stood near him. Sarah sat in the rocker, near the fireplace. She sat very erect, not moving. Tolly could not see her face, only her body.

He looked around the yard and saw the opened barn door. He stepped to the porch of the house.

"Rachel," he called.

He saw the figures in the house stiffen as their faces whipped toward the window and the voice.

"Rachel, it's Tolly Wakefield," he said in a strong voice.

He saw Michael move from his chair and to the door. The door opened and Michael stepped onto the porch, followed by Rachel and Dora.

"It's good you're here," Michael said seriously. "I — I've killed the Benton boy."

Tolly stared at Michael and then moved his eyes to Rachel's face.

"I had to do it," Michael said. "He come at me with the knife and I had the pitchfork I was mending. He was ravin'. I did my best to talk him down. I couldn't."

Tolly's eyes drifted to Dora and then beyond her to Sarah, who was standing inside the doorway.

"He's in the barn, Tolly," Dora told him. "In the room." She added, "I looked. He's dead."

Tolly turned and walked to the barn. He stood for a moment at the door, listening. He heard a rat sprint across a rafter. He stepped into the barn's darkness and struck a match and saw the room, with the door closed. He moved cautiously to the door and pushed it gently open, and he could feel the weight of Owen's body on the door and hear Owen's feet drag lightly across the floor.

He stepped into the room and struck a fresh match and stood looking at Owen's body, hanging like a grotesque ornament, and thought of the chill that had engulfed him on the back porch of the Caufield house. His eyes circled the room and he saw the candle and lit it and placed it on the stove, and then he removed Owen's body from the door and stretched it across the floor and pulled a blanket from the bed and covered the body.

He blew out the candle and stepped through the opened door and walked from the barn to the house, where Michael and Rachel and Dora waited for him on the porch.

"I'll go to town," Tolly said. "Bring back the doctor and sheriff."

"That'd be helpful," replied Michael. "I was about to do the same, but it's left me heartsick, what I done. I wish you'd found him instead of me in the woods today. He'd be alive now. I trusted him, Tolly. It almost cost me. I still find it hard to believe."

Tolly did not reply. He stared at Michael's bandaged left arm and the hunter's instinct tightened in his chest.

"Sarah?" he asked. "She all right?"

"Upset, but all right," Rachel answered softly, looking back at Sarah.

Tolly nodded.

"Don't go back to the barn," he said. "Leave it for the sheriff."

He turned and walked hurriedly away.

\*   \*   \*

Owen's body was taken from the barn at sunrise. It was wrapped in blankets and placed across the back seat of Garnett Cannon's car and Garnett began his slow drive into Yale.

No one had seen it happen, but Garnett had walked behind the barn after viewing the body and he had vomited. It was the first time he had ever become ill in the presence of death and he knew it was because Michael had told a horrifying account of the demon that had raged in Owen like a terrible madness.

It was not possible, Garnett told himself. He had tended the boy, talked with him, examined him with care. If there had been a demon in Owen, Garnett would have felt it with his fingers. He trusted what his fingers told him and they had discovered nothing in Owen but the trembling of a battered child.

Yet the Irishman had known Owen well — perhaps better than any of them. The Irishman had coaxed him from his coma of silence, and had defended him before his own father. The Irishman had trusted Owen on the night that he escaped, and had urged his safe return, and there were the other considerations: the knife and the report of Owen's preoccupation with the legend of Eli's money, and the details of Owen appearing at the barn, vowing to bleed the truth of the money from Rachel. There was the cut on Michael's arm — a swiping cut, not deep, no need for stitches — and the anguish of Michael's remorse as he wept unashamedly over the tragedy of his act. All of it was evidence that Michael was right, that a madness had possessed Owen.

Garnett drove slowly, easing his car over the hard ruts of the road. If only Tolly had been there earlier, he thought. Tolly might have seen Owen going into the barn. Tolly might have stopped it. But that would have been ironic, a one-in-a-million chance, Tolly being there. At least he had been right: Owen did not go south, as Michael had described. Or he had circled back. And, Christ, he had had the nerve to hide in the house where Lester and Mary Caufield had been murdered. That alone was an indictment of his guilt. There was a demon in Owen, Garnett thought. A demon that had slipped from the thrusts of his fingers with the teasing facility of a matador. If only Tolly had been earlier. But the fact was that he hadn't. By the time Tolly arrived, Owen had been dead an hour or longer. There was nothing he could do, he had said, and it was a simple, sensible explanation, and Tolly had said nothing more about it. Still, Garnett wondered if Tolly knew something he would not tell until he was alone with the sheriff. He had remained solemnly quiet during Curtis's questioning of Michael. If so — if Tolly did know more than he told — Curtis would soon hear it: The two men had left for Frank Benton's house to deliver the news of Owen's death.

Garnett realized he was perspiring and his mouth was dry. He was deeply depressed. He tried to dismiss the sight that Tolly had described: Owen pinned to the door with a pitchfork driven through his throat and into the wood with enough force to hold the slender body. The prongs of the fork had penetrated the trachea and punctured the carotid artery, but Garnett was not convinced Owen had died from the wound. It could have been the trauma of a shock that had locked his heart in mid-stroke. But however Owen had died, it was brutal.

He looked over his shoulder at the wrapped body. It was such a tiny bundle to contain a man.

"Goddammit," he muttered aloud. He beat against the steering wheel with the heel of his hand and looked at the mountains around him. The early sun feathered across the valley. It would soon be autumn, he thought. The mountains were beautiful in autumn. Colors that boiled and spilled like brilliant rivers pouring into the funnel of the valley. He loved the mountains, but he needed to be away from them. He needed to renew himself in a great city like New York or Boston. He needed to hear the music of an opera, dine in a fine restaurant, speak with other doctors about medicine — medicine, not patchwork mending. He needed to sleep with a woman who had soft, perfumed skin. He had been too long in the mountains and he needed to be away from them. But he knew he could not leave them before autumn.

\*   \*   \*

Owen was buried the following morning, on Wednesday, in graveside services attended only by his family, the old minister, the doctor, the sheriff, and, because the sheriff had insisted, by Tolly Wakefield. There was no sermon, no praise of Owen's life, no attempt to invoke God's mercy. Frank Benton's vision had been confirmed: His son was a murderer. He would serve his agony in Hell. God would not listen to lies about the good of Owen's life. God would not be merciful. The old minister read Scripture, hurriedly, almost in shame, and Owen's coffin was lowered into the grave. The minister pronounced a prayer to benefit Frank and his children. Frank said nothing during the service. There was no emotion in his face. None of the children cried. It was as though they had been drugged. Garnett knew what had happened: Their father had preached the power of his vision to them, and they had believed him. Garnett could not have understood them when he first arrived in Yale; now he did, and he knew they had retreated into a silence that was as killing as a lobotomy. Owen's name would never again be mentioned in the Benton family.

\*   \*   \*

A calm settled over Yale and the Naheela Valley after Owen's funeral. Yes, it was tragic that he had died as he did, but it was also just. He had murdered Lester and Mary and had tried to hide it, but Good and Right — those twin soldiers of the inevitable — had trapped him. Eye for an eye. God's law. Irrefutable. Hard as a rock. Just as God had revealed the truth to Frank Benton, God had made it impossible for Owen to escape the punishment of his act. Too bad about the Irishman. He had believed in the boy. God knows, he had. He had convinced the entire valley that Owen was innocent, and then Owen turned on him. Lucky the pitchfork was in his room for repairs. It might have been different. The Irishman might have been the one dead.

But it was over. The valley was safe again. And the Irishman was the man to thank for it.

*     *     *

On Monday, a week after he had killed Owen Benton, Michael appeared in Garnett's office. His eyes were puffed and he seemed deeply morose. He had not slept well, he said. He could not sleep, though he had moved from the barn into the house. Rachel had insisted on it, because there would be ghosts for him in the barn. She and Sarah and Dora had taken the bed from the barn and set it in the living room. They had comforted him in every way they could, assuring him that Owen's death was not his fault. And he had tried to believe them, but still he had not slept. He had not worked on the fence. He had sat and relived Owen's death, fragment by fragment, word by word. He could not erase Owen from the gallery of faces in his memory, he told Garnett. He did not mean the demon Owen. No. He meant the boy Owen, the Owen who had listened to his stories and songs, who had smiled shyly at his frivolities in the jail. He had wanted to attend the funeral, he confessed, but he did not, because the ceremony would have been a ceremony of pain. He had wanted to go to Frank Benton and ask forgiveness, but he knew Frank Benton's mind was sealed with his sense of triumph, and his words would be wasted, like a song for the deaf.

"It's been a Hell, sure enough," he said quietly. "I've had scrapes, Doc. Too many of them, I'm sorry to say. And there's been broken bones and blood, but I've never killed a man. Never. And the sad thing is, it wasn't a man I killed; it was a boy. But I can't fault him. Not the boy. It wasn't him that came to the barn; it was a madman. Somethin' took him over, sure as God. Sure as God, Doc."

"You know that, then live with it," advised Garnett. "There's enough voodoo in the world. Don't let it haunt you."

Michael paced the floor in Garnett's office. He squeezed his hands together and nodded agreement.

"You're right," he said, "but if it was easy done, I'd be out with the lads — Teague was by the farm, askin' me — and I'd be celebratin'." He rubbed his eyes with the knuckles of his hands and then combed his fingers through his hair. "It's not easy done, Doc," he whispered. "Not in the least. Not with loose ends floatin' around in my mind like balloons."

"Such as?"

Michael faced the doctor.

"Whether or not people believe me in what happened."

Garnett pushed his swivel chair away from his desk with his feet.

"What makes you think that?" he asked.

"No reason," Michael replied. "Just somethin' I feel."

"Who from?"

Michael shrugged.

"Well, Doc, you, for one," he confessed. "I keep gettin' the feelin' you want to say somethin', but you don't. I felt it that night at the farm."

Garnett leaned back in his chair and propped his feet on the edge of his desk. A frown of concern crossed his face and he stared at his shoes.

"No questions," he said after a moment. "I guess I've wondered why you couldn't disarm the boy, weak as he was, without having to kill him."

"He had the knife, Doc."

Garnett nodded thoughtfully.

"He did, yes," he said. "But I keep seeing what you did to Teague that night at Pullen's."

"I tried to talk the boy out of it, Doc," Michael replied earnestly. "I tried. But when he came at me with the knife, I had to do what I did. I had to."

Garnett locked his hands behind his neck. He began to rock slowly in his chair and the chair squawked in a heavy, dull rhythm.

"Well, forget it," he said. "I don't doubt you. Guess I just wish it could've been prevented." He laughed cynically. "Hell, if I'm the only one you've got to worry about, Irishman, you could be out in the middle of the street dancing one of your gaudy Irish jigs, or whatever it is you people do. You should know by now that nobody around listens to me, unless they're dying and I'm the only person around who looks halfway intelligent."

"There's Tolly Wakefield," Michael said deliberately.

Garnett stopped his rocking. He looked quizzically at Michael.

"Tolly?" he asked.

"Past couple of days I've seen him up in the woods, across the road from the farm. Just standing in the edge of the woods, watchin' the house."

"Tolly? You sure?"

Michael nodded.

"It's almost as though he wanted me to see him," he said.

"If you saw him, you're damn right it's because he wanted you to," Garnett replied. He dropped his feet from his desk and pulled his chair forward. "I don't know what he's doing, but I'll ask Curtis. Maybe he knows."

"No need," Michael told him. "I don't know why he'd be there, but it's no bother to me. I think he's still upset about me bein' in the woods, lookin' for Owen."

"Could be," agreed Garnett. "Tolly's a stubborn man. From what people say, he doesn't like for anything to get the best of him. I remember when the Caufields were killed, he could find only one sign and that was a step going into that little branch beside the house. He thought someone had been in the barn, but he wasn't sure. Anyway, he spent days out in the woods, but it rained a lot a day or so after he started looking and if anything was there, it washed away. Forget Tolly. He's that way."

Michael thought of Tolly in the woods in March, chasing him.

"If he's got suspicions, I wish he'd say it out," Michael said.

"He will," promised Garnett. "Don't worry about it. Come on, I'll give you a ride back to the farm. You need to quit brooding. Get out. Do some work. Finish that damned fence, before even I start to thinking you're blood kin to Eli, like the rest of the people around here."

Michael laughed easily.

"I will, Doc. I will. Talkin' it out helps," he said.

\*   \*   \*

In the afternoon, after Garnett had driven him back to the farm, Michael began work on the fence. The last push, he called it. One last section to tie it together and then the cows could be turned to graze. And it would be done without interfering, he declared enthusiastically. Sarah would watch over the cows above the house, Dora would help him set the posts, Rachel would stay at the quilting.

"Can't stop everythin' for a couple of strands of wire," he told Rachel. "You do the quiltin'. Winter'll be here before you know it."

\*   \*   \*

Rachel stood at the window in Dora's room and watched the work in the field. She did not know what had happened during

2

36 ]

Michael's visit with the doctor, and she had not asked. If he
wanted to tell her, he would, in his time. It did not matter. He
was at last relaxed. The gloom that had shadowed him since
Owen's death was gone. His eyes were again bright and the lilt,
the song, was again in his voice. His whistling had filled the
house and he had remembered stories of the circus that were
grander even than the performances of those nomadic people.
He talked of the fence with an obsessed eagerness. The fence
would be his triumph over the tragedy of the summer; it would
be a finished thing, something to mark his presence. And he
would not be like other men of the valley, spending his energy
and time in Pullen's. He had had enough of the daily trips into
Yale, he said. And he did not want to hear the questions that
would surely be asked of him.

"I'm wantin' to stay home," he told Rachel.

Home. In a single word he had announced his intention.
Rachel understood, and she did not object.

She stood at Dora's window and watched him work, setting
a row of posts that he had cut and split from the blackgum trees
near Deepstep Creek. She smiled at a playful exchange between
him and Dora as he sighted the straightness of a post against
the fence line. It was an exaggerated mime of hand signals that
Dora could not read, and Michael threw back his head in
laughter and dropped comically to his knees. Rachel thought
about Dora. She now followed Michael like a servant mesmerized by his commands. Michael had disarmed her with his voice
and his gestures and manliness, and the suspicions that had
soured in her for years had turned into a giddiness that was very
often embarrassing. Rachel knew Dora was infatuated. She
could see it in Dora's eyes and in her innocent attentions, which
could be easily defended as friendliness. Dora was like Sarah
around Michael, and Sarah had become almost possessive in
her jealousy if Michael's attention wandered from her. Rachel
wondered if Dora had dreams of making love to Michael. Her
mind saw them together, embracing, and a quickening pulse of

anger ran through her. She turned in the room and her eyes searched the furnishings for the ghost in her imagination. It was uncomfortable being in Dora's room, she thought. Dora had always demanded privacy. She looked at the high bed, which had belonged to their mother and father. It was covered by a sunflower quilt she and Dora had made earlier in the summer. She stepped to the bed and touched it and she could see a shallow indentation in the mattress, the curled outline of Dora's body in sleep. Her eyes wandered to the night table beside the bed, covered with a daintily embroidered cloth. Dora's Bible was on the table, and a kerosene lamp. Rachel picked up the Bible and opened it and turned the pages slowly, scanning the passages of hope, or truth, that Dora had underlined in order to fix God's mighty voice in her memory. Dora had always been afraid of God. God would roar fiercely over the slightest error, and his vengeance would be awesome. It was odd, Rachel thought: Dora did not talk of God, yet the specter of his presence hovered over her like an unblinking eye. Her anger was God's anger; her suspicions, God's suspicions; her bitterness, God's bitterness.

In the center of the Bible, Rachel found a yellowing photograph of her parents staring into the barrel of the camera in a stiff, formal pose. She smiled gently. She had forgotten about the photograph. She placed it back in the Bible and turned another page. Then she saw it: the paper shamrock Michael had given them. Her hands trembled and she quickly closed the Bible and replaced it on the table. She had found her ghost. She fought the biting anger that rose in her and she whirled contemptuously from the table and looked again out the window. She saw Dora holding a post that Michael packed solidly into the ground with the handle of a shovel. Suddenly, Rachel was ashamed of her anger and jealousy. It was such a small thing, she thought. Yet it was all that Dora had. And as great as her secret desires might be, it was all that Dora would ever permit. She was too afraid to take the man in the field. Dora needed only the illusion of being loved. The illusion could not hurt Dora.

Rachel walked from the room and returned to her work on the quilting frame. She picked up a square of material and placed it over the linings that had been stretched across the frame and stuffed with cotton. Then she began to stitch. Her fingers moved expertly, bowed at the joints, darting nimbly at the material with the needle. She thought of Michael at work in the field. She remembered what he had said about staying at home, and the sound of it was good in its echo. She wondered if Dora's God would be upset for the stirring that moved restlessly in her. Probably. If Dora asked him. She wished suddenly that she could feel guilty, that some outside force would condemn her with the same threat as Dora's God.

She finished the stitching of the square and looked for another. There was none. She pushed back the quilt divider separating her bed from the quilting frame and walked to the chifforobe and opened it and removed a bundle of squares that she had cut and sorted into a pattern. She looked at the quilts folded and stacked in the foot of the chifforobe. They were the first quilts she had made to sell in Fred Deal's store and Eli had bought them from Fred Deal and given them back to her as a present. For Sarah, he had explained. Because it was right that Sarah should have them when she married. Rachel knelt before the quilts and touched them, and then she realized they had been moved. They were not stacked as she had left them and she had turned them only the evening before. She could feel her heart leap. She stood and looked at the quilts. How could it have happened? she wondered. She had been in the garden all morning with Dora and Sarah, gathering beans for canning. Michael had slept late and then left to walk into Yale. How could it have happened? Only Michael could have done it, but Michael was asleep. And why would he do it? There was no reason.

She closed the door to the chifforobe and walked across the room, past the quilt curtain to the doorway leading into the living room. She looked at the bed where Michael had slept. Why would he do it? she asked herself again. Or was she wrong? Was something happening to her? No, she thought. There had been other things. Small disorders. A piece of furniture moved inches. Canned goods awkwardly stacked in the storeroom. All of it so insignificant, so unnoticeable, that it had never mattered. If the house, the farm, had not been part of her as her arms were part of her body, she would never have realized it. And it had happened since Michael had arrived. It had begun in the barn. Michael had changed everything in the barn — to clean it, he had explained. But the barn had been in order. Was she right? Or had his being there made her forget how things had been? Had his presence changed things without anyone recognizing it? The weight of his step as he moved through the house like a parade, could it not jar things out of place? She was suddenly confused. Perhaps it was only her imagination that the quilts were not stacked as she remembered them. She often turned them to fluff the wool stuffing she had used in making them. And the patterns were similar. Yes, she decided, that had to be it. She was mistaken. Michael had not bothered the quilts. He had slept. She was sure of it.

# 20

CURTIS HILL arrived at the farm after supper, in the purple light of evening. He spoke politely to Rachel and Dora and Sarah and then asked to see Michael privately.

"I'll be back in a few minutes, ladies," Michael said. "But you're not to be worryin'. I've made my promise: no more wanderin' off to Yale, even if this good man doubles my wages." He laughed cheerfully and followed Curtis outside, away from the house.

"What's the trouble?" Michael asked quietly. "Is it the Benton man? Is he swearin' vengeance?"

Curtis shook his head and began a deliberate roll of a cigarette.

"No trouble," he replied. "I was talkin' to the doctor. He said you'd been to town."

"I have," Michael admitted. "Came in today. I've been bothered about the boy. Just needed to talk it out."

Curtis offered his pouch of tobacco to Michael.

"Smoke?" he asked.

"Got my pipe," Michael replied. He pulled his pipe from his pocket and began to pack the tobacco in the bowl.

"Doc says you've seen Tolly up at the edge of the woods," Curtis said. "Thought I'd see about it."

Michael held a match over the bowl of the pipe and drew fire into it. He sighed thoughtfully and his face wrinkled into a frown.

"Well, I have," he confessed. "But I said it didn't bother me. I was just curious, that's all."

"Where was he?"

Michael motioned with his pipe.

"Over there, across the road," he explained. "Up near the tip of those pines. Just standin' there, lookin'."

Curtis did not answer. He pulled from his cigarette and let the smoke seep from his lips.

"No reason to worry about it," Michael added. "I think he took offense when I suggested that maybe Owen didn't stay in the Caufield house, like he thought. It could've been a wanderer, you know, not knowin' about the house, and findin' it empty."

"Could've been," Curtis agreed.

"Anyway, I didn't see Tolly today. Maybe he got tired and went home."

"Hard to know what Tolly's doin' most of the time," Curtis observed slowly. "God knows, it's whatever he wants to. Don't guess there's ever been anybody follows his own mind as much as Tolly. Anyway, I'll ask him about it."

"No reason, like I said," Michael replied.

Curtis looked evenly into Michael's eyes.

"I know that," he said quietly. "It's for me, not for you. Just thought I'd stop in on my way by here and ask about it."

Michael smiled brightly and nodded and drew on his pipe in short, quick puffs.

"Well, I'm glad you did," he said. "Helps to look things over. While you're here, come on in and have some coffee. We'd like the company."

Curtis dropped his cigarette and stepped on it.

"Maybe next time," he replied. "Gettin' late. I better be goin' on in." He walked to his car and opened the door and slipped beneath the steering wheel. Michael could see a question in his face, but Curtis did not ask it. He started the motor and nodded and drove away.

Michael watched the car as it turned left into the road leading to Yale. An alert signaled in his mind and he fidgeted nervously with his pipe. The instinct to run shot through him like a scream. He looked at the black line of trees where Tolly had stood and he remembered his own surveillance of the Pettit house and the house where Lester and Mary Caufield had lived. He pulled hard on his pipe and the hot tobacco seared his tongue and the pain calmed him. He began to hum softly, then turned and strolled back into the house.

\*    \*    \*

Curtis guided the car to the side of the road by the bridge at Deepstep Creek and stopped the motor. He opened the door and stepped out and stretched and realized he was still bruised from the shove Tolly had given him. He smiled to himself. He was bruised, but not lame, like George. He saw the sudden attack again in his mind. God, he admired Tolly. Tolly did not give a damn that he was in the county jail when he moved against George. Tolly simply did not care.

Curtis looked at the woods around him. He said, "Come on out, Tolly. I'm by myself."

Tolly stepped from the ink shadows of a tree. Curtis did not hear him move.

"You find out anythin'?" Tolly asked.

"Nothin'," Curtis answered. "Didn't expect to. You got him nervous, I could tell that."

Tolly walked to the bridge and stood on the heavy boards and looked into the creek swirling in silver pools below him.

"What d'you think?" he asked.

"Don't know," Curtis replied. "If I didn't put so much trust in you, I ain't sure I'd be out here right now."

Tolly kicked a pebble off the bridge into the water. It splashed with a thud.

"Maybe I'm wrong," he admitted. He paused, then added, "Maybe."

"He's moved into the house, all right," Curtis said. "I saw

the bed put up. Talks like he's taken over, like it was his house."

"Yeah."

"You sure about that hole in the ground?"

Tolly nodded.

"Don't know why I didn't see it right off," he said bitterly. "It was plain as day. The same hole that I found down by the Caufield house, and there it was in the woods and he was the one who made it."

"A walkin' stick," Curtis muttered.

"What it was. I couldn't figure it out before and wouldn't've now, if I hadn't seen him with it."

Curtis remembered the single step in the clay bank of the stream that ran beside the Caufield house, and the sharp, strange hole beside it. He stood beside Tolly on the bridge and folded his arms and stared into the water. The sound of the water was like a rushing wind and the creek banks squealed with the shrill violin cry of crickets.

"How long we been knowin' one another, Tolly?" Curtis said at last.

"Long time."

"That's right, and there's somethin' else botherin' you that you ain't said. What is it?"

Tolly did not move. His face did not change expression. When he spoke, his voice was angry, but tired: "The man lied."

"How, Tolly?"

"If the boy come at him, moved on him, with a knife, the Irishman couldn't've stabbed him to the door with a pitchfork. The boy'd have to be standing against the door."

"I don't know, Tolly."

"Did you see that pitchfork? Wadn't nothin' wrong with it."

Curtis looked up at Tolly. He was surprised at the age in Tolly's face.

"Nothin'?" he asked. "It wadn't broke?"

"Never had been," Tolly said.

"Goddammit."

"The man lied," Tolly said again.

"Maybe. We better tell the doctor."

"Up to you," Tolly replied. "I'm goin' home."

$$* \quad * \quad *$$

Michael denied there was any trouble with the sheriff —
"Wanted to know if I was feelin' all right," he explained —
but Rachel could sense his worry. She led him into a story of
the circus and he stretched across his bed in the living room as
the three women sat around him in chairs and listened attentively. It was a rambling story about a midget who wooed and
married a woman with a trained dog act and then learned the
woman always slept with the dogs in bed with her. And when
he finished the story, he tucked his hands behind his head and
fell asleep fully clothed while Dora was describing a dog she
had had as a child.

"He's asleep," Rachel whispered. "Leave him be."

"I told him to slow down some today," Dora said. "Told him
he'd be wore out." She motioned for Sarah and the two left for
their rooms through the kitchen.

Rachel pulled a blanket over Michael. Even in sleep, his face
was clouded with worry. She wondered why he was bothered,
and if the sheriff had said something about Owen that had made
the terror of Owen's death return.

She blew out the light in the kerosene lamp on the side table
and crossed the room quietly to the doorway leading into her
bedroom. She stood for a moment looking at Michael and then
pulled the door closed behind her. She paused with her hand
on the doorknob and then opened the door slightly. She knew
it was a foolish thing, but the opened door made her feel closer
to the sleeping man, and the opened door was an admission that
no longer shamed her.

She undressed in the dark and pulled the cotton nightgown
over her and buttoned it to the throat. She stepped to the quilt
divider that separated her sleeping from her work and parted

it and pushed a chair against it. From her bed she could see the narrow slit of the opened door. She listened to the heavy, even stroke of Michael's breathing and the need for him touched her with a feather lightness. She thought of Sarah and Dora. They were infatuated with him. They would not understand her need. She had had Eli. But Eli had been gone so long, so very long. She closed her eyes and tried to imagine Eli close to her, but she could not. It was Michael's face that she saw. She pressed the palm of her hand over her abdomen and could feel the fluttering inside her.

\*     \*     \*

Her body awoke suddenly, fully, with each of her senses tautly aware. Her eyes flew open and focused on the face above her, staring at her with a steel gaze. It was Michael. She moved instinctively, pulling the cover to her, her eyes flitting over him. Then she saw the knife in his right hand, its cold blade turned up. A short gasp caught in her chest and died in her throat.

Michael signaled to her with the palm of his left hand. She watched horrified as he turned slowly in the room, peering into the darkened corners. She realized her hands were frozen in a frantic grip on the bedcovers over her.

Michael stood for a moment, looking into the room and listening. Then he slipped his knife into its sheath on his leg. He eased onto the edge of the bed and leaned close to her.

"I thought I heard a noise," he whispered.

"What — what time is it?" she asked quietly.

"Three, I suppose," he answered. Then: "I didn't mean to frighten you. I've been a bit touchy since — " He let the sentence drop. He looked at her, then began to pull away.

"Wait," she said.

She reached for him and touched him on his neck. He rolled his face to her hand and kissed it gently across the tips of her fingers. Her palm opened in a fan and her fingers danced slowly over his lips. She pushed her head back into the pillow and lifted her breasts high and toward him. He pulled away the covers and slipped his arms beneath her back, cradling her. He thought of Sarah and how he had held her exactly that way. His face dropped to her breasts and he began to nuzzle gently against her. She swallowed the sound that cried with its own voice and her hands moved to the buttons across the front of her gown. She picked awkwardly at the buttons, opening the gown to his face, and then she caught his neck with her hands and moved her face to kiss him, and her kiss was hungry and blind and she did not know that Sarah stood beside the quilt divider and watched.

Sarah did not cry out. She said, very timidly, "Mama."

The thin voice of her daughter exploded in Rachel's mind. She pushed hard against Michael, rolling him from the bed.

"Mama?"

Sarah reached for the quilt curtain and tried to balance against it. The curtain pulled loose from the ceiling and she sank to the floor on her knees. Her eyes were fixed in a paralytic stare on Rachel's opened gown. She tried to speak again, but she could not breathe. A shallow, gagging whimper sputtered in her throat and she could feel the blood draining from her face. She fought to sit upright on her knees. A hot pain, like a blow, knotted in her stomach. She felt her mouth fill with a cold secretion. She wrapped her arms tight around her stomach and breathed deeply, quickly, swallowing the horror that screamed inside her like a piercing whistle.

Rachel scrambled from the bed. She pushed Michael, shoving him, and stumbled to Sarah, gathering her in her arms. Sarah's body shuddered. Her arms squeezed around her waist. She began to swing her shoulders angrily, pounding against her mother. Rachel held her, burying her face.

Then, suddenly, Sarah relaxed. She let her face rock against the pillow of Rachel's shoulder and she began to sob quietly.

"Baby," Rachel whispered gently. "Baby — "

Michael watched the scene intently, nervously. He had made the mistake that he feared — a single blunder of eagerness. His mind flashed to the visit of the sheriff and the phantom voice urging him to run. Now he had no other choice. He could not kill them. Killing them would be his blood signature to guilt. He wondered what would be said between mother and daughter. He needed to think.

"Rachel," he said softly.

"No," Rachel answered. "Just — just go on. Leave me with her."

"Yes," he said. He walked past them into the living room and lifted his coat from the wall peg and opened the door and left the house.

\*     \*     \*

Her face was warm against her mother's shoulder and Sarah rested with her eyes closed. She breathed evenly as Rachel stroked her hair and rocked her like a baby who had had a frightening dream.

"I'm sorry, baby," Rachel whispered. "You know that, don't you? I — you know your mama's sorry, don't you? I didn't mean nothin' by it. Nothin'. Sometimes I — I don't know how to say it; sometimes I feel like givin' in. That's what I was doin'. Givin' in. I've missed your daddy. For a long time I've missed him. I was givin' in."

Sarah snuggled closer to her mother. She nodded into Rachel's shoulder.

"Mama," she said quietly, "I been with him, too. Did you know that, Mama?"

Rachel's body stiffened. Her hand trembled on Sarah's neck. She remembered the birthday party, and the jealousy that had been only partly hidden in Sarah's eyes.

"He — he said it was me, Mama," Sarah continued. "He said it was me he wanted." She paused, then added, "But I knew it was you. I — I could tell, the way he'd be lookin' at you. I knew it. I don't know why I knew it, I just did. Sometimes, when we was workin' out in the field and I'd carry him water, he'd talk about how good you was. He said you was a friend, somebody who understood who he was."

"Shhhhhhh," Rachel said gently. "Hush, baby. You have to know there's them kind of men, Sarah. He's a — a hurter. I guess I always knew he was. I guess I knew it from the first, the day he was bit by the snake."

"Why, Mama? Why? Why'd he have to do it?"

"It's his way," Rachel answered. "He's one of them people that hurt you, and you let him hurt you because — because you can't help it. It's like — it's like a gift with him."

"What's he want, Mama?" Sarah asked innocently.

"I don't know. Maybe just to prove somethin'. Maybe it's because of the money people keep sayin' your daddy hid. He talked about that some, after the Benton boy ran away."

Sarah pulled from her mother's shoulder and looked at Rachel. Her eyes were swollen and moist.

"He used to tease me about diggin' for buried treasure, puttin' in the fence," she said. "I never thought about them stories, about Daddy."

Rachel brushed away the hair from Sarah's forehead with her fingers.

"Don't be thinkin' about them things," she whispered.

"Mama?"

"Yes."

"Was there any money? Did Daddy leave some here, and you been keepin' it?"

Rachel smiled. She caught Sarah's face in her hands.

"If there was any money, baby, it'd be yours, for when you need it," she said. "Just think of it as somethin' your daddy made up."

A door closed in the house and Rachel lifted her head to the sound. She instinctively pulled Sarah close to her.

"Michael?" she said. "Is that you?"

She heard footsteps cross the living room. She knew it was not Michael; it was Dora.

"Dora," she mumbled to Sarah.

"Mama — "

Dora stepped into the room and looked at Rachel and Sarah on the floor, huddled beside the fallen quilt curtain.

"Sarah?" Dora said. "What's goin' on?" She stepped closer.

"Nothin', Dora," Rachel replied curtly.

"Nothin'?" Dora asked. "Where's Michael? What happened, child? Tell me."

"Nothin' happened, Dora," Rachel said firmly. "Leave us alone."

Dora stepped closer and stood above them. Her face turned suspiciously to look at the room. She saw the bedcovering thrown aside. Her eyes drifted back to Rachel and she glared at her opened gown.

"You let him at you," Dora said coldly. "You let him lay with you, ain't that it?"

"Dora, leave," Rachel commanded.

"Get away from her, Sarah," Dora shouted angrily. "She's been whorin' with him. She's been whorin'." She caught Sarah and dragged her away from Rachel.

Rachel twisted on the floor and jumped to her feet. She grabbed Dora by the shoulder and turned her forcibly, pulling her away from Sarah.

"Get out! Get out of here," she snapped. "She's my child. You been tryin' to take her away from me for years, but she's mine, damn you."

Dora stood, staring, her face ashen in the dim light of the room. Her lips curled into a sneer and her chin quivered.

"The child found you layin' with that man," she said quietly. "Ain't that it?" Her voice rose. "Ain't it? You been layin' with that man, and she found you. I know it."

Rachel's hand lashed out, slapping Dora across the face.

"We both been layin' with him," she shouted. "You hear

that? We both been layin' with him. That's what you want to know, damn you. And don't tell me you ain't been wantin' the same. I've seen you lookin' at him, wishin'. Wishin' he'd touch you."

Dora's face changed. It aged in a sad hurt. She placed her arms across the front of her gown, in an X, as though covering her breasts. She looked at Sarah and her mouth opened and closed. Tears began to well in her eyes. She turned and ran from the room.

"Dora," Sarah called. "Aunt Dora."

Dora did not answer. She stumbled blindly through the living room to the door leading into the kitchen. She pushed with her shoulder against the door and it opened quickly and she fell through it. She looked around as if lost. The room was hazy. It swam in her head like an uncontrolled dream. She could feel tears sliding over her face and she put out her hands and began to follow the corridor leading from the kitchen. Her fingers walked the wall until she touched the door to her room. It was open and she turned inside the room and slammed the door behind her. The sound echoed throughout the house like the crack of a gunshot. She leaned heavily against the door with her back. Her hands dropped to her sides and spread open against the door paneling. She threw her head back and her mouth opened and her face twisted into a contortion of great pain. Then she pushed away from the door and fell across the room to her bed. She crawled over the bed until she reached the nightstand beside the headboard. She lifted her Bible and turned onto her back, holding the Bible close to her chest and staring into the ceiling. Then she opened the pages and carefully removed the paper shamrock. She dropped the Bible and it slipped from the bed to the floor. She held the shamrock above her and looked at it, and then she pulled it to her and rubbed it tenderly across her face, over the ridges of her lips. She breathed on it softly. The tears streamed from her face and down her temples and into the pillow. Then she again held the shamrock above her and began to tear it apart — deliberately, carefully. And the tiny paper bits fell from her fingers onto her face.

*    *    *

Rachel sat on the floor with Sarah, holding her in a blanket. It was nearing sunrise. Outside a rooster crowed arrogantly, and Sarah moved against her mother.

"You know, Sarah, it's true," Rachel whispered.

"What is, Mama?"

"What Eli used to say," Rachel replied. "He used to say his baby was his wife made over, a baby Rachel, he said. He used to say no child was ever more like her mother." She paused and smiled. "Maybe it's not as true as I'd want it to be, but that'd make me happy when he said it," she continued. "Oh, that'd make me happy. I guess that's somethin' I missed more than anythin' else about Eli not bein' around. He was a sight around you. Last time he was around you — that was a long time ago, now — he kept callin' you his sweet angel. You had a doll then and, oh, Eli was a spoiler with you. One time, when you was just a baby learnin' about things, Eli woke us both up about this time, about sunrise, and we all went tiptoein' to the kitchen window. He said he wanted to show us the prettiest sight in the whole world. You remember that? It was a bunch of wild canaries. They'd lit out by the woodpile. The prettiest yellow birds you ever saw. Singin' and chatterin'. First time I ever saw any wild canaries. And the last time. Funny. Now that I think of it, it's funny. Eli said they was wanderin' birds. Never stayed long enough for people to see them." She paused and pulled Sarah closer. "He left home soon after that," she said. "Just up and left."

Sarah lifted her head in surprise.

"I remember that," she said. "I do, Mama. Yellow birds. I thought it was a dream, maybe. I never guessed they was real."

Rachel nodded.

"Mama, what'll we do now?" Sarah asked suddenly. "About him?"

"Nothin'," Rachel replied. "It's over. We'll let it be at that. He won't be comin' back."

"What if he does?"

"We'll tell him to go."

"Did he have to kill Owen?" Sarah asked hesitantly.

"I don't know, baby. Don't think about it."

"But I do, Mama."

Rachel thought of Owen Benton. She thought of the story Michael had told. She thought of the doctor and the grief she had seen in his eyes.

"So do I, baby," she confessed.

# 21

THE SMOKE from the chimney was a blue curl against the shell white of morning. It was as thin as a string and rose high above the house and spread into a veil, like a net of silk.

Michael knew the fire in the house was hot: pine kindling and hardwood. It was a quick fire on a clean grate and it would warm the kitchen and the heat would drift into the living room and along the corridor leading to Dora's and Sarah's rooms. The smell of coffee would be heavy.

Michael pulled the collar of his coat around his neck. He squatted beside a bush in the hem of the woods above the house and crossed his hands inside his coat, with his palms pressed against his chest. The night had been cold and he could not have a fire.

He did not know what had happened at the house, but he was calm. It was finished and he would not again be a fool. He would wait, be patient. From the distance, he was safe. He did not have to run. He smiled. He did not *want* to run. Not without Eli's money, and the money was there, in the house. He would not leave without it; if he did, it would be a failure — a small failure — and it would linger with him. Rachel had hidden it with cunning. It was not in the quilts, as he had believed, but it was near her. Not even Eli could have found it. Eli, he thought. Was it the reason Eli left? Angry because he could not find the money he had stolen and given his wife? It would have been a fight, all right. Enough to make a man take a fit and storm out, if not kill her.

He looked over the roof line of the house to the hills opposite him. He wondered if Tolly Wakefield was there, waiting, watching. Tolly Wakefield was suspicious, but he had nothing he could prove. He was an annoyance, nothing more, Michael thought. Still, if Tolly Wakefield interfered with him he would split him open like a melon.

The door of the kitchen opened and Michael moved forward against the bush. Rachel and Sarah hurried across the yard to the barn lot. He watched as Rachel bridled the mule and led it to the fence. Sarah climbed the fence and straddled the mule and took the reins from her mother and rode away toward Floyd Crider's house. He was puzzled. Why Floyd? What would she tell him? There was nothing to say, except to confess the intimacies, and they would never do that.

*    *    *

Rachel knocked lightly on the door leading into Dora's bedroom.

"I want to talk to you, Dora," she said.

"It's your house," Dora replied from inside.

Rachel opened the door and entered the room. Dora sat in a chair beneath the window, over which the curtain had been pulled. She was still dressed in her gown. She held her Bible in her lap.

"Dora, I'm sorry for what I said, what I done," Rachel told her.

Dora looked away. Her hands played over the gold-edged pages of her Bible.

"I can't live your life for you," she mumbled. "It ain't for me to say. You'll have your judgment, like he will, like everybody else."

"I know that," Rachel replied quietly. "But I don't want to talk about that. I've got to tell you somethin'."

Dora did not answer. She sniffed the air and waited.

"I sent Sarah up to Floyd's on the mule," Rachel said.

"What for?"

"I remembered somethin' this mornin'."

"What?"

"Michael, he — he said he killed Owen because Owen was cuttin' at him with the knife he stole when he run off at the jail."

Dora stared at her. She did not have to ask the question.

"It wadn't the truth," Rachel explained. "Michael had the knife on him the night before that happened."

"How do you know?" Dora asked bluntly.

"I saw it. It was in his pants leg. When we was havin' supper, he leaned back and I saw the top of it. I remember it because I'd seen it before, when he was carvin', and that was the first time I ever saw him wear it on his leg."

Dora sat forward in her chair.

"Maybe they was two knives," she said.

Rachel shook her head.

"There was only one. It was that one. He let me hold it one night, when he was carvin'. Said it was the only one in the world like it. Said a man from England made it special for him."

"Didn't you think nothin' about it?" Dora demanded. "He'd told us about the boy stealin' the knife."

"I don't know," Rachel admitted. "I didn't. I just didn't. It didn't come to me until this mornin', when Sarah was askin' why he killed Owen."

Dora stood and walked to the table beside her bed and placed the Bible on it. She looked at the shredded pieces of paper shamrock scattered across her pillow.

"What does it mean?" she asked.

"I don't know," Rachel said. "Tolly — Tolly didn't believe him. I could tell."

Dora remembered Tolly's silence and the way his eyes had stayed on Michael. She thought of Sarah, alone.

"And you sent Sarah out by herself?" she asked angrily.

"She's on the mule. I told you."

"What's she supposed to be tellin' Floyd?" Dora said bitterly.

"That Michael run off. We don't know why. He just up and left. I told her to tell him I'd feel better if he'd come over and help me check and see if he took anythin'."

"You should of told me before she left," Dora snapped. "It ain't right, her bein' out there by herself. You tell her about the knife?"

"No," Rachel answered. "I — I couldn't."

Dora thought of Michael with Sarah, whispering soft, soothing promises, taking her.

"What if he catches up to her?" she asked.

"He won't do anythin' to her. Anyway, she's on the mule. He won't catch her."

"What he won't do is come back here," Dora said coldly. She moved to her dresser and began to pick among her clothes.

"What you doin'?" asked Rachel.

"I'm goin' to take the gun and go after her."

"Dora, there's no need in that."

Dora turned to Rachel and stared hatefully at her.

"It's somethin' I'm doin'," she said. "Ain't nothin' you can do about it. That girl may be from your own flesh, and she may have sinned her way right into Hell with that man, but she's mine, too. I ain't lettin' anythin' happen to her, if I can help it."

Rachel knew it was senseless to argue with Dora. Dora was angry. And Dora's God was angry.

"All right," she said softly, and then left the room.

*　　*　　*

Michael saw Dora leave the house carrying the shotgun. He nodded to himself. She was after Sarah, to protect her. Dora knew. Dora knew it all. And she would gladly kill him. Poor Dora. She had been such a fool, such an ugly bitch of a fool, following after him like a child. Now she knew and she wanted to kill him. But she had left Rachel alone in the house. He settled against a tree and rubbed against its rough bark. He was pleased with himself. He had waited and the waiting had rewarded him. He was not like other men, he thought. Other men would have panicked.

\*    \*    \*

He saw her through the kitchen window. She sat at the table, holding a pan of beans that she snapped methodically. She seemed serene. A trace of a smile that was cupped in memory rested in her face and her eyes floated over her moving hands as though gliding in a fantasy. He looked around him, then stepped to the door and opened it quietly.

"Rachel," he said.

She looked quickly to him. Her eyes widened and then softened. She smiled warmly.

"Michael," she replied. "You're back."

She placed the pan of beans on the table and moved to him, folding her arms around his waist and turning her face into his chest.

"I'm glad you're back," she whispered. "I been hopin' — "

He pulled her close and held her.

"Rachel, Rachel," he said gently. "You're a good woman, Rachel. I'm sorry. I'm sorry about what happened. I'm the bastard of bastards. It's a weakness in me. A curse. It runs in the men of my family. Blarney, they call it in Ireland. A curse of the blarney. I — I didn't mean it with Sarah. Sweet Sarah. Wantin' to be a woman and me around, and weak like I am. I'm askin' your forgiveness."

Rachel lifted her face to him. She kissed him on the corner of his mouth.

"No need explainin' it, Michael," she told him. "I'm a woman. I understand a woman's needs. I talked it out with Sarah. No reason to forgive what's easy enough to understand."

Michael studied her face. He could see nothing hidden in it. He kissed her on the eyes.

"I been achin' all night to come back and take you up close like this, like we was last night," he said. "Up in the woods there, tryin' to decide about leavin' before seein' you again — before apologizin' — I kept tellin' myself to go, but I couldn't do it, and then I saw Sarah leave on the mule and Dora after her, carryin' the gun. And I knew what she was wantin' to do, and I couldn't blame her. But I knew I'd not have another chance to see you."

"It's all right, Michael. I just sent Sarah off to visit, just to let her get away for a while. Dora got scared and went after her."

Michael held her tight. His hands rubbed over her back and shoulders, searching for the surprise, the lie, that his mind failed to hear. He thought of his audience, wondered if their faces could tell him anything, but he could not call them out of his deep senses where they rested.

"But I have to be goin', Rachel," he said at last. "You know that. And the pain of it crushes me. Just when I was beginnin' to feel like I belonged, like there was a chance of takin' Eli's place." He laughed quietly. "You won't believe it, but I was makin' plans. Yes, it's true as the day's long: I was thinkin' about hirin' on with Teague and the sawmill gang after I finish the fence. Me, Michael O'Rear, workin' out wages, because I knew we'd be needin' the money."

She said it very easily, very casually: "You needn't be worryin' about money, Michael."

The words struck him like a slap. He would not have to force her, he thought. She was about to tell him. He cupped her face in his hands and let his eyes draw her into him.

"You're a lovely woman, Rachel," he said. "I swear I've never met better. You'd give me the last cent you had. You've proved that. But I know you live from day to day, and — "

"No," she protested, interrupting him. "It's not my money, Michael." She paused. "It's Eli's," she added. "Like we talked about, but I never told nobody about it. Never. Not even Dora or Sarah. That's why I told you it was a lie."

"Do you mean it?" Michael asked eagerly. "There was money? It's not just a story?"

She shook her head and touched his lips with her fingers.

"No, it's not just a story," she answered. "There's money. It was stole and I never touched it. Never. I always saved up the quilt money. But I helped Eli hide it. I know where it is."

"Why, Rachel? Why not spend it? It'd take you places you've never seen, buy you things you've never thought about havin'."

"Because," she answered hesitantly, "it was stole, and it wouldn't matter where it took me; this is where I'd come back, and nothin' else ever seemed to matter, knowin' that."

"Why?"

"It was somethin' my daddy said when I was little," she replied. "I heard somebody callin' us hill people one time and I asked him what they was sayin', and he told me to be proud of that. I think I learned what he meant."

"What?" Michael asked patiently.

"It's like when Mama Ada died," she told him. "The preacher said he'd shuddered when he heard about it. And that's what it's like, livin' here. You die, somebody shudders a little bit. I guess we all know that."

Michael nodded seriously. He pulled her to him again and put his face against her face. She could feel the energy racing in him. She kissed him on the cheek and he nuzzled her neck. Suddenly, she felt the presence of Eli anxiously watching her. She closed her eyes. Eli, she thought. She smiled easily.

"And comin' back's what I'd be doin', given the chance," Michael whispered. "That's the Hell of leavin', Rachel. Knowin' I'll be wantin' to come back every day I'm gone."

"Take it with you," she said. "The money. If it'll help to bring you back, I want you to have it."

Michael stepped from her. His face burned with excitement.

"It would," he whispered. "Yes, it would. As soon as things calm down a bit, when Sarah has time to get over it, I'll be back. I'll use the money to get started in somethin', so I can come back a full man, not a beggar."

"Eli — " Rachel began.

"No," interrupted Michael. "Eli's gone. He's gone. After Eli, there's just me, Rachel. And I've got to be goin', before Dora comes back with her shotgun."

Rachel stared at him, her eyes searching his face. She knew that he had murdered and that it had been easy for him, but she was not afraid. Was it because of Eli? she wondered. She had never felt Eli in such a way, standing off, watching her, awed by her. She was not afraid.

"It's in the well," she said easily. "About halfway down. There's a rock shelf Eli cut out when he was diggin' the well. It's like a little cave. He put the money there, in a heavy box. He said nobody'd ever think of lookin' in the side of the well."

Michael laughed and his eyes brightened. He lifted Rachel and whirled her.

"In the well?" he exclaimed. "Now, that's as good a hidin' place as a man could find. Eli was right. Nobody would think of it."

"You'll need a rope," Rachel told him. "That thick rope in the barn. And a crowbar to take off the top of the wellbox and a trace chain to put around the box. That's how Eli got it down. It's got a handle on the side for hookin' the chain on."

"Why the rope?" Michael asked.

"To get down in the well. That's how he did it. Tied big knots in it to hold on to, then lowered himself down and I dropped the box to him on the well pulley."

"I'll get them," Michael said. He stepped to the door. "It'll bring me back, Rachel. I promise that. I promise it." He opened the door and jogged across the yard to the barn.

"Yes," Rachel whispered to herself. "Yes."

*　　*　　*

The rope was heavy and strong and Michael tied knots into it at two-foot intervals and then he tied the end of the rope securely to a support post holding up the roof of the shelter and tested it against his weight.

"Strong as steel," he announced. "Now all I'll have to do is manage to hold on, or I'll be swimmin' my way to China. Give me the crowbar and I'll take off the top."

Rachel handed the crowbar to him and watched as he pried loose the oak shelving of the wellbox and slipped it to the side. He then dropped the rope into the well and peered into the black tunnel.

"Good enough," he judged. He looked across the field in front of the house. He sensed the need to rush.

"The trace chain," he said. "Do I tie it to the well rope?"

"Yes," answered Rachel. "Take off the bucket."

"Best to cut it off," he said. "It's wet." He pulled his knife from the sheath tied to his leg and sliced through the rope and tossed the bucket aside. Rachel stared at the knife.

"Better let me hold the knife," she said quickly. "You might drop it."

Michael handed her the knife and slipped the end of the rope through a link of the trace chain and tied the rope into a double knot, pulling it tight.

"Ready," he announced eagerly.

"I'll take it," Rachel said, reaching for the trace chain. "I'll hand it to you when you get on the rope."

"You'd better," he laughed. "I'll have a devil of a time just keepin' my balance."

He climbed onto the wellbox and lowered himself into the well on the rope.

"It's a bit shaky," he said, laughing nervously. "Hand me the chain."

"Not yet," Rachel replied. "You have to get used to bein' in the well. You lose sense of where you are. Eli told me that. Said you could look up in the sky in the middle of day and see stars, like it was night."

"I'll take the advice," Michael said. He slipped lower on the rope. "It's strange enough, all right," he added. His voice echoed. "Drop the chain."

"Just a minute," Rachel told him. "Let me get it untangled. I'll loop it so it can fit over your arm."

Rachel lifted the chain and slipped the line of links through the latch loop and pulled it. She caught the handle of the winch and turned it until the rope tightened on the chain. Then she locked the winch and stepped to the wellbox, beside the rope ladder.

She looked into the well. He was two feet below her, holding on to the rope. One foot was braced against the opposite side of the well. He smiled up at her.

"Come up a little piece," she said. "Give me your hand and I'll slip the chain over your arm."

He pulled up on the rope, climbing with his feet against the clay wall of the well. Rachel picked up his knife and placed it on the stone of the wellbox, near the rope. She held the chain loop open, above him.

"Close enough?" he asked, looking up.

"Close enough," she said. She stared at him and did not move.

"What's the matter?" he asked. "Why're you starin' at me like that?" His left arm was extended toward her.

She grabbed the rope ladder suddenly and began to shake it and Michael caught it with both hands and struggled to hold. He cried in surprise and his eyes flared in shock as he saw the wide noose of the chain slipping over his head. He shook against it and it fell around his neck. He clawed at it with one hand and began to pull up on the rope.

Rachel turned the handle of the winch until she could feel it tighten and then she locked it. She turned quickly and grabbed the knife and began to slice across the rope ladder. The knife was sharp and it cut quickly.

"No," Michael shouted desperately. "No."

The rope severed and as Michael fell the chain clattered tight around his neck.

Rachel pushed away from the wellbox. She could see the

chain quiver, and she grabbed the winch handle and pushed against it with her shoulder. The wedge lock clanked sharply and held and the pulley beam creaked and sagged. She heard a short, hollow sputtering, like air escaping from a ruptured lung, and she turned and looked down into the well at Michael. His hands clutched weakly at his neck. His legs danced frantically and his head bowed forward, and then his body slumped against the chain and she heard a dull snap. His head jerked twice and dropped to his left shoulder and his arms fell limp at his sides and he began to turn slowly around on the chain, like a toy on a string.

Rachel stepped away from the well. She walked across the yard to the fig bush Eli had planted for her. She looked back at the well. She could hear the squeak of the pulley as the chain turned lazily.

She could feel Eli watching her, smiling his approval. Eli was dead, she knew that. She wondered where he had died, and how.

# 22

RACHEL SAT on the front porch and snapped the beans she and Dora and Sarah had picked from the garden. It was late in the morning, nearing noon. The August sun had warmed the northwest air that flowed like a silver river along the trough of the mountain valley. The smell of the earth was in the air — soil and plants and trees and wild flowers and the crops of Floyd Crider's fields. And the pollen from the ripening of those growing things floated in a translucent cloud of dust, and swarms of tiny black bugs — their whole complicated bodies no larger than pencil dots — swam through the haze like schools of feeding fish. Everywhere there were birds.

Rachel felt suspended in the cool, green day and in the earth's perfume and in the festive music of the birds. She liked the work of her hands, cupping the beans, breaking them into links by the feel of her fingers. It was the same as holding a needle and working at the quilting frame. Her hands performed their tasks from memory. Her hands did not ask questions of her mind and her mind was free to dream. She did not think of what she had done, or what she must do. She had only to watch the road and wait.

\* \* \*

She saw the wagon as it topped the hill a quarter of a mile away. Even from the distance, she knew that Dora sat beside Floyd on the driver's seat. Sarah was behind them, in the body of the wagon. Jack sat at the back, legs dangling, as he always did. The mule Sarah had ridden was tethered to the wagon by a rope.

She placed the pan of beans on the porch floor and stood and smoothed her apron with the palms of her hands. She thought of Floyd. He had been patient and faithful. She did not like lying to him, but she knew she must, and she knew Floyd would believe her and do as she asked. She stepped from the porch and walked slowly to the turnoff into the main road, watching the wagon. She saw Dora nudge Floyd and the flip of Floyd's arm as he rippled the rope rein across the back of the drag mule hitched to the right side of the wagon. Floyd would be afraid, she thought, but he would not show his fear; he would show nothing she had not seen in the years of their Wednesday conversations. He would listen and nod and roll his cigarette and look away.

* * *

The wagon pulled to a stop at the turnoff.

"Rachel," Floyd said in greeting.

"I'm glad you could come, Floyd," Rachel replied.

And then she told Floyd about the knife, that she had remembered Michael having it before Owen was killed. She told him that Michael had searched her quilts and she knew it was for the money that people believed Eli had hidden. She told him of the visit from the sheriff, which had worried Michael.

"I don't know what was said," she explained. "I just know he got up and left in the night." She paused and looked at Sarah. "I wouldn't be worryin', except for the knife," she added.

Floyd rolled his cigarette. His face was furrowed and he nodded in a slow, rocking motion.

"Can't never tell about a man," he said gravely.

"I'd appreciate it if you'd go on into town and get the sheriff," Rachel told him. "I think he ought to know."

"Uh-huh," Floyd mumbled in agreement. He looked at Rachel, then quickly dropped his eyes back to his cigarette. "I'll leave the boy," he said.

"No," Rachel insisted. "We've got the gun. But I wish you'd take Sarah with you."

"Mama — "

"No, Sarah, I'd feel better about it if you'd stay with Mr. Crider," Rachel said firmly.

"Your mama's right," Dora agreed. "Not likely he'll be comin' back, but if he does, it'd be easier if you'd go on with Floyd."

Sarah said nothing. She settled against the wagon body. She could sense a secret in her mother.

"You're sure you don't want Jack to stay?" asked Floyd.

"No," Rachel told him. "We'll be all right."

Floyd nodded and lit his cigarette. He would not argue with Rachel. He knew he could not dissuade her.

"It'll be a while before we get in," he warned. "May take some time to find the sheriff, if he's out somewhere. Be best to stay in the house and keep the doors locked."

"We will," Rachel promised.

Dora climbed from the wagon and handed the shotgun to Rachel. She then untied the tethered mule and led it away.

"I don't like askin' you to do this, Floyd," Rachel said. "Takin' you away from work. But I thought it was best."

"Ain't no bother," Floyd said quietly. He clucked to the mules and the wagon pulled away.

*   *   *

Rachel and Dora watched the wagon until it disappeared around the road above Deepstep Creek, and then they began walking toward the house.

"Why'd you tell him about the knife?" Dora asked.

"There's no need to worry about anythin'," Rachel answered simply. "Not any more. I got somethin' to show you."

"What?"

"You'll see."

Rachel led Dora to the well. Michael's body still dangled from the chain. Dora stared at it without emotion.

"I had to do it," Rachel explained quietly. "He would've killed us, if it was needed."

Dora touched the chain with her hand. The body swayed slightly.

"What'll we do with him?" she asked. "Leave him for the sheriff?"

Rachel shook her head.

"No," she answered. "We'll bury him. I been waitin' for you to come back with the mule, to drag him off. We'll just keep sayin' he left and never came back."

"I'm glad Sarah didn't see him," Dora said. "What was he after?" she asked after a pause.

"The money," Rachel replied calmly. "Eli's money."

"There ain't no money," Dora said.

Rachel looked into the well. She smiled slightly and stared at the dark side of the well below Michael's feet.

"There ain't no money," Dora said again.

*       *       *

It was late afternoon when Curtis Hill arrived with Garnett and Tolly. They sat at the kitchen table and listened intently to the rehearsed story told by Rachel.

"We figured he was lying," Garnett said when Rachel had finished. "The knife's only part of it. Curtis told me about something that Tolly had seen, but damned if I believed him when he said it." He paused and drew a deep breath and fanned his face with his hat. Then he added, "It could be the Irishman was the man who killed the Caufields. Tolly thinks so."

Dora's body stiffened. She looked at Rachel.

"And the Benton boy?" Rachel asked. "What about him?"

"It was just Frank," Curtis said. "Him seein' things about those children. The boy talked some about Lester, and Frank started seein' things. The boy couldn't've done it. I never thought he did."

"Dear God," Dora whimpered. "Him dead and did nothin'."

"The Irishman had to have planned it all," Garnett said. "He took the town, everybody in it, including me. Had us all believing he was the boy's friend, and our friend. Damned if he didn't. I still believed him even after Curtis told me what Tolly had seen." He placed his hat on the table and tapped the top of it with his finger in disgust. "I think it's time you told that he wasn't a cousin of Eli," he said to Rachel.

"I'm sorry about that," Rachel admitted. "I thought it was best at the time. He'd helped Sarah — or I thought he had."

"Nothing to worry about," Garnett replied. "People'll get over it. Hell, we'll say he lied about it." He looked at the sheriff and Tolly, and the two men nodded agreement.

There was a silence in the room. Curtis cleared his throat. Tolly sat erect and stared out the kitchen window. Garnett tapped at his hat. Rachel looked through the door leading into the living room, to Michael's unmade bed. She thought of him sleeping, and then standing over her with his knife, and then cradling her and tipping his face like air against her breasts.

"He's gone," Rachel said evenly. "I'm sure of it."

"Maybe," Curtis said, "but we'll look around." He stood and looked through the window. "Not much of daylight left," he added. "Tolly can start now, if he wants. I'll take the doctor back and get some more men." He pulled his hat on his head. "Floyd'll be by soon with Sarah," he told Rachel. "I didn't think about bringin' her with us until I was almost here. Slipped my mind when I went to get Tolly. I'm sorry."

"It's all right," Rachel replied.

"There'll be some men around tonight," Garnett said, "but it might be best if you go spend the night with Floyd's family."

"We'll think about it," Rachel promised solemnly.

*    *    *

Tolly saw the tracks immediately. They began at the edge of the
yard, in the field grass. The mule's step was deep and the
runners of the woodsled had plowed into the soft ground. He
scanned the yard casually and saw the fanned pattern of a brush
broom on the white sand, leading from the well to the field,
erasing the tracks. He knelt to pick up a twig. He knew he was
being watched from the house, but he did not need to examine
the tracks closely; they were too clean, too fresh, too obvious.
He stood and turned deliberately, pretending to study the landscape above him. Then he moved quickly away from the direction of the tracks. He knew they would be easy to find again,
when he could no longer be seen from the house.

He walked in a steady, climbing gait along the beach of sand
that had been sifted by rains from beneath the bed of needles
and leaves that spread in a skirt from the woods into the cleared
field. Halfway up the mountain, he turned left into the woods
and disappeared behind a knoll that ran like a spine above the
house. He then turned right and followed the knoll until it
dropped and crossed into the field and dipped sharply into the
bottomlands of Deepstep Creek. He knew he was covered from
the house, and he stepped from the woods into the field and
walked slowly, peering at the ground. He quickly found the
tracks, where he imagined they would be. They led from the
field into the woods, down a narrow logging trail, and he followed them to the stand of blackgum trees Michael had cut for
fence posts. And then the ruts of the runners stopped and he
could see where the mule had stood, pawing at the ground,
stepping at the bite of horseflies. His eyes circled the ground,
following the turnaround of the sled, where the runners had
skimmed lightly across the ground. He knew the weight that
had been on the sled had been removed.

He picked up a limb cut away from one of the blackgums and
then pulled his knife from his pocket and whittled the tip of the
limb into a point. He began to circle cautiously over the area,
probing at the thick bed of leaves and needles covering the
ground. The light was failing and he could not read the signs

he knew were there. He moved closer to the soft clay bed near the creek line, jabbing the ground with his stick. And then he stopped and stood erect. A log had been rolled, with its decaying side turned up. He circled the log, studying it. The worms that had fed from its decaying heart still crawled over it, their white membrane bodies stretched full by their slow feast. He caught the log and lifted it and pulled it aside and then he dropped to his knees and began to dig into the dirt with his hands.

Two feet down, his hands touched the body and he pushed the dirt back over it and packed it. He stood and lifted the log back into place. He had found Michael O'Rear. He kicked easily against the log, then turned and walked away.

*   *   *

Tolly could not see the sun in the west. He could see only the color that spread its feathered fan across the bowl of the horizon. It was the color of fire, with flames licking high above the ball of heat. He stood on the hill above the house, among the trees, and watched the women at work in the garden, in the last hour of day.

They were strong people, he thought. He remembered Eli. Eli. Laughing Eli. Off all these years, chasing after a ghost that teased him with promises of immortality. And the women, left to wait, pinned to their place by the days and the years, enduring the mutterings of pity that had followed them like a disgrace. They had stayed and waited because it was expected of them. It was their duty. And all of that time had been lost, because they had done what was expected of them.

Tolly wondered if they knew he would find Michael. Perhaps they even wanted him to. It would then be a shared secret— known but never spoken. It was their way; his way.

He looked across the field to the fence the Irishman had almost finished. There was only one span left unconnected. One span, a gap, like an unkept promise. His eyes wandered back to the women, then over the house and to the road. He saw the dust from the sheriff's car boiling in the same rust-red as the flames of the sun. He raised his hands above his head and laced his fingers behind his neck and pulled hard. It felt good, being in the woods. He looked again at the women in the garden. They stood still, watching the funnel of dust from the sheriff's car.

And then they drifted from the garden into the house.